A History of Vampires

of Vampires

A New Queen

Amanda Lewis

A History of Vampires

A New Queen

Amanda Lewis

Also by Amanda Lewis

The Levander Brothers Series

The Weight of Birds (2020 Silver Medal Winner,
Contemporary Christian Romance, Reader's Favorite
Awards)

Still Waters: Peter's Story

A History of Vampires Series

A History of Vampires – A New Queen

A History of Vampires – Legends & Lore (Pre-order
now!)

Goodwater Ranch Series

The Cowboy – A Goodwater Ranch Romance

The Movie Star – A Goodwater Ranch Romance (Pre-order
now!)

For Kayla, Kelly, Diane & Daphne

My unicorn tribe

And the high mountains will be shaken, and the

high hills will be made low,

And will melt like wax in a flame

Enoch 1:6

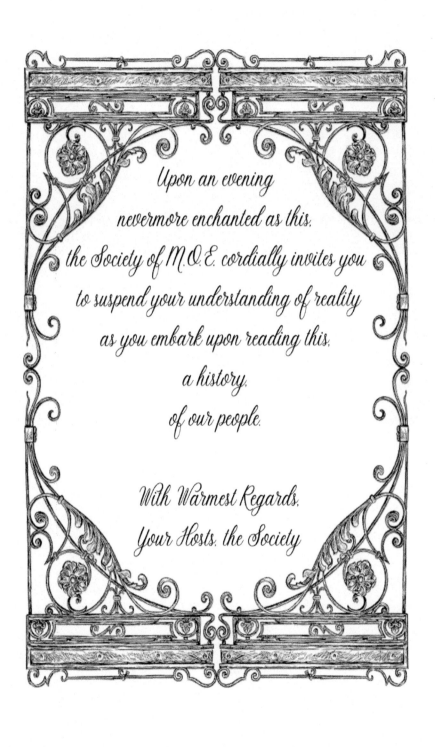

Upon an evening

nevermore enchanted as this,

the Society of M.O.E. cordially invites you

to suspend your understanding of reality

as you embark upon reading this,

a history,

of our people.

With Warmest Regards,

Your Hosts, the Society

Prologue

New Orleans, Louisiana. September.

It's lunchtime at the Café du Monde, the weekend of the latest festival. Amidst the sea of excited chatter, fresh coffee and fried dough scents consume the crowd.

His presence lingers in the air, hovers over all of her senses, floats in the electricity of tourists. Through the hustle and bustle he's barely visible, but she knows he's there in the corner, observing.

Waiting.

They've met before, several times actually. Each moment as thin as a sheet of paper. He's been following her for quite some time, yet she knows instinctively there is nothing to fear from him.

Just a glimpse of the man in the corner is visible

as a waitress bumps into a table, tripping over the corner of a fancy boutique shopping bag. The woman it belongs to glares at the help, as if she was a bug that had failed to be squashed. The waitress lurches forward momentarily before catching herself, her eyes wide in fear. A snow of powdered sugar falls onto Angelina's hand and into her coffee.

"I'm so sorry!" the waitress squeals as she tries to dust the sugar off with her already coffee-stained dishtowel. Angelina notices the creased brow lines on the waitress, the pleading in her eyes to please not yell at her. She smiles and slips the waitress a $20 for her struggles. *Maybe that'll help make her day a little better.*

A shadow shimmers in the corner. He's starting to move. If she doesn't approach him, she'll have to wait for the next time, whenever that may be. She can't wait that long again, for the uncertainty. Not anymore. She has to know why.

Angelina gets up, carrying her sugar-dusted coffee. She bobs and weaves through the crowd, making a beeline across the covered patio, to his table. He won't get away from her this time. His eyes are on her, observing her the whole time, until she's standing in front of him. A curious, yet unhurried, expression adorns his handsome face.

"May I sit?" Angelina asks. He motions with a long, pale hand, welcoming her to the chair across from him. She sees him clearly for the first time. Before, there were only glimpses, whispers of a man. He's devilishly handsome. He's leaned back in his chair, and dressed superbly. Obviously wealthy, but arrogance is not a word he's familiar with.

Well-tailored dark gray vest, white shirt, gray pants, and shiny, black pointed shoes. Casually crossed ankles jutting out into the walkway. The corner isn't as busy, and he's not hindering anyone's actions. He reminds her of a Tom Ford ad. His white shirtsleeves are carefully and precisely rolled up to his elbows, and, underneath the vest, it is unbuttoned at the top two buttons. Curly black chest hair spills out. Proper but casual. A carefree gentleman.

He looks foreign, but she can't place from where. Spanish, maybe? That would fit.

His eyes are gray, or maybe they just reflect his clothing. An exotic gray, like sands in the moonlight. His wavy dark hair is slicked back, like a black ribbon eel. The length is just below his ears. A short beard frames his face, accenting his jawline and red lips. The beard hasn't been trimmed in a few days, making him look rugged and sexy. A little too sexy. No, actually, a lot too sexy. Beneath the table, Angelina subtly runs her palms against her shorts to remove the perspiration that is not weather-related.

He's olive-skinned, only just so. He should be darker in this August New Orleans sun, but his translucence reminds her almost of skimmed milk. Skimmed milk, blended with a smooth, medium amber caramel.

He takes a sip of his coffee, as black as his hair. They watch each other a few seconds longer. A lion and a gazelle at the watering hole. Angelina is not the lion. A dozen beats pass between them before she speaks again.

"You've been following me."

"I've been following you." His head nods slightly in agreement as he repeats this as a statement of fact, rather than a question.

Chapter One

The first time she caught a glimpse of him, he was dressed as a security guard. Angelina was just about to leave the French Embassy in Washington, D.C. Descending to the lobby, she noticed the usual team of security guards was standing by to usher her to her vehicle.

Frustrated at her failure to get permits for the next excavation site, Angelina's mind was elsewhere when she missed the last stair. She tripped and nearly fell flat on her face, her slingback pump flying off in the opposite direction to her body. Her head whipped around to check how many people might've seen her clumsy misstep. Angelina stood up straight, brushed her suit back into place, reclaimed her shoe, and tried to regain her composure.

There, in the shadows, she noticed a guard that didn't quite fit in. His suit, though black, was a different style, and he wasn't wearing an earpiece. Then he was gone, blending in with the hustle of suits in the lobby. It barely registered in her mind as she ran out the door and into the awaiting transportation. Until she saw him again a few months later.

Barcelona, noon, hot July summer, almost two months ago. She had meetings at the consulate's office, trying to get paperwork in order. It hadn't taken all day like she'd planned on, and she'd decided to take a scenic stroll through the capitol's bustling streets.

It was hot, a little too hot for comfort. She'd packed some shorts and sandals in her backpack that morning, just in case she got a chance to go sightseeing. Angelina slipped them on in the bathroom, double checking to make sure she looked cute yet professional. That was her style, business casual with a hint of fun. The black sandals she'd chosen complemented khaki, pleated shorts and a black halter top, all of which complemented her olive skin. She pulled her long, dark brown hair back into a ponytail before going outside to meet the Cabify driver, who would take her to her dream destination,

La Sagrada Familia.

That morning, Angelina had grabbed a tourist map at the hotel and quickly made a to-do list of the most important places to see while she was there. La Sagrada Familia made the top of the list, without competition.

In college, way back when, she had taken an architecture class as an elective. Gaudi's designs and dreamlike buildings had garnered a special place in her heart, and she knew if she was ever in the area, she'd journey to as many as she possibly could.

There was a park across the street from the entrance of La Sagrada Familia that she decided to go to first, to relax and take in the atmosphere and smells from the city in order to immerse herself in the culture. Angelina first grabbed a sandwich and soda from a snack stall, along with a new baseball cap for the collection. Some people collect T-shirts, some pins, some bells. Caps were her thing. She slid it on to help keep the hot sun off her face, pulling her ponytail through the back, and strolled onward.

Other than the heat, it was a beautiful day. Warm sunlight and uplifted moods rang throughout the park. Random little birds were hopping around eating crumbs and whatnots. She had imagined it wouldn't be busy during a weekday—it was Tuesday, after all—but then she remembered it was still the summer. A melting pot of tourist families ebbed and flowed all around her.

Angelina came to a crowded intersection, with three walkways to choose from. She picked the middle one that sported a shaded bench, free from people and housed underneath a nice tree with purple blooms on it. It was just off the main intersection of all the walkways. She sat down and dug into her sandwich while watching the groups of tourists and passers-by mingled through the park.

In the crossing there were several different performers entertaining anyone who was interested. Two men were playing flamenco music just across from her. As they strummed their guitars furiously, several small children danced and hopped about in front of them.

An elderly couple to her right was slow dancing to the music, wide smiles spread across both their faces. The lady's bright orange shawl with red fringe swayed back and forth, her orthopedic shoes barely leaving the ground as she and her husband shuffled slowly around in circles.

On the other side of the crossing, a bubble artist was blowing huge bubbles of various shapes and lengths. This had attracted even more children, who were squealing and popping them enthusiastically. Their parents looked on with relief and appreciation for the bubble artist who was keeping their children entertained, if even for a moment.

Many other tourists passed through, carrying various bags from their many excursions from the day. As Angelina downed the last bite of her sandwich, a strange feeling settled over her shoulders. She looked around. There were dozens of people around her, but none noticeably stuck out. She dismissed the feeling as being paranoid, and decided to head over to La Sagrada Familia. She bought a ticket, and started over to the entrance with her self-guided tour tape.

Stepping inside was an awe-inspiring act in and of itself. Angelina gasped, her breath getting caught up in the marvelous architecture that surrounded her. She removed her cap in favor of a full and unobstructed view. Walking in a little further, the cool, colorful air hit her skin. All around her was a kaleidoscope of rainbows, on every visible surface. As she walked further into the nave, on either side towers stretched upwards and branched outward to the heavens to support a canopy of jagged stone, Gaudi's palm forest. It was afternoon, so the sun was on the west side, streaming in bright vibrant hues of reds, oranges, and yellows.

The eyes were on her again as she stood there, helplessly looking at the landscaped ceiling above. She turned to the east corner, the blue and green windows lining the cathedral on this side. The cool side. Someone hovered in the shadows, behind one of the towers in the darkest corner. A mysterious, shadowy man, solemnly watching her. Angelina blinked and he was gone.

After she had done sufficient sightseeing and had observed every unique article of design, she headed towards the door. There, in between the entrance and exit doors, was a massive wall, reminding her of an open book, with words in a language she was unfamiliar with.

Angelina stopped in front to observe, read, take it in. The sculpture, if it could be called that, was covered in bronze, the patina aging the letters written in the Catalan language. She stood there, reciting quietly the relief-etched words that she did not understand.

"'Vingui a nosaltres el vostre regne; faci's la vostra voluntat.'"

"'… així en la terra com en el cel.' On earth as it is in heaven,"* someone whispered the next line as if on cue. A deep, smooth voice, with a subtle foreign accent. She felt a wisp of wind on her neck as she turned around.

There was only a family behind her now, painfully tourist in their appearance, as if they'd meant to go to a beach instead. The dad, dressed in orange shorts and fisherman hat, a bright blue Hawaiian shirt, and flip-flops, handed his camera to Angelina and asked her to take a picture of them.

The next day was entirely free and devoted to being Parc Güell Day. In all its Seussical wonderment, Angelina was eager to spend as much time as she could taking in all of Gaudi's minute, precise details. At the entrance, she took a selfie with Gaudi's dragon fountain. The cool water splashed her shoulder while she leaned in as close as possible. Then, Angelina continued on, meandering aimlessly throughout the gardens and mosaics beautifully laid out around her.

Angelina wandered through the hallways of stonework that had been magnificently handcrafted to resemble nature, running her hands along their walls until she stopped suddenly. The feeling settled upon her yet again, and she looked around, trying to identify the source.

At the end of the hallway, he was there. Frozen in place, and gazing out over the gardens. He had no one accompanying him, that she could readily see. The sunlight shone through his black hair, fluttering in the wind. From his profile, she knew he was handsome, but no other physical details offered themselves up from the distance where she stood.

And yet, there was something about him, some slight familiarity she couldn't place. Had he been at the consulate's office? Did he work for the government? His posture changed as he felt her presence. He turned to look at her, and their eyes locked. Shivers went up Angelina's arms as she gasped, though she wasn't sure why. She took one step closer, more intrigued by this stranger than the historic park they stood in. He took a step forward and vanished into the crowd.

Chapter Two

Angelina was secretly thrilled that she'd finally managed to catch him, like a lightning bug at sunset. Always present but not always visible. *Or had he let me catch him?*

"*Why* have you been following me? Who are you?"

"It's more a matter of who *you* are, Dr., Ms. Arbonne. It is Ms., correct?"

He said this without reserve, like he only asked questions he already knew the answers to. He knew her name, and what else? "Yes, Ms. Well, Dr., first and foremost. I think you probably knew that, though. And if you took the time to find out beforehand, you're probably a man who doesn't appreciate small talk and casual conversation. What else do you know about me?"

He took a sip of his coffee. Unhurried, unbothered by her presence. Confident.

"You are Dr. Angelina Arbonne. You were born here in New Orleans, an only child. You didn't grow up here, not the first twelve years of your childhood, but you live here now because it's the only place you've ever felt like you belong. Your parents died in a car crash when you were twelve, leaving you to be raised by your aunt. She was an activist in her free time. Now she resides in a nursing home.

"In high school, you joined every club you could use to your future advantage. Debate, culture, student government, Beta. You volunteered at Big Brothers Big Sisters on the weekends.

"You're well read and well educated. You've always tried to understand the world and the people around you. You received full scholarships, and double majored in Archaeology and French in college. You already knew you wanted to travel the world to unearth history. French came easy to you; your father and aunt were from France. Your name, Arbonne, means 'good things from the earth.' Fittingly, you feel most at home doing field research, unearthing forgotten times.

"That empowers you, makes you feel like it is your mission in life to give back. You work for the university, but really you would gladly work anywhere that you could benefit and help others to understand their surroundings.

"You're beautiful, strikingly gorgeous. Cameras notice, as do men. Powerful men. You've gained a small platform on the world's stage just so they can watch you talk, but you're not just a pretty face. You've got the machismo to back it up, to make them sit up and take notice. You're starting to be influential just on your name and reputation alone, what you've always wanted. With your job, you could live anywhere, but you chose New Orleans. You always come back to New Orleans." He said all of this assuredly. It was unnerving how he knew her details, and she still knew nothing about him.

"Did I miss anything?"

"Do you work for the CIA? Did I piss off the wrong people and you've been sent to track me down?" Angelina asked. He shook his head no, a slight smirk on his cherry red lips.

"You know my whole history. How is it that you know so much about me, but I know nothing about you? No, I take that back. I do know some things."

He raised one eyebrow, amused and questioning. She continued, slightly unnerved at the lack of edge she currently had. "Yes, I do know some things. I can profile the profiler. I know that you're a world traveler. I've seen you; I saw you, in D.C. You were pretending to be a security guard. I saw you over in the shadows and then you were gone, but I did catch just a glimpse of you.

"Then in Barcelona, you followed me for at least two days. You were there in the park, watching me eat my sandwich. I know you were. Then you followed me into La Sagrada Familia. I did see you in the shadows and then you whispered to me.

"Again, the next day, we made eye contact before you disappeared. Were you scared of me? You should be, I know people." She was almost pleading in her tone, trying to convince herself more than this stranger of the power she possessed.

Angelina, who was composed and fearless when she spoke in front of auditoriums full of people, sat on her hands to try and disguise her nervous shaking at confronting this one handsome man. She certainly wasn't used to being caught off guard in such a colossal manner.

The waitress came around and refilled their coffees. She looked a little less frazzled this time. She smiled at Angelina as the stranger said, "May we order another round of beignets for the lady?"

"Oh, I don't—" Angelina started, as he interrupted her.

"Yes, she does." He smiled at the waitress as she left. Then he focused his eyes back to hers, and Angelina felt the shiver and curiosity again that she'd felt at Parc Güell.

"You always order beignets at the end. You tell yourself every time that you won't, but then the atmosphere takes you over, as the afternoon street melodies float through the air. You remember why you love this city, the music, the vibes, the art, the culture, the religious heart of it, and then you think, 'Maybe just one more time.'" He sat up, putting his elbows on the table and resting his chin on his crossed fingers.

"So, this is the end of this encounter?" Angelina asked, irritated that he was on point with his observations. He'd been following her much longer and closer than she'd realized.

He smirked, his gray eyes glinting in the sunlight.

"It doesn't have to be, Dr. Arbonne."

Chapter Three

The beignets arrived, and Angelina eagerly watched the waitress place them in front of her on the table. She studied them, moving her head around in a slow, circular motion until a smile crossed her lips when she found what she was looking for. *They're delightful. Fresh, sizzling grease, caramelizing the powdered sugar on top. This is what dreams are made of. Sometimes if you order beignets, if they're just a minute old, you don't get to see that sizzle.*

It's not because they're not fresh, they absolutely are, but there's just a fine line between sizzle and stop. It should be classified as a delicacy. She felt her mouth water as she licked her lips, forgetting present company.

"Your green eyes glitter every time they arrive," the stranger said, jolting Angelina out of her sugar trance and back into her potentially uncomfortable situation.

"Exactly how long have you been watching me? And are you going to tell me anything about yourself, anything at all? Start with your name."

"Jude."

"Just Jude?" she asked, as her mouth hovered over the coveted first bite. It instantly blistered her tongue as she bit down on the beignet, causing her to flinch. A puff of powdered sugar floated up into her nose.

"Just Jude."

"How long have you been following me, Jude?" she rephrased her question.

"Long enough to know."

"Know what?" Angelina said snappily. Her sore tongue was pulsing, making his short answers slightly irritating as well.

His eyes twinkled at her, amused and unoffended. "When you leave, you'll cut across the street, over to Jackson Square. If there's art, you'll stop, maybe buy something small. You like things with cats, or various animals. Tigers are your favorite.

"Then you'll head over to the St. Louis Cathedral. You only go in on cloudy days, though. Rain changes the smell inside and you love the shadows the clouds create. You feel closer to God in the rain. Rain reminds you of power, of uncertainty, of life. If it's sunny out and you didn't get beignets, you may head to one of the tourist shops to get a praline. An old-fashioned one, like your mom used to make when you were little. Then, you'll walk to your apartment."

"And then?" Angelina was leaning forward, nearly on the edge of her seat as he described her life with his invitingly accented voice. She was intrigued and wanted to hear more. She would've been more alarmed at having being confronted by a stalker, but Jude was different. Somehow, it wasn't strange or odd that he knew so much about her, about her details, the little things she liked and how they made her feel.

He had seduced her, and in a matter of minutes. The way his voice lingered on his words, and the way his lips moved as he spoke, made her think of how crème brûlée felt on her tongue. Rich and sensual, smooth and addictive. Considering Angelina had such high standards for men, being seduced in broad daylight over beignets was not something she was used to in the slightest.

She realized she was licking her lips and stopped. He had certainly noticed.

Jude grinned seductively, his cherry red lips glistening in a stream of sunlight. "Well, I don't know, Dr. Arbonne. I've never been inside your apartment. However, around 8 p.m. every night, you do open the windows on your balcony to let in the music of the streets."

He scooted his chair out and got up to stand. A little piece of her heart broke. She was completely entranced and didn't want this to end. He held out his hand, and her pulse quickened when she offered hers in return. He pulled her up in one quick motion, and they made their way through the crowd of people.

Angelina couldn't help feeling a little bit giddy. They walked down the sidewalk, to the steps which had really just been repurposed into a makeshift amphitheater. A group was doing some break-dancing routines to a crowd of onlookers as they passed, heading up the steps and over to the waterfront.

The heat from the concrete blended with the breeze off the river swirling all around them. Angelina was getting sticky and uncomfortable, imagining herself sizzling bacon on a stovetop pan. She pulled her shirt out and away from her back, trying to fan the beads of sweat collecting down her spine.

"It is quieter here, but I didn't realize how excruciatingly humid it would be. Let's walk back to the park, shall we?" Jude said, reading the drops rolling down the crook of her arm. Angelina raised her hands to her brow, shielding her face from the sun as she looked at him. There wasn't an ounce of perspiration to be seen.

They turned around to walk back, and Jude placed his hand on the small of her back. As a guide, or as a comfort, she wasn't sure. But she liked it.

They found a shaded bench at Jackson Square and sat down. Looking around at the tropical plants, Angelina couldn't help but feel a parallel to the day in Barcelona. Only this time, she knew who was staring at her.

Now that there wasn't a crowd of chattering people around them, Jude stared ahead, his eyes fascinated on something in the distance. His perfect face and body were on full view for her, as if he wanted her to decipher him. He stayed still, like a marble statue on display in a museum, while her eyes roamed him freely, taking in more of his details. He was wearing a light cologne, something manly yet sweet. His cheeks were slightly flushed, a side effect of the heat, though much less than Angelina's. His lips were an even brighter red, and Angelina couldn't help but stare at them.

The breeze had let loose a few strands of his wavy black hair, which gave the appearance that he was frazzled. His demeanor said otherwise. He leaned back on the bench, and propped his arms up on either side. One was draped completely around Angelina, his fingers just brushing her arm opposite him.

Again, she felt like a schoolgirl anytime her crush said her name. His legs were as in Café du Monde, stretched out in front and crossed at the ankles. Angelina sat upright, rigid, self-conscious, and aware of how she'd been staring at him. She adjusted her shorts, folding and unfolding the hemmed edges. He'd said not a word since they'd entered Jackson Square.

He looked over at Angelina suddenly with his gray eyes, and she felt her breath hitch in her throat for a split second.

"How are you feeling, Dr. Arbonne?"

"Curious."

"I'd like to be completely honest with you, in our relationship, for as long as it may last."

She swallowed hard. "More curious." Now it was a relationship? Thirty minutes ago it was a predator/prey situation. *Maybe it still is.*

He smiled, his ruby red lips framing perfect white teeth. Completely entranced, Angelina fought the urge to lean over and kiss him.

"Dr. Arbonne, may I cook dinner for you later this evening, at my house? I would like to further discuss our relationship."

Yes! She hadn't had a date since she could remember, and she was already infatuated with this handsome stranger. A tiny voice in Angelina's head said something was slightly off about the whole encounter, but she couldn't pin it down, so she ignored it. Jude had mesmerized her, and she felt oddly at ease around him.

"I take it from your wide-eyed silence and smile that's a yes?"

"Oh yes, I'm sorry. Yes, that'll be fine."

"Lovely. I'll send my driver to pick you up about 7 p.m.?"

Oh, he has a driver?

Angelina chose a short black dress, strapless, that came up to mid-thigh. Feeling extra seductive and alluring, she paired the dress with strappy stilettos. Her dark chestnut hair was parted to the side, draping down her shoulders and back. Glancing in the mirror, she couldn't help but giggle. She looked more like a trophy wife from a reality show than herself. To add an extra punch, Angelina had applied smoky eyeshadow and just a drop of perfume, Chanel No. 5. *Classy and sassy.*

When she got downstairs, a man in a classic chauffeur's uniform was waiting for her at a car that could only be described as gangster fabulous. A black 1940 Packard 120 four-door sedan, this car was breathtaking in and of itself. Angelina recognized it instantly, only because her dad had been obsessed with classic cars. She'd kept some of his books after he'd passed, and he'd been particularly fascinated with cars from the 1930s and '40s. She also knew it was extremely pricey to keep a car like that in such pristine condition. *What exactly am I dealing with?*

The man in the chauffeur's uniform looked about eighty or so. Short, so short that his pants had been rolled up several inches and hemmed at the bottoms, creating a hoop of fabric around his ankles. His fluffy white hair stuck out underneath his hat, like the feathers on a newborn baby bird's head. His wrinkled cheeks and beaming smile were framed by large, wire-rimmed glasses. He was adorable, and charming in a little-old-man sort of way.

"Hello, ma'am. I'm Harold, I'll be your chauffeur this evening."

"Good evening, Harold. I'm Angelina. This is a mighty fine car you're driving. Have you worked for Jude long?"

"About forty years or so. He's a good man, Mr. Jude is."

Poor thing. He must have a touch of dementia. Jude couldn't have been much older than her, if even, and she had only just turned 35. *I hope he doesn't forget where we're going.*

They drove maybe thirty or forty minutes she estimated, until the car slowed in front of two massive iron gates. It was nearly sundown and she had no clue where they were. They hadn't passed many houses on the way, and there had been no subdivision signs or anything that would clue her in as to where Harold had driven her to.

"We've arrived at the Estate, ma'am," Harold said, reading the questions on her face. He tapped a small remote control attached to the roof of the car that she hadn't noticed until just now. The towering iron gates, shining and twisting like strands of black licorice in the headlights of the car, slowly swung open as Harold inched the car through them.

On either side of the driveway, massive live oak trees sprawled up towards the sky, their branches stretching out as if to support the stars above them. The Spanish moss swayed in the wind, like women dancing to some bayou song only they could hear. In the shadows, Angelina could make out the outlines of palm plants in the distance, and from the perfectly shaped shadows, what she could only assume was well-landscaped grounds.

Harold turned right on the driveway, beginning on a well-lit circular path. There were hanging lanterns on either side of the driveway, every eight feet or so. They were on wrought iron posts, reminding her of Victorian England, but really they fit in perfectly with the French Quarter. Small fleur-de-lis were caught inside the iron scrollwork on the tops of the posts, their little shadows barely visible against the bright lights from behind them.

As the car neared about a quarter of the circle, a massive house started to appear. It wasn't a traditional plantation style, like Angelina had been expecting here in the Deep South. It was more like an abstract plantation, modern combined with old to create a style unique to only Jude.

Where the massive white pillars should've been, wrought iron ones stood. Eight huge, sprawling pillars—each one at least eight feet around, etched with vines and ivy—supported the covered walkway the car was now pulling up into. On either side of the walkway were five enormous windows, at least two stories high. Looking through, Angelina noticed matching crystal chandeliers aligned central to each window, indeterminately bright that they illuminated their respective rooms, plus the driveway and hedges they had just passed. The car came to a stop, and Angelina watched Harold slowly walk around to open her door.

Angelina stepped out onto a cobblestoned walkway, immediately feeling like she hadn't left the French Quarter at all. The large, round iron pillars grew into regular-sized iron columns, which led through two glass doors into an almost solid glass room, like a Victorian conservatory, which doubled as a foyer. Only instead of Victorian, it was more along the lines of French Quarter chic. Iron veins with detailed decorations ran up the seams of the panes; tiny bugs and animals were hidden anywhere and everywhere she looked.

Below her feet, mother of pearl mosaics covered the floor, with swirls and random patterns of the shells arranged in coordinated chaos. To the sides and in front, various potted tropical plants were in the four corners of the foyer, with a copper fountain in the very middle. There was a solid white cat sitting on the side of the fountain, watching her silently. Angelina said 'hello' to him. He sized her up, assessing this new stranger in his home, before meowing back and jumping down to entwine himself between her legs.

She could've stayed in this room for hours, and she would've moved in and lived here if given the opportunity. It reminded her of the Crystal Palace in Madrid, which was everything she'd ever dreamed of, and far more luxurious than she'd ever been used to. Angelina was too busy staring at the glass ceiling to notice Jude, who had appeared from the other side of the fountain. "I see Harold got you here OK."

Her eyes traveled down from the ceiling to the man standing in front of her. He had changed into a more casual black turtleneck, with white pleated pants and the same shiny black shoes. All afternoon after he'd left her, Angelina had tried to tell herself that she'd been caught up in the moment. Surely he wasn't as handsome and stunning as she'd made him out to be, and he couldn't possibly look as good as she'd thought he had.

Her bottom lip quivered at the sight of him.

"You look … ravishing," Jude said, hanging on his last word. *I bet you could ravage me*, Angelina thought, before shaking the mental image out of her head, in case he somehow knew what she was thinking, even though her blushing cheeks betrayed her mind. She had never been the boy-hungry, desperate kind of girl and she wasn't going to start now. Even if this Adonis was standing here, with his smoldering eyes and cherry lips, practically begging her to make a move.

She tried to focus on something, anything else, instead of looking directly at him and rendering herself nearly speechless. "Jude ... this is *your* house?"

"Yes and no. Do I live here right now? Yes, in a room in the back. Will I live here for a long period of time? Probably not. Maybe. That all depends on ... circumstances."

He was growing more mysterious by the second, and Angelina was unaware of what to make of the situation. He stepped closer to her, and the smells of glorious herbs flowed around him and into the foyer. Garlic, rosemary, tarragon, marjoram, chives, all the greats now consumed the air around Angelina, and instinctively she reached a hand up to her stomach as it rumbled.

Jude grinned knowingly, and put his hand on her lower back, as he had done that afternoon. Tingles of electricity raced throughout Angelina's body. He opened the massive glass doors on the other side of the foyer, and led her into another smaller, darker type of foyer. This one had a hallway on either side, with a crimson red carpet, and gold wallpaper stretching up as high as the windows in the front had been. A series of ornate double doors lined the walls on the front sides of the house, as if to cater to large groups.

"Ballrooms," Jude said, following her gaze.

Just then, Angelina heard a scuffle to her left and turned her head in response. A short young man, in his early to mid-twenties, popped out of a door. He was carrying a stack of papers which fluttered to the ground as he tripped on the carpet. He had a mop of deep-red curls and was dressed much plainer than Jude, in ripped jeans and a washed-out band T-shirt. He certainly didn't fit into the surroundings.

"Dr. Arbonne, this is John Keats. He's my … roommate."

"Oh! Just like the famous poet! Please, call me Angelina." She'd always loved reading Keats' poetry.

John stopped and looked at her, rudely rolling his eyes. "Sure, just like the famous poet." He muttered something under his breath and scurried on his way.

"Did I offend him somehow? I didn't mean to," she said apologetically.

Jude laughed hesitantly. "Don't mind him, he's having a bad day. Tortured artist, and all that," he said, as he continued guiding her through the house.

They entered another giant room, two stories high with light olive-green walls. This one, which Angelina guessed was supposed to be like a living or common room, was more like a hotel lobby. There were multiple couches and recliners arranged into several separate seating areas, but there was enough room that they could easily be rearranged into a giant circle if need be.

There was another greenhouse-type room along the back wall, with a shorter ceiling. Inside it were several glass-top tables and some fancy-looking chairs, probably enough to seat fifteen to twenty people. Angelina wondered exactly how much entertaining Jude must do to have a place like this.

Along the left wall was a row of bookcases each at least ten feet high, a deep, rich cherry finish and glass doors on all of them. Directly above them and running around all four walls were rows of paned glass windows, to let in the natural light throughout the day. On the wall to the right of Angelina hung an enormous painting which she recognized immediately. She darted past the couches and furniture to take a closer look.

"*Destruction* by Thomas Cole! He's practically a master! The burning of the Library of Alexandria was such a tragic loss for humankind."

"It was. It really was. I was there, but there was nothing I could do," Jude said reflectively. This was not the first odd thing she'd heard today since meeting Jude. Angelina tried to correct him, in order to make sure she herself wasn't going crazy.

"It happened in 48 BC. You mean you've been to the archaeological site?" Perhaps this was how he'd been able to follow her around the globe. If Jude, too, was in the archaeological field, they would have all sorts of acquaintances and work sites in common. Still, though, Angelina was certain if she'd crossed *him* at work, she would've remembered. Archaeologists didn't frequently look like they'd walked straight out of a magazine photoshoot. She decided this was the most logical explanation, and continued talking.

"That's really, really neat! That's one thing I'm going to try and focus on, seeing more places like that on my bucket list." Jude still hadn't responded to any of her comments, and Angelina could feel herself starting to take over the conversation. She stopped talking and looked up at the painting.

"How do you like your steak cooked? And would you like coffee?" Jude asked, changing the subject and diverting her attention from the painting.

"Medium well; some pink is fine as long as there's some char on the outside. Coffee and water, please." She followed him through a door beside the bookcases, and was again astonished at the room she had entered. It was a giant kitchen, fit for a television cooking show.

A huge island, twelve feet long if not more, with a white marble top sat in the middle, with about eight barstools on the walkway side and two separate racks of copper pots hanging over it. The pots were completely unmarred, like they'd never been used at all. A twelve-range burner and gas oven combo, another stacked oven, at least thirty feet of white marble counterspace, and a sink nearly large enough to take a bath in all lay before her.

"Jude! Is this seriously your home?" He chuckled at her shock and awe.

"I'm going to sell it, or rent it out, I haven't decided yet. I'm in real estate, I have properties, many properties like this all over the world. I rent most of them out, for hotels, conferences, bed and breakfasts, bachelor parties, work retreats, you name it. This one isn't quite finished yet; when it is then I'll decide what's next."

"Oh. Then you're not also an archaeologist?"
Angelina asked, quickly rerouting her brain to figure
out a new alternative.

Jude turned to her. "No, I'm in real estate."
Then, reading her quizzical expression, he answered,
"My job allows me to travel all over the world. I have
properties everywhere." The tension in her forehead
eased up a bit.

He patted the last two barstools at the marble
island, and Angelina noticed that two place settings
had already been fixed next to them. She walked over,
secretly pleased that the heels she'd chosen to wear
would allow her to gracefully slide onto the high
barstool, rather than flap around awkwardly and wiggle
onto it like a fish out of water.

Jude disappeared behind the island only to
return a second later with a beautifully plated meal.
Filet mignon, lightly charred, surrounded by grilled
and seasoned asparagus and roasted potatoes sat
before her. The aromas of the potatoes, meat, and
herbs surrounded her, making her mouth water.
Looking at Jude's plate, he had portioned himself two
rare filets. Completely, straight-out-of-the-refrigerator,

rare. He had given himself two pieces of asparagus and about four cubes of roasted potatoes.

"Do you not like potatoes? You really didn't have to go through all this trouble for me, I'm not picky. It does smell amazing, though."

"I try to stay away from carbs in general. I don't like how they make me feel. I do make some wicked, glorious roasted potatoes, so I may eat a few more," he said, grinning as he cut into his cold beef. His confidence in his culinary skills was adorable, and Angelina smiled to herself.

Taking a sip of her coffee, she realized that she hadn't put any sugar or creamer in it, and there was none sitting out anywhere that she could see. Angelina gracefully slid out of her chair, the pointy heels making stable contact with the floor. *Nailed it.*

"Is everything OK?" Jude asked.

"Oh, everything is perfect, I just need some creamer is all. Can I get you anything while I'm up?" She was at the refrigerator door before he could stop her. Angelina didn't hear him say anything. She hadn't even heard his chair move, but suddenly Jude was directly behind her.

She smiled at him. "It's OK, I can get it. You've gone to enough trouble." His gray eyes sparkled. They looked lighter now while he was standing beside the white marble surface.

Angelina opened the refrigerator door and stood there searching. Inside, there was almost nothing but packs of filet mignon. Fifteen, maybe twenty packs, and they all looked fresh. For a second, she thought maybe she'd accidentally opened the freezer. She opened the second door. The other side was definitely the freezer, but there was nothing inside but a bag of ice. *Weeeeird.* "Um, if you don't have milk or sugar it's totally fine."

"It's actually just down at the bottom," Jude said from behind her. His nearness sent shivers down her spine, and she became hyperaware of every movement he was making. Though everything about all of this was strange, Angelina couldn't help but be turned on. He wrapped his arm around her waist for support and reached all the way down to the bottom of the door to pick up a single serving bottle of milk. Not a gallon, not a half gallon, but a single serving like you'd get in a convenience store to wash a donut down. That was the most he had, and that was the only other thing in the entire refrigerator, besides a field's worth of cow. He raised himself back up, squeezing her tighter to him for support as he did so. Angelina was transfixed by his cherry lips as he said, "Help yourself." *Who knew milk could be so sexy?*

Chapter Four

Jude didn't eat any more potatoes. In fact, he only ate one or two of the cubes he'd so delicately arranged on his plate. He did, however, eat both of the cold filet mignons before Angelina had finished her plate. "I'll be right back," he whispered in her ear, before walking away.

She sat there for a few minutes, finishing her food. It really was quite delicious. He knew his way around the kitchen, so it was odd that he'd gone to so much trouble for something he wasn't even going to eat. She hoped he hadn't gone to all that trouble for her. She wasn't really a fancy person and she'd never needed the pomp and circumstance of dating and all that came with it. Maybe that's why she never dated.

Plus, she was horrible at flirting, and it didn't matter anyway. In between degrees and globetrotting careers, there had only ever been a small handful of men that she'd deemed worthy of her time and effort. But Jude? She'd only known him a few hours, but he just might be worth including in her plans.

Jude was taking too long. Maybe the bathroom, if that's where he'd even gone, was on the other side of this palace. Angelina decided to get up and explore. Along the whole back length of the building, or what she assumed was the whole length, was a glass patio overlooking the backyard. The portion of the patio visible in the great room had continued onto the kitchen, to as far as she could see on the other side.

Originally, it looked like there were just enough tables and chairs for maybe twenty people, but now she saw there was high-end patio furniture in the extended sections as well. This truly was a conference center, or a retreat center. She imagined a botanist conference or something similar, a group of people who really felt at home in earth's natural glories.

It was pitch-black outside, but Angelina decided the backyard must be just as manicured as the front lawn appeared to be. There were two glass doors leading outside to another patio, dimly lit in the moonlight. She opened one of the doors and then closed it almost as quickly. The night's humidity raced in as a blast of cold air behind her rushed out. She decided not to irritate any of the mosquitos that were undoubtedly looking in at her with salivating jaws.

Jude appeared again, just as she was turning around to go back to the kitchen. "Dr. Arbonne, shall we dance?" He led her back towards the front of the building. Angelina couldn't help but be drawn in to the bookcases when they walked past them. She hadn't stopped to read the titles earlier, but now she noticed that nothing in the last one hundred years or so particularly stood out. Ancient and dusty, but in perfect condition, instinctively she knew these were all rare and highly valuable first editions. *Dracula, Frankenstein, On the Origin of Species, Don Quixote*. Old, familiar friends all reached out to her as Jude and Angelina glided past.

They turned down the red-carpeted hallway and entered through the first of three sets of large, ornately decorated double doors into one of the giant ballrooms she had seen from the car. Angelina's eyes adjusted to the dim lighting, while Jude took her hand and led her to the middle of the ballroom.

The chandeliers were turned down, faintly glowing orbs of light stretched throughout the room.

There were candelabras placed around, and classical music was playing softly. Golden walls and golden-marbled floors stretched before her. Lining the wall with the doors were large gilded mirrors, as high as the ceilings. Angelina felt like she had stepped into the Hall of Mirrors at Versailles. And she might've been completely fooled except that in the far-off distance, there was a pile of buckets, ladders, and various cans of paint and sponges with a drop cloth thrown over to try and disguise them.

"These rooms are almost finished, just a few more details," Jude said, following her gaze. "Dr. Arbonne, please forgive me. It's been quite some time since I've dated anyone and I seem to be a little bit out of practice." Jude lightly wrapped his arm around her waist and pulled her into him. They began slowly swaying to the music.

"It's all right, I'm out of practice, too. You should know, this isn't like me. I don't usually date and I *never* go to someone's house that I've only just met."

Jude smiled. "Dr. Arbonne—"

"Please, call me Angelina."

"Angelina, if at any time you feel threatened or

unsafe, Harold is waiting outside to take you back to your apartment. I want you to feel comfortable, relaxed, and I want to be completely honest with you." He'd mentioned that earlier in the day, how honest he wanted to be with her. *Odd.*

"You keep saying that. What deep, dark secret are you hiding? That you're not really a millionaire and you broke into this house? I have to say, I might be willing to play along with that just for one night." Angelina laughed, but Jude didn't. He stared at her with those gray eyes, the tiny reflections of the candelabras creating golden flecks in them. Her arm was draped around his shoulders as they danced, and she could feel his muscles tense up. His brow creased as he let out a sigh. Whatever it was, he was deeply troubled by it and thought she probably would be, too.

Angelina felt comfortable with him, maybe too comfortable, and she rested her head on his shoulder to calm his silence, her body snuggling into his. His tension eased, and he laid his head against hers. Finally, he spoke, stopping to look at her as the words left his beautiful cherry lips.

"Angelina, there's much that I need to tell you. So much that I want to share with you." He was nothing if not dramatic. "I need you to be open, to understand everything I'm about to say. There's no easy way to say any of it. Please just promise me that you'll think about it before you answer, OK?"

"I promise," she said, meeting his intense gaze. He looked like he might break down and cry.

"I've been married twice. I've been divorced twice." *That's all?* "I chose wrong, very wrong. I needed someone to share in this life with me, to help me carry my burdens. The first was a queen, she was radiant and beautiful. She was brilliant, but she was also rude and spiteful. Single-handedly the most self-absorbed woman I've ever met in my life. We were married for thirty years. We still fight all the time and I truly hate her. I've made many mistakes, Angelina, and I am truly sorry."

Hold up, thirty years to a queen? Angelina was starting to think maybe Jude was high on a little more than life, and she certainly didn't have time for that. She subconsciously took a tiny step back and moved her arm down just an inch from where it had been across his shoulders. Jude noticed the subtle change in her demeanor, a trace of panic rising in his voice. "Don't go, Angelina, please hear me out.

"My second wife and I were only married for

two years. She was never in love with me, she was just using me. I didn't know that or I wouldn't have married her. When the love of her life was murdered, we had only been wed just over a year. It was too much for her to bear. I thought she was in love with me, but she admitted that she never had been. She wanted to change him, spend the rest of her life with him, which was the only reason why she agreed to marry me." *That made no sense at all.*

Angelina was about ready to go home at this point. She wasn't going to put up with drugs or crazy, no matter how shiny the wrapping paper was.

"Angelina, I don't mean to unload all my baggage on you, but I have to tell you that to make you understand everything else. That's why I followed you. I had to make sure you were different, that you were better than them."

"Wait. How long did you follow me? None of this makes any sense at all."

"Three years."

"*What?!* Three years?!" She'd only remembered seeing him several times in the *last year.* More perplexed, and even more keenly aware of how bad her stilettos were hurting her feet, Angelina reached down, whipped them off, and ran out of the ballroom to sit down. She found a well-cushioned couch, front and center of Cole's painting. Jude followed close behind her, sitting on a chair that was a good distance away, to give her space. Angelina's mind was spinning. She'd thought maybe the last several encounters had been coincidences at most. In her heart of hearts, she hadn't really believed he *was* actually following her.

"Why did you follow me for three years? Three years! Explain yourself! Are you really a stalker? Why am I here?" She was practically shrieking. He raised his hands up in surrender, and lowered his voice to an apologetic level.

"Angelina, please, calm down. Just hear me out. If you'd like to leave after I've finished, you can. You're under no obligation to stay here. I just want you to be comfortable."

"Answer the question, Jude," she said harshly, cutting him in half with her tone of voice. If looks could kill, that would've been a throat punch to him.

"I followed you for three years because I had to make sure you were a good person, a deserving person. I want to marry you, Angelina," he said, instantly ruffling his brow and shaking his head. Backtracking, he continued. "I mean I want to date you as well, but it's all or nothing. There's no tactile way to say this, so I'll just say it …"

He paused, hesitantly watching her. Angelina nudged her eyebrows up to urge him to continue.

"I'm a vampire."

"No, you're not. I'm not stupid. Do you think I'm stupid, Jude?"

"No, you're not stupid. I am a vampire."

"No, you're not! I met you in the sunlight. You drink coffee, not blood. You eat filet mignons, albeit cold and rare, which is freaky, but still, you ate them. You're just a ferociously attractive, wealthy weirdo who has nothing to do but stalk women all over the world."

"All of your preconceived notions are just myths. Put forth by myself and a dear friend several centuries ago to distract from our true nature. You don't believe me because his writing was widely accepted as truth. He was brilliant."

"Now you're telling me that Bram Stoker is

your best friend, and you expect me to believe that? I guess John Keats was the real John Keats, too?"

"Was one of my dear friends, yes. He didn't want me to turn him. And, yes, he was the real John Keats."

"Are there others?" Angelina was intrigued enough to go down the rabbit hole now, to indulge in his brand of insanity for a few minutes longer. Jude still didn't exactly feel threatening in any sort of way. Despite what he was saying, his passive demeanor said otherwise.

"Yes, there are. There are many others. In fact, our annual Society Convention will be held here the week after next. I'd like you to attend."

Angelina burst out laughing. "You're telling me you're a twice divorced vampire king who holds annual vampire conventions? Do you put that on your business cards? *Now* I've heard it all! What do you discuss? Blood types? The latest in dentistry?" She worked herself up into a maniacal laughter with occasional snorting, only half-believing the conversation she was having right now.

Jude smiled, relieved that she was starting to

relax, if even just a miniscule amount. "No, we discuss world events, politics, human and immortal rights, how we can influence, who we should influence, that type of thing. I am the king, and I need a new queen. I would like you to be my queen, Angelina."

Wide-eyed, Angelina just stared at him. She had the passing thought that maybe she'd gotten stuck in a really bad soap opera, which had to be the reason why Jude was out-of-this-world insanely attractive. She lowered her head into her hands, cradling the migraine that was forming between her temples and trying to remember if she'd ever signed up to be on any cheesy reality shows.

"Did I say too much? I didn't mean to scare you. I'm so sorry. That was never my intention. I'm really not good at dating and I tried to be ever so careful this time. I really wanted to get it right. If you'd like to leave, Harold can take you home. If you'd like to stay, there's plenty of extra bedrooms for you to choose from and Harold can drive you home in the morning."

Jude's voice was pleading, begging her to forgive him for all of the events and actions he felt he'd done wrong. The sadness in his voice, like he'd already given up, possessed her thoughts and sympathy. Angelina looked up at him. He was perched on the edge of his chair, the sorrow from his anguished years spread across his beautiful face. His eyes, gray diamonds, sparkled behind his sea of grief. Then the tears rolled down his cheeks. Her heart softened towards him instantly.

She didn't know vampires cried.

Chapter Five

It was nearly midnight when Angelina decided to take him up on his offer of a room. Ever cautious, she picked a room on the opposite side of the palace from Jude's room to make herself feel more secure.

On the second floor, this room was unfinished as well, but only just so. The smell of new paint lingered in the air, maybe a few weeks old at most. The ceiling was high, with gilded gold and white trim. The walls were a light salmon color, with gold accents. There was no carpet in this room, only a giant pink and mint green rug spanning nearly the entire floor. It was intricately detailed and certainly must've cost a fortune.

There was a huge white canopy bed in the middle, with an elaborately laced mosquito net draped over it. The lace was pretty, but more fitting to be a tablecloth in a tea room. It was a little too old and gaudy for Angelina's taste. The decorator should've just stopped at the canopy bed and moved on, instead of beating a dead horse.

Additionally, there was a white and gold vanity, armoire, and several marble side tables supporting antique lamps. The room was in the back corner of the mansion, with tall cathedral windows on two sides to let in the morning sun when it came. Not a good touch to a room that looked like a jewelry box had vomited inside of it.

The mattress was fluffy and comfortable at least, and Angelina was asleep before she could even give a second thought to anything Jude had said or what she was going to do about it.

The next morning, she didn't have time to plan anything, either. Angelina awoke to the sun beaming straight into her face, accompanied by a horrible shrieking sound coming from the downstairs kitchen area. She opened the door and stuck her head out, trying to figure out what was going on. A man's voice that sounded like Jude's echoed throughout the hallways, and something that sounded more like a banshee than an actual woman castigated him mercilessly.

"I hope you're happy! I can't even get my stockings because you can't keep your kidney buster to yourself! Those are my special stockings!"

"Shut up! Shut UP! You bumbling twat! No wonder everyone hates you! Your own husband hates you! I haven't so much as looked at anyone in the last fifty years, let alone dated anyone! Not that it's any of your business anyway, you repulsive shrew! You always dress like a prostitute, I'm sure you've got a spare pair shoved up your—!"

Angelina quietly crept to the top of the stairs, trying to hear more. A third, deeper voice interrupted them. "All right, everyone, let's calm down. You can get them later. You do have several extra, more than suitable, pairs."

"You're just going to let him talk to me like that, Flynny?! I'm your *wife*!" The banshee was somehow able to whine and scream at the same time.

"And I can undoubtedly tell you, he is sorry about that!" Jude said.

"One of these days, I'm going to shove my foot so far up your ass, I'll kick your fangs out! Let's go!"

"We'll see you at the Convention. Have a nice day, Jude," the man with the deeper voice said.

From where she was standing, Angelina saw a tall, older, and dashingly handsome man escorting out a short, petite woman with white curls piled on top of her head. Angelina thought the man looked vaguely familiar, but she couldn't place how she knew him. Flynny, as he'd been called, was practically steering his wife out the door before she could cause any more of a scene.

The woman's face was turned halfway towards Jude, probably sneering at or cursing him, if not both. She was dressed in a silver flapper dress, with silver, sparkly heels to match, sans stockings. Even from Angelina's distance, she could see that the woman was wearing enough eyeshadow to cover a family of raccoons. Jude was right—whoever she was, she did look like a lady of the night. Angelina had definitely heard her use the word "fangs," though, and all of a sudden, she was snapped back into her present situation.

She lightly padded down the stairs when she

heard the glass door to the foyer slam in the distance. Jude was standing on the outside patio, his back to the mansion. The aroma of coffee told her it was already brewed. Giving herself an extra moment to compose her thoughts, she poured both of them a cup, leaving his black, how she knew he preferred it.

Opening the glass doors, she couldn't help but notice how defeated Jude looked. Wearing blue pajama pants and a plain blue T-shirt, his shoulders were slumped and his head was hanging down a little. He'd seemed confident yesterday, suave and sure of everything. He'd even said he was the king of the vampires, whatever that meant. He didn't look like a king now. Past the patio and down the hill, the river churned, the sound of its rushing waves possessive over the silence of its surroundings.

Angelina was still in her black dress, the only outfit she had with her. She had considered asking for a T-shirt or something to sleep in last night. Now she was glad she hadn't. The banshee might've gotten even more pissed.

"Good morning," she said, as she handed him the coffee.

"Is it?" Jude replied, the same sadness from last

night still on his face. His wavy black hair wasn't slicked back anymore, it was all messy and wild like an artist in the middle of a creative streak. It made him look even sexier than he had done yesterday at Café du Monde. As if that were possible.

"Who was that stark raving lunatic?" Angelina asked lightly, trying to make him smile.

"My first wife. I told you, we hate each other. I really mean that."

"She seems like an absolute nightmare. And I'm guessing I picked her room to sleep in? I'm sorry I caused you any trouble, Jude."

"No, really, it's fine. She doesn't even live here. I haven't seen her since the last Society Convention. She just has a knack for showing up and ruining my day at the most inopportune times. I think she must have a censor installed somewhere in the house that alerts her in case I'm in any type of good mood, so she can drop in and ruin it."

"But she has her own room here?"

"No, not really. She insisted on designing her own room. She's never even slept in that bed. I didn't even know she had left anything here. She pushed me until she got to design the ballrooms, too. They look much nicer than the bedroom, but every time I walk in there, I have to resist the urge to shatter a mirror."

Now that it was daylight, Angelina looked more closely at the rest of the mansion. The patio was lined with big, earth-toned stones, like a riverbed, and had a matching waist-high wall running around it as well. She turned around to sit down on the wall, and Jude sat down beside her. Close, but not too close. The banshee had torn his confidence down in one swift blow.

Angelina decided to build him back up.

"I think you need to start over. From the beginning. Let's start with why you've been following me for three years and add the details in as we go. Does that sound OK? My instincts tell me you're a good man, Jude. I'm willing to listen to what you have to say."

Jude's face lightened, and he smiled shyly.

"Yesterday, with the waitress, that was when I decided it was time we should meet."

She thought back but couldn't remember. "You mean, when I said I didn't want beignets?"

Jude chuckled. "No, when you tipped her after she spilled sugar all over you. She wasn't even your waitress. You're kind, and good. I've tried to create an organization to influence a better world, and I need that in my partner. Obviously, I've messed up a few times, but a lot of times I got it right.

"I first saw you on TV, on some telethon. You were advocating for donating to children in poverty. They kept showing clips of you in a makeshift hut, handing out water bottles, handing out food rations, helping the children. I ran a search for you online, saw all you'd accomplished. When I looked back at the screen, you were staring at me, through the camera. Your emerald green eyes, something about them made me think that you were going to be the one."

"I remember that. We'd been at a dig site, and realized the conditions that surrounded it. My colleagues and I took it upon ourselves to try and bring awareness to the issues of the people living there. It was only right that after we scrounged around in their land that we should use our resources to try and get wells built for towns that didn't have any running water. Just a few days later, an anonymous donation of $1.5 million came in. We were able to help out quite a few villages with that." Angelina stopped, the realization hitting her. She turned her body inward towards him, subconsciously inviting him into her space. "Wait. Was that you?"

"It was," he said. Hearing the humility in his voice, she could've kissed him right then and there.

"Jude, thank you so much. I don't know what to say."

"I've come to understand that I'd do anything for you, Angelina."

She stood up, sitting her coffee cup down on the wall. She held her hands out to him. "I don't think we finished our dance last night."

"There's no music," Jude said, suppressing a cheesy grin as he wrapped his arms around her waist.

Angelina draped both her arms over his shoulders and ran her hands through his ruffled hair. "We'll just use the sounds from the river."

Chapter Six

They danced and swayed to the rhythm of the water, twirling and box-stepping, fox-trotting and tangoing the day away. Jude was in his pajamas, Angelina in her black dress, the both of them barefoot on the river-stoned patio.

The daylight had long given up the rest of the night's secrets. Massive live oak trees Angelina hadn't seen in the darkness now shaded the patio and the entire upper backyard. Emerging from the river-stoned wall were stone steps connecting to a path leading directly down to the river.

Her head was resting on his chest when she realized they hadn't talked any vampire business in several hours. "Jude?" His handsome face was tender and soft as their eyes met. Angelina once again fought the urge to kiss him.

"Can I see your fangs?"

Jude laughed, his eyes twinkling before he parted his cherry lips. Two little white pointed teeth slowly appeared. They were adorable and almost normal-looking. Even if he'd had them out before, they would've been nearly unnoticeable. Anyone unaware would've thought they were slightly pointy, regular teeth.

Angelina giggled. "Oh wow, that's not what I expected at all!"

"Do you believe me now, that I am what I say I am?"

"You're definitely something all right, but I'm not sure what name I'm going to give it yet." She paused, lost in her thoughts on the subject. "Are you going to bite me?" If he was indeed a vampire, he'd had more than plenty of opportunities to munch on her neck if he'd wanted to.

"No, we don't feed on human blood. That's another myth. We have a very limited diet, or I do at least. I only eat filet mignons and drink black coffee. I try to keep my system purified. It makes me feel better health-wise, and I like to set an example.

"Others eat less restricted diets. My ex-wife, for example, loves bonbons, even though they make her wretchedly bloated. We don't process any foods normally. It gets easier over time to manage our diets, but we still have to be careful."

"Are you actually dead? I'm fascinated to know how all of this works. How many others are there like you?" Her mind was racing with questions she'd always assumed she'd known the answers to. Had the classic vampire stories everyone had grown up with had just been smoke and mirrors all along?

The noonday sun was starting to disregard the live oaks keeping it at bay. Angelina could feel the sun zeroing in on the black fabric of her dress. "Do you mind if we find a more shaded spot?" Jude took her hand and guided her down to one of the trees to a double swing, wide enough for two, attached to one of the sprawling branches. They sat down, letting the wind from the river designate their movements.

"To answer your first question, I suppose I'm kind of dead. I'm not fully alive, and I'm not fully deceased."

"Are you a zombie?"

Jude laughed and wrinkled his nose, pretending to be offended. "No. Zombies are completely dead and can't think for themselves. Plus, they don't exist, silly goose." He nudged her shoulder with his before continuing.

"We have a heartbeat, but only a heart beat. As in, one per day. Our aging is dramatically slowed down. That's how we can still process some foods. I don't know why I was created, but I have to believe that I wasn't created to be a monster. I have used my life to make more like me, people better than me. People who were prominent figures and authorities who did good in the world, inspired people and helped them, who could continue to influence moral law and human decency. I feel that was my original, intended purpose."

Angelina was becoming curiouser and curiouser. "You're the original vampire? Who created you? Where were you born? Who were your parents? Did you save them, too?"

"I don't know who created me. I don't remember much, just pieces here and there. I think the man who made me was a scientist or doctor of some sort. I can remember that I was nearly dead before he turned me." He got quiet, a solemn expression on his handsome face.

"I only have flashes of my parents. They were farmers, maybe? I really don't remember much of my life before. I was a soldier; I know that from my scars and wounds. Occasionally, I'll have a flashback or nightmare, usually about being in a battle I can't much recall. I always end up on the stone slab with the scientist looking over me.

"And I don't know if I was the original. As far as I'm aware, only my line exists in the world. But if I've learned anything, it's that anything is indeed possible."

It was strange, she did believe him, yet he was nothing like she would've imagined or expected the king of the vampires to be. Even from yesterday, he went from being this ethereal and complicated man to a humble and even semi-remorseful soul who was beating himself up over not having been a better vampire. He was still so inexplicably … human, even after living as long as he had and having seen everything he'd seen.

"Are you the king because you're the first, or do you hold elections and appointments? How does the vampire patriarchy work?" she asked. She had to know if there was a vampire government.

"It's not a patriarchy, far from it. It's really a bureaucracy, I would say. I've tried to create beings who are better, smarter, more influential than I. To give us a better name. I royally messed up with my first two wives, rose-colored glasses and all that, but everyone else I've done pretty good with. We hold the Convention every year. Really my biggest role is to supply the venue—which will be here this year—give an opening and closing speech, and welcome any new vampires.

"Anne handles the rest. She's brilliant, and irrationally organized. It's mind-blowing, really. Throughout the year, she delegates me the Turn Requests, out of respect for my seniority. If she ever wanted to do them, I have complete trust in her judgment and ability. Otherwise, I'm free to continue to work in real estate without having to worry about what the community is doing."

"Who is Anne? One of your ex-wives?"

"Oh goodness, no. She was only fifteen when I turned her." He wrinkled his nose as if she'd offended him, before remembering that all of this was new to her. "She's the vice president of the Society. She organizes everything from her home in New Zealand. John, who you met earlier, is her assistant and writes the monthly newsletters."

Angelina smiled at the thought. A vampire newsletter was something she hadn't heard of before, either. "What's a Turn Request? Is it what I think it is?" She was trying to take a crash course on a whole subculture that she never knew existed.

"Yes, probably. All of my line has the ability to turn any warm-blooded creature. They have to ask their permission, of course. We have a moral code that we uphold, we never turn anyone that doesn't want to be turned. That's just polite. A Turn Request is sent in to me, nowadays through forwarded emails from Anne. It's a formal agreement between the two parties, saying that they've discussed the options and the living would like to be turned. They send in a copy of their résumé as well, listing their achievements and how they hope to change the world with their future ambitions."

"Wow. That all sounds so ... organized. I had no idea that vampires were so regulated. What happens if they turn someone without their approval or yours?"

"That's Anne for you. No one has ever turned anyone without their permission, or without my permission. Everyone in my line is linked to me; each one could not be made had I not ventured to make more than myself. They respect my blood. We have to keep our secrecy. Can you imagine if everyone suddenly wanted to be immortal? How exhausting that would be! Anyone that gets turned, you're going to literally have to see for the rest of your life. Even if it's only once a year, you can still end up fighting."

"Can you manipulate normal people, hypnotize them with your eyes? Make them want to turn?" she had to ask. The feelings she'd been having since she'd met Jude were rare for her. Now, Angelina wondered if her feelings were based in reality or some extension of an alchemical trance.

Jude laughed a deep, hearty laugh. "No, that's another myth. We are skilled at reading people and predicting behaviors. We've been around so many people collectively throughout the centuries, it's only natural that we should be good at reading them, too. I still question my abilities, and I have to test them out.

"For example, yesterday. You allowed me to lead you around the entirety of Jackson Square, trusting of the intentions of a complete stranger who you knew to be following you. Still, you left the safety of the café and the crowd, and came with me. You let me guide you to the park, in the public, yet alone, even though you would've been right to question my behavior. That is how I knew you would feel safe enough to trust me if I invited you to dinner." *Clever little trick.*

He was right, though. She *did* trust him, despite all the weirdness she'd experienced. The sun was starting to set, and she knew she had to be back at work the next day. "Jude, this has really been … eye-opening. I've honestly had a really good time. I do need to be going, though; I have to go back to work tomorrow."

Jude sighed and nodded slowly, and she got the feeling these last two days had gone nothing like he'd imagined. His shoulders dropped slightly, a returning hint of the defeated man she'd seen that morning. Maybe he'd perceived himself as someone who could sweep her off her feet instantaneously with his suave charm and allure. He'd done a pretty fantastic job to start with, but Angelina wasn't going to give her heart away to someone she'd only known for two days. Not yet anyway. Jude might be a king, but he was still a man who would have to win her heart.

An extremely handsome, normal, vampire man.

Would she see him again? Probably, if she were a betting woman. They walked, hand in hand, through the mansion and outside to the Packard. He opened its door for her as she turned to face him. "One more question for now. I really have to ask."

"Go ahead, Dr. Arbonne."

"Can you fly? Like the vampires in the movies? If you were following me, you would be able to fly, right?"

Jude smiled, his pouty red lips looking irresistible.

"No, I have my own private jet. If I've been exercising, I can walk really fast, though." He demonstrated by walking around the car faster than Angelina could take a breath. "That's why I keep my system pure. If I eat junk food, it slows me down and I have to walk at a normal pace."

She nodded in understanding. *Fascinating. A vampire who worries about physical fitness.*

"Will I see you again, Jude?" she asked, reaching to hold his hands in hers. A brief flash of shock registered across his face.

"Do you *want* to see me again, Angelina?" He had not officially asked her if she wanted to be turned, but he had said he wanted to marry her. That was basically the same thing, right? Maybe he'd said more than he meant to, and had meant to save that proposal for later. Maybe that's why she got the impression he felt as if he'd blown the whole date. Angelina couldn't help but feel pity for him. It had been hard enough for her to find a decent companion in her adult life, and this poor guy had been trying for centuries.

"I would. I had a really nice ... and strange, time, but I would like to get to know you better." She leaned up to kiss him on his cheek, his surprisingly soft beard brushing against her face.

Jude smiled broadly. He hadn't looked happier in the whole two days she'd known him.

"Then you shall see me again, Dr. Arbonne." And with that, he raised her hands to his lips and kissed them softly, closing his eyes as he did so. A rush of adrenaline coursed through her body.

Chapter Seven

A loud screech from a peacock resounded somewhere in the distance as Harold inched out of the covered walkway. Seeing everything illuminated clearly, Angelina looked around at her surroundings. Jude really had outdone himself with his landscaping decisions. The well-manicured lawn looked more like a tropical resort than a New Orleans plantation home. It was definitely not a plantation-style structure.

Angelina had been bouncing around in her head what to actually call it—a home, a building, a resort, a venue, a mansion, a palace. None seemed to fit, and all seemed to fit. She decided to classify it as "palatial venue." Classification was important, it always had been. As a doctor, an archaeologist, and a researcher, you're nothing if you don't know what you're talking about. The most technical and specific of terms can make all the difference.

As they started back down the other side of the rounded driveway, she noticed something else she hadn't seen the night before. In the middle of the circled driveway was a pristinely manicured landscape of brightly colored lilies and various flowers. In the middle was a sculpture. She knew the subject immediately, and the understanding behind it resounded through her body and caused goosebumps.

Atlas was kneeling down, the weight of the world on his shoulders. His face and body appeared young and fit, similar to Michelangelo's *David*, rather than the old man she was more accustomed to associating with the Greek god. The world on his shoulders, a deep green patina, was hollowed out where the water should be, exposing only the continents. Actual water washed over from an unseen fountain at the top, filling in its respective areas. It collected into a pool below the platform Atlas was sitting on. Around the pool were detailed, sculpted embellishments, reminding her very much of the Trevi Fountain in Rome.

Harold, noticing her awe from the rearview mirror, said, "Ah yes! Mr. Salvi sculpted that! He didn't get to finish the other one, so he made this one extra nice!" *The* Salvi? The one who had supposedly died before ever finishing the actual Trevi Fountain? *What had I gotten myself into exactly?*

The shadows from the previous night also made themselves known as Harold drove. On either side, beneath the live oak trees, the driveway was aligned with azalea bushes as large as hay bales, their bright, fuchsia-covered blooms popping out like floral confetti. Arranged behind them, as if to give the illusion of being a little closer to the beach than the marshland, were Chinese fan palms among other spiky plants, sticking out like dozens of jittering jazz hands.

Angelina made sure to keep track of where they were and how far they'd come. While taking note of landmarks and road signs, she glanced up towards Harold. The silver chrome of the dashboard amenities reflected the sunlight onto his fragile and whitened face, making him appear even more ghostlike. He was driving with his black leather-gloved hands in the ten and two position, checking all his mirrors every twenty seconds or so. He was incredibly alert for such a little old man. A content smile lay across his face.

"Harold, can I ask you something?"

"Yes, ma'am, go right ahead."

She opened her mouth to speak and realized she'd backed herself into a corner. It was a weird subject to bring up—how should one even mention it? What if Harold didn't know? Surely he did; he'd said he'd worked for Jude for years.

"Harold, um … are you … did Jude ever …"

"No, ma'am, and yes, ma'am, he did." He read her thoughts, as if this wasn't the first time he'd had to answer these same questions.

"Mr. Jude took me in after my wife and daughter died in a car wreck. I was real depressed for a while, and I got fired from my job because of it. I was mighty down on my luck when Mr. Jude found me. He offered to turn me, but it just didn't seem like a thing I should do, living an eternity without them.

"Mr. Jude's been right good to me, loyal. Can't say the same for every job or boss. So, I take care of Mr. Jude 'til it's my time to go, like he's taken care of me. He's a real good man, that's what he is. Mr. Jude is the kindest, most respectable person I know. I've seen him help so many people with so many things."

"That's good to know, Harold. Thank you for telling me. I … I'm really sorry about your family. My parents died in a car crash when I was young, too. I know how lonely it can be."

"Yes, ma'am. It was lonely for a long while, until Mr. Jude. A job isn't a replacement for a family, but not a lot of folks can say they've gotten to travel the world for free, either, so that's somethin'. I count my blessings each day."

When Harold dropped her at her apartment, there was an embarrassingly large arrangement of lilacs, sunflowers, and amaryllis with vines of honeysuckle accents waiting in front of her door with a note that simply said 'XO.' Almost tipping over the large vase they sat in, Angelina stuck her face into the soft blooms as she tried to pick them up. A honeysuckle vine went up her nose, causing her to sneeze while she opened her apartment door.

A rush of old building smell greeted her inside, temporarily blocking out the envelope of floral air she was walking in. Mostly empty except for souvenirs from her travels and a window full of aloe and other various harder-to-kill plants, she hadn't spent much time trying to make it a home. Angelina preferred it like this, uncluttered. The openness gave her a sense of calming and relief compared to her hectic life.

She decided to do some baking before going back to work. Baking had always been the best way for her to enter a meditative state to clear her head. Jude had given her a lot to think about, but how did she truly feel? And could she even comprehend the answers to half of the questions she'd asked?

She still had many thoughts, insights, and curiosities to consider. Would he bite her neck? He hadn't really said, but she thought not. Was turning people as gross as it was in the movies? Why couldn't he fly? If he couldn't fly, was he also not able to transform into a bat? What other areas of history had he influenced, altered, or completely changed? If he knew Bram Stoker, who else did he know? How old was he really?

She'd always thought the vampires of legend were on the ridiculous side, artificial monsters who were carnal and gluttonous in nature. In the few days she'd known him, he was nothing like she'd ever assumed vampires to be.

His ex-wife had seemed all the things that vampires should be, but Jude was a gentle and tender soul. He seemed almost fragile in his existence as an immortal, so adept at human emotions and the passage of time that his spirit had nearly been broken, yet his body lived on.

Plus, the way Harold so adoringly talked about him ... speaking that highly of someone after being witness to the ins and outs of their life for so long is a rare treasure. Angelina wanted, needed, to know more.

The next day, she went to work. Then, she came home.

The next day, she went to work. Then, she came home.

The next day, she went to work. Then, she came home.

The next day, she went to work. Then, she came home.

The next day, she went to work. Then, she came home.

Five days later, she still hadn't heard from him since leaving the palatial venue. No phone call, no text, no more flowers, and no mysterious hunk waiting for her when she walked out of the university.

Walking up the narrow, ancient steps to her apartment after a long day at work, Angelina started contemplating if maybe she'd just dreamed the whole thing. She fantasized for a minute that she might write a book about it, a nice little short story about a vampire who wasn't really a vampire.

She walked into her apartment, cold and uninviting except for the sweet aroma of honeysuckle seeping out from the bouquet of flowers that had been delivered days before. The only memento that Jude had been real, every bloom was still a vibrant, thriving symbol of the life it had represented, and there was still not a blemish amongst them. She decided right there what her next move would be.

Angelina Arbonne never has and never will wait for any man.

Chapter Eight

She pulled her phone out and started tracking down the street signs she'd seen. Narrowing it down quickly, she was able to do a map terrain search and see Jude's estate. *Thank goodness for technology!* She changed into a nice green blouse, jeans, and strappy sandals. Her Uber showed up, and away she went.

It was about to start raining. The sky was dark and gloomy, casting a shadow over the grounds. Angelina panicked momentarily, hoping she wouldn't have to scale the fence if the weather turned bad. Luckily, the iron gate was wide open, and her Uber driver turned and started creeping up the long driveway.

The closer they got to the building, the more her mind raced. *Is this maybe a little too forward?* But Jude had said he'd wanted to marry her. You really can't get *more* forward than that on a first date. She decided not to overthink her approach and to instead focus on being her confident, accomplished self.

The car pulled up to the iron pillars, and Angelina couldn't help but feel like a princess when she stepped out of the car. Two peacocks walked up to her, one on each side, and fanned out their feathers as if on command. The palatial venue was abuzz with energy today, with seemingly more life pouring out of every crack and crevice of the cobblestone walkway and iron pillars despite the cloudy weather. No one was visible, yet she got the sense that the house itself was very engaged in whatever was going on inside.

She walked through the glass double doors. The same white cat with a nub tail who had greeted her the week before was sitting on the copper fountain. He gave a slight meow to her as he hopped down. He walked over and nibbled her leg, not hard, just testing her out. He looked up at her with his mouth slightly open, and two little white fangs made themselves known. Seemingly accepting her as a friend, he entwined his fluffy body in between her legs and started purring.

Angelina was leaning down to pet him as Jude appeared from the other side of the fountain. He was more gorgeous than she had remembered, or thought should be allowed for any man. Her heart skipped a beat, and she wondered if his one heart beat for the day had skipped, too.

"Did you … smell me?" she questioned, failing to remember all the things he'd told her and how they diverted from the narrative in her head.

"No, I heard the car door," Jude said, smiling as he walked up and kissed her cheek. On a roll with her stupid questions, she then asked, "Is your cat a vampire?"

"Yes. I got him from the pound. He was found in a dumpster, emaciated and clinging to life. I showed up right as they were bringing him in, and I knew he was mine. His name is Neville."

Forgetting she was supposed to be irritated at his silence, Angelina fell a little more in love with his gentleness. Jude took her hand and guided her into the house. There were workers, painters, and construction workers buzzing about around them. Another step in, and the most glorious music echoed through the house to greet them.

"What's going on, Jude?"

"Evidently, I epically lost track of time and yesterday everyone showed up to start getting the venue ready for the Convention next week. I apologize that I haven't gotten back to you, it wasn't my intention," he said, as he brought her hands to his pouty, ruby red lips. *Oh heck, I'll give him the benefit of the doubt.*

"There are some people I'd like you to meet." He guided her into the ballroom on the right side of the foyer, where the beautiful sounds were coming from.

Walking through the gilded doors, at least a dozen people were swarming about. There was a stage, and a fancy podium painted in gold and white to match the room. Angelina did a double take at a very tall man dressed all in black, who was directing the workers rather vigorously. The air smelled like new lumber and fresh paint all around them.

They walked towards the corner where the music was coming from. There was a grand piano, certainly the grandest she had ever seen. It was massive, with a cherry finish. Carved into the front two massive legs on either side was a woman holding a wreath of flowers, her skirt flowing down and turning into the leg itself, among other adornments around the sides of the piano. It must've cost a fortune, and the only other time Angelina had seen any piano so elaborate was on a tour of the Newport mansions.

The man playing was not nearly as well adorned, simply sporting flip-flops, khaki shorts, and a faint green button-up shirt, loosely pushed up around his elbows. He was completely entranced as he played some modern version of the "Moonlight Sonata." His locks flopped in time to his key strokes, and he was oblivious to their presence. Jude cleared his throat, pulling the man out of his enchantment. He turned around, and Angelina gasped. If Jude hadn't already captured her attention, this was a man she would've definitely taken a second glance at.

Wavy, light brown hair framed a heart-shaped face, with full lips and green eyes that were almost white they were so light. He had a smattering of soft freckles across his handsome expression, and a strong jawline framed with a scruffy beard. He stood up to greet her, revealing that he was equally as tall as Jude.

"Ludwig, this is Dr. Angelina Arbonne. Angelina, I'd like you to meet Ludwig van Beethoven," Jude said, stating the fact as serious as anyone could be. She burst out laughing. This man had easily been in his early-to-mid thirties when he'd been turned.

Beethoven was much older and frumpy when he died.

"OK, seriously? 'Keats' and now 'Beethoven?' I know that Beethoven was much older than you, and definitely didn't look like you at all. And you're most certainly not deaf, as we all know Beethoven was," Angelina said, covering her mouth in case he was, instead, an excellent lip reader. "You play rather well, I'll give you that, but what's really happening?"

With the subtle trace of a German accent, he said, "Ah yes, my dear friend. I had nothing more than a bout of tinnitus when I was turned. Coincidentally, he was diagnosed almost immediately after and succumbed quickly to the full loss of his audible sense."

Angelina's mouth fell open. Nothing he'd just said made any sense to her whatsoever.

"Semantics, Dr. Arbonne. You're someone well educated. I have no doubt that you only accept concrete facts," Ludwig began. "Surely you know not to believe everything you read in history books, given how easily they can be influenced and tweaked? How humans can be manipulated with a little placebo?" He winked at her and grinned, disarming her defiance instantly. Even if *the* Beethoven really was standing in front of her, Angelina was absolutely not prepared for what was about to happen next.

"Jude! Jude! My King!"

The tall man who'd been directing the workers had noticed Jude from across the room. He yelled towards them as he hopped down off the stage. He saw Angelina, and his eyes grew wide as his mouth dropped. She mirrored his actions, equally in shock. He was a dead ringer for the real thing. The man was taller than Jude and Ludwig, and wearing a long black coat and suit from the 1800s. His black hair and sad eyes, his squared face and rectangular nose, gave her chills at their familiarity.

Angelina would've known his face anywhere, at any point in time. She'd spent a year teaching in Baltimore, and his presence was a veil over the entire city. He ran up to her awkwardly, haphazardly, like a spider missing a leg.

"My Queen! My Queeeen!" the man screeched.

"I'm not a queen."

"I know a queen when I see one, madam, and you most certainly are," the man said, awe oozing from his voice. His sparkling obsidian eyes, like black glitter, closed slowly and his head bowed in respect as he took her hand in his. "Edgar … Allan … Poe …" he said slowly, as he kneeled to the floor. When his knee reached the ground, he stated just loud enough for the three of them to hear him, "At your service, until the last breath I breathe."

Angelina looked at Jude, the full weight of present company sinking in. *What else do I not know? What part of history is a lie? Is all of history a lie?*

Ludwig was smirking, as if reading her thoughts. Jude was looking at her, deciding if she were about to pass out or not, and changed his stance to prepare to catch her if need be.

"Oh, so *him* you believe?" Ludwig asked teasingly. "Even with all the dramatics, which I can assure you, never end. You're not special."

"She most certainly *is* special, Ludwig! You should talk to her with the utmost respect!" Edgar snapped, turning his body to face Ludwig in a protective gesture.

Ludwig and Edgar were both highly entertaining if nothing more, and Angelina knew right then and there with their playful banter that she was going to be good friends with this brotherly duo.

"I'd know him anywhere. I spent a few semesters working in Baltimore. Do you ever go and visit? There's a football team named after your poem and your portrait hangs all over the city! How are you alive? Or, a vampire? We studied you in school. Your death is still a mystery to this day. They did autopsies of you, for crying out loud!" She was hysterical and excited. Angelina wanted, needed, to know everything now.

Taking his cue to leave, Jude kissed her cheek and then excused himself to work on Convention matters. He'd clearly heard Edgar's story more than several times before.

"Incorrect, my Queen. They tested my hair only. When they tried to move my body, which wasn't really my body at all, you see, they gathered locks of my hair that had been placed in the coffin prior to burial."

Angelina was dumbstruck as Edgar continued.

"It was a dark and stormy night!" Conveniently, the rain of the afternoon had now convened directly over the palatial venue. Lovely New Orleans weather, always changing at the drop of a hat. Perfectly scripted, deafening thunder cracked and lightning lit up the ballroom around Edgar's pale face.

Ludwig, with an amused expression, sat down on one side of the gilded piano bench. "Here we go. You'll need a chair," he said, patting the empty half beside him.

Edgar, ignoring him, turned his eyes up to the ceiling as if stargazing. He lifted his hands out up to his sides rather dramatically, as if he were waiting for a hug from the skies.

"It was a dark and stormy night when I decided to end my life!"

Chapter Nine

He had been on his way to Philadelphia, to attend some business. Though Edgar had been sober for quite some time, a fit of depression had overtaken him, and he sidetracked to Baltimore. At the natural halfway point, he decided to rest his thoughts a moment before venturing further.

It was a dark and stormy night, and the wind was blustering about as he ambled on down the sidewalk. Cold and feverish, Edgar stopped into a tavern to warm himself. The usually dark and crowded space was fully awake. The election was in three days, the air inside reverberating with excitement and anticipation from the raucous horde of patrons.

This was the last night he was to be fully human, though he did not yet know it. Edgar pushed through the crowd of caterwauling men and found a table in the back. Hanging his wool coat on the back of his chair, which now carried the stench of drenched, sullied sheep in a field, he noted the details of the rest of the room. The tavern didn't smell much better, a damp mustiness of piss and rainwater permeating the air. He ordered a glass of cognac and nursed it quietly in the corner.

Edgar was not drunk, not drunk enough to fail to acknowledge the man who came to sit at his table. The man was not offered a chair, but merely took it, uninvited and uninviting. His back was to the crowd of rambunctious drunkards, blocking them out from the conversation that was to come.

For a moment, Edgar thought that he must be more inebriated than he realized, and that he had somehow crossed a dimension and ended up in England. The man before him was a right young chap, dressed in a brown tweed suit with a strangely round, little brown hat. "What a funny hat you have," Edgar stated.

"It's a new invention, a friend of a friend passed it on to me," the man replied. Though his clothing was British, his accent contained a hint of German.

The man was completely dry despite Edgar's being soaked to the bone, and he was the oddest person he'd seen for a time. Disengaged from the busy surroundings, the man fixated his eyes upon Edgar's.

"What is your name, sir?" Edgar asked.

The man replied, "You would not believe me if I told you."

Edgar was slightly unnerved at the sight of him, something he couldn't quite place his finger on. He was younger than Edgar, no older than his late twenties to early thirties, at best. He was pale, several shades lighter than even Edgar, which the latter had never considered possible. The man's eyes stayed fixated on Edgar, calculating his moves, down to the subtle ticks on his face. Even with the lights behind him, casting his face in shadows, the man's eyes were nearly white. They were the lightest shade of jade Edgar had ever seen.

"Do you need a drink, Nameless Sir?"

"I'll have a cognac, as well. I smell a good year."

"You smell a good year?"

"Yes, I have an excellent sense of smell,"

Nameless Sir stated factually.

"Might you consider drinking it and then go on about your way, Nameless Sir?"

"No, that would not be in your, or my, best interests. You see, I have a proposition for you, a job agreement if you will."

"I'm not looking for subsequential employment," Edgar said, and signaled for another glass.

Nameless Sir downed his glass in one gulp, and then signaled for another one as well.

Friendly conversation commenced, nothing personal. Edgar assumed he was a fan; he'd received a little more attention from strangers in the last several years after his poem's success. It wasn't anything unusually odd to be accompanied by a total stranger in a tavern. Edgar was not in the mood to entertain, but Nameless Sir seemed to be quite in his element and conditioned to doing the entertaining. They bantered back and forth for quite some time, frittering away the hours until Nameless Sir changed the subject completely.

"How did you feel about the President's untimely demise?"

"I thought it rather sad. I'm of the opinion that a man should be able to enjoy his life, rather than dying as soon as his work is finished."

"Yet, you are drawn to death. You are a master of prose and illusion of what should be and what never was. Tell me, what would you do if you had an infinite amount of time?"

"I suppose I'd spend a few months in California trying to strike gold."

"And after that?"

"With the gold I found, I would build the grandest house for my love. She would worry no longer about such matters. She was my first love then, but a widow now. Her husband put a stipulation in his will, that, should she remarry, she would lose most of her fortune. Can you imagine? How preposterous! I would assure she was well provided for above all else."

"What if I could provide you with that, Mr. Poe? What if I told you I could make you an immortal?"

"Then I would not believe you, Nameless Sir. Such things are only written about, dreamed about. To be immortal is to exist in the minds of others, and nothing more."

"Such things are written and dreamed about because they are attainable for the lucky few. I'm here to offer you the chance to be one of the few. My name is Ludwig van Beethoven, and I'll be eighty years old in December."

Now, remember, Edgar had been taking laudanum for his feverish state, plus all of the cognac he'd been consuming as they talked. To say he was coherent would be a fabrication. Nameless Sir, who now wanted him to believe he was Beethoven, was offering immortality? All Edgar could think was what a great story this would make, true or untrue! He decided to humor Nameless Sir.

"Nameless Sir, do you mean to say that you are *the* Beethoven?"

"The very one!"

"Sir Beethoven, but you are not aged a day past

thirty, if that!"

"Theatrics, my dear Poe. Simple theatrics. You mustn't believe everything you've come to know about reality."

Edgar pondered this for a moment, the words twisting themselves around in his mind. He decided to entertain the gentleman's wild notions a little further. "Sir Beethoven, what are the rules for immortality? Surely there must be some, for no one shall live without consequence."

"Please, call me Ludwig. The selection for immortality is based upon your work as a living human. If you have contributed greatly to your field, at a genius level shall we say, a representative may consider turning you. Should you be considered, you will be contacted. I have followed your work for many years, and I believe you would make a sizable contribution to the future of humankind.

"The rules are simple. We work as a secret society. Can you imagine if every human wanted to be an immortal? What a mad and chaotic world it would be, and certainly no good would come from overpopulation. We don't turn anyone over the age of fifty. We can, but their bodies don't process it quite as well. The body is a funny thing, indeed.

"There is a consumption of blood, a Toasting Ceremony, if you will. The blood is healing. If you have an ailment in life, it will heal you. My ailments have disappeared since being turned, but I beg you to please not tell my ex-wife.

"You may still eat what you want, but try to keep it light and simple. You will have more energy if you stay clean. If you eat unhealthily, this will slow you down.

"You may never, ever, turn a member of your own family. To do so would cloud your focus of the mission—which is to provide a better world for future generations. Worse still, it would surely kill them if they are of your own blood. This has been attempted only once, with dire consequences.

"If you are killed, the blood will heal you, but only if you have taken it within twenty-four hours of your passing. You cannot bring anyone back from the dead if they have not had the blood in that time length.

"You must fake your death, to allow the world to grieve and know that you are no longer. That, my friend, is where you may choose to be creative with how you go out!" Beethoven stood up from the table and cleared his throat. "Provided that you have not been previously sentenced to die from public execution. It's a lot to muster over, I'm well aware. I will meet you back here tomorrow night to discuss your choice."

"I don't need another night to think about it. I agree to your conditions." Edgar signaled for another round of cognacs for himself and his new historical friend. He had nothing to lose from entertaining the ramblings of a mad man madder than he. Perhaps, at the very least, inspiration for a new story would be gained.

Beethoven asked for an extra glass, and the waitress brought a sparkling chalice. It wasn't crystal, it was too heavy. Crystal would never survive in an atmosphere such as this one. Nonetheless, it was fitting, fancy, and representative. Edgar downed his newest acquisition of alcohol.

Beethoven reached for Edgar's wrist, and raised it to his mouth. Two alabaster points sprouted just below his upper lip, and then he bit in. It was a subtle, almost tickling sensation. Edgar would've thought it was a horrid mosquito had he not been witness to the action itself. Edgar resisted the urge to scratch as Beethoven returned his wrist. Then, biting his own wrist, Beethoven squeezed a few drops of his blood into the chalice. The red liquid trickled down the side of the chalice, pooling into its cup. He proceeded to pour a bit of his cognac into the glass, the amber liquid mixing with the crimson to create a rich cherry color.

Beethoven slid the chalice to Edgar's side of the table. "A toast to good deeds and great futures!"

Edgar raised the chalice to toast, and then downed the sweet nectar of immortality. His bulbous head fell to the table promptly, and he remembered not a thing until several days later.

Chapter Ten

"How much blood was it?" Angelina felt queasy at the thought of drinking a cup full of blood.

"I would say no more than a teaspoon, to give a visual."

"And then what happened?" She was captivated by Edgar's storytelling. Literally on the edge of her seat, she was eager to learn more about this mystery that had haunted generations of historians.

"Then what happened was I carried him out," Ludwig chimed in beside her. "I didn't know how much laudanum and cognac he'd actually consumed. When my blood hit his bloodstream he was left in a drunken stupor for days, a life-sized rag doll that I had to haul around Baltimore slung over my shoulder. Can you imagine? He still hasn't quite recovered, or maybe this was his natural personality all along. It's hard to tell sometimes.

"The day of the election, October third, he was still soft-headed and soft-bodied. I was afraid to leave him by himself. Even immortals can still get beaten up pretty badly. I had changed his clothes, which in retrospect was probably a mistake.

"Semi-conscious, Edgar was at least able to move his legs with assistance standing up. I wrapped my arm around his waist and his arm around my neck, and we headed to the polls. You can imagine the sight of us, two bumbling idiots trying to make it down the sidewalk. I had to feign drunkenness because he wouldn't quit babbling on. Every time someone passed us on the sidewalk, he would start muttering to them, and then I'd have to start muttering to lessen any suspicions that we were just two immortals walking around Baltimore.

"When we got to the polls, I propped him up against the building. I didn't think anyone would notice him; I thought they would just assume he was another drunken, miserable beast. I went inside, and when I came back out not thirty minutes later, he was gone. Into thin air."

Edgar cut back in, their words flowing seamlessly together how stories from old friends often do. "When I became coherent again, I was in the hospital, surrounded by familiar faces. The last recollection I had was of Ludwig's blood pouring down my throat. I was in and out of consciousness, trying to piece my thoughts together. They were as delicate as lace, as fragile and transparent as a dragonfly's wings. As soon as I'd recall a clear image, I'd be out again.

"I could hear the doctors and nurses in the room talking about me. 'Colorless,' 'lifeless,' 'shallow breath,' were all words used to describe my state. I realized that I was coming more and more into my consciousness if I could recall these words, and just a moment later, it seemed, Ludwig showed up.

"I had been left alone to rest for a while, when I heard footsteps approaching my bedside. My eyes fluttered open, and standing there before me in a full doctor's uniform was Ludwig. I said to him, 'My old friend, Death, has returned.'"

"'You slipped away from me, but now I'm back. What do you remember?'" Ludwig carried on the conversation, as if they were back in the hospital room.

"'Your amber-colored blood oozing into my veins, a hideous dressing, and the pains of being unaware. Death has come to collect. Are you a ghost, or are you here?'"

"'I'm here, Edgar. I'm afraid I wasn't aware of the contents of your blood before I gave you mine. I apologize, I should've given you the day to recoup. The turning knocked you into a delirious state for several days, of which you are finally recovering from.

"'You will be preserved in this state, never aging. Edgar, you must sell the act. Unfortunately, you don't get a grand show of death, now that everyone has seen you.'"

"'Ah, Death, I will not fail you!'" Edgar shot his arms back up to the ceiling. The thunder clapped all around him again, on cue.

Edgar continued, "Early that morning, I waited. When the doctor approached my bedside to check on me, I raised my arms, took a deep breath, and proclaimed loudly, 'Lord, help my poor soul!' And with that, I went limp. I hissed a breath out of my chest for good measure, to give the appearance of deflation, and then the doctor covered my face with a sheet. I lay there, stiff as a corpse, which in fact I now was. More or less."

"That's … astonishing. Really, it is. The circumstances and rumors around your death have been going since, well, since you died."

"Yes, my Queen. It's my greatest story yet!" He closed his eyes slowly and bowed his head down, signaling the end of his elaborate retelling of his death.

Angelina glanced over at Ludwig, who was starting to have a distant look in his eyes, despite playing his part in the retelling. "I take it you've heard this story before?"

"Only several hundred times. But if you think about it, I'm the hero. So, it never gets too boring," he said, winking at her with his jade eyes. "Besides, he left out the *fun* part," he said sarcastically.

"Oh? What's the *fun* part?"

"When I had to dig him out of the ground after his funeral."

She hadn't been expecting that, and burst out laughing a little too hard and let out a loud snort.

"I had always had a particular fear for being buried alive, but I daresay I found it rather … excitable is not the word I would use. Adventurous would be more like it."

Missing Jude, Angelina stood up to excuse herself. Edgar bowed another deep and dramatic bow as Ludwig stayed seated on the piano stool, unimpressed by whatever formality Edgar was obeying. Angelina felt their eyes on her as she walked out, and she could hear Edgar whispering enthusiastically.

In the great room, painters and workers were all abuzz with large ladders everywhere. Dusting, painting trim, detailing the room perfectly. Over in the corner with a clipboard in hand, a small girl with concealed eyes watched Angelina intently from behind one of the palm trees while she made her way to the back patio. She was wearing a bright yellow sun visor, and had it not steadily turned along with Angelina's movement across the room, she probably wouldn't have noticed her.

Angelina opened the glass doors and stepped onto the patio. It had grown dark after the storm, almost nightfall. Only a light drizzle remained, closer to a mist than a drop. She'd been so captivated by Edgar's storytelling that she hadn't realized she'd already been there for quite so long. *Time sure does fly in the company of vampires.*

Large, old lanterns adorned the gardens and walkways, creating the most romantic, candlelit appearance Angelina could've imagined. She didn't remember them all being lit up the week before on their first date, but now in the darkness, a clearly illuminated pathway down to the river stretched out before her. There were flower beds all around the trees, as well as ornate beds bordering the patio that hadn't been there before. An entire crew of landscapers had obviously been hard at work in the last week.

Angelina's eyes roamed the palatial venue in its new lighting, exploring the things she hadn't paid attention to before. Her eyes wandered all the way to the end, where Jude had said his room was. There was an ornate balcony lit up in candlelight at the end, connected to the house but not to the patio itself. She wondered if he ever used it, if that was where he took all of his women. How many women he must've had before her …

She snapped back, not letting her mind go down that rabbit hole of bitterness. She was smart, she was sexy, she was confident, and she wasn't jealous. *Much.* She was not going to be jealous of things she couldn't change.

Jude's voice drifted up the wall from below, and Angelina peered over the patio wall to watch him. Jude was on his hands and knees, picking earthworms off the river-stoned steps. He delicately placed them in his palm, all the while talking to them and reassuring them everything would be OK. He crawled over the flower bed closest to him, dug a hole, and placed the worms in it.

"There you go, now you're free to worm the earth as you see fit, little buddies."

She giggled silently at his pun. *This man cannot be real, he just can't.* Vampire or not, sexy and gentle is a lethal combination. He looked up and smiled when he noticed her walking towards him. Angelina felt her knees go weak at the sight of that wicked, inviting smile.

"Hey, you."

"Hey, yourself. You left me alone in there with *Edgar. Allan. Poe.* I can't believe it! Who else is a vampire? George Washington? I've always wanted to meet him!"

Grinning, he said, "No, George Washington isn't a vampire. I thought it was best for you to hear

Edgar's story. He tells it with such enthusiasm, he's basically my celebrity spokesperson. The way he explains it, and with Ludwig's comedic anecdotes, is more entertaining and informative in a short time than I could ever be. I'm thinking about making a welcome video starring them."

"Oh, you absolutely should! That'd be just the best thing ever!"

"Will that be your first project as my Queen?" Jude smiled adorably at her and Angelina blushed. Just then, he stood up and wrapped his arms around her waist, surprising her. Her eyes went wide at the contact of his lips on hers, and then they rolled back into her head as he kissed her. It was soft at first, and then she tasted sweetness on his pouty cherry lips, like he'd been eating Jolly Ranchers. She kissed him back feverishly, accepting her fate with open arms. They were both clearly enjoying the moment until someone behind them cleared her throat obnoxiously.

"AHEM. Jude, can I have a word with you?"

Startled, Angelina didn't even look at her. She felt ashamed, like she'd been caught being naughty with the girl's dad. And hadn't she, technically? Somehow, Angelina knew it was the little girl in the sun visor who now stood behind her. She'd gotten the impression before from the way the girl had steadily watched her walk through the room that she held an upper edge and was not afraid of confrontation. Angelina continued to hide her face as Jude peered around her.

"Not now."

"It's really kind of important," the girl said pointedly.

"Whatever it is, I'm sure you can handle it. I trust you completely."

Angelina didn't see it, but she could feel the power behind the girl's massive eye roll. She turned her head just in time to see in her peripherals the girl spinning on one heel and walking away.

"She hates me."

"No, she's just protective. We've been through a lot together and she's like my daughter."

"I don't think she feels the same way."

Jude playfully huffed, dismissing their newly developed feud as insignificant.

"Where were we?"

"I think you were telling me about being queen of the worms? My mind went blank after y—" He kissed her again. At first his lips were as light as feathers, teasing the air between them. Then he was seriously kissing her, his lips turning slow and sensual as Angelina felt his touch deep into her core. *This* was something she could definitely get used to.

Chapter Eleven

"Would you like to take a walk down by the river?" Jude asked, pulling away from her lips. Angelina's body instinctively leaned into him, searching for more.

"Of course," she breathed, her mind dizzy.

He took her hand as he stepped down onto the cobblestone sidewalk leading to the river. She paused, using his shoulder for balance, and took her shoes off. They walked side by side in the grass, the feeling of the wet earth squishing between Angelina's toes. She'd always liked that sensation for some reason.

"A penny for your thoughts? How are you feeling?" Jude interrupted her momentary lapse in earthy reality.

"Honestly, I don't know. I'm pretty blown away by everything."

"Can I take you away for a week? Can you get off work for that amount of time to spend with me, just the two of us? There's somewhere I'd like for you to see, at the edge of the world."

The cicadas sang out loudly in the trees all around them, their rhythmic chirps competing to drown out any thoughts she was struggling to grasp.

She wanted to say yes, to get lost in his gray diamond eyes forever and not worry about a thing. "I, um, no, I can't get away for a week. I still have to work, Jude. I have obligations. I don't have the luxury of time standing still for me."

"I know. I'm sorry. I just meant that I would like to date you," Jude said, kissing her again before she could stop to breathe.

"OK," but it came out as more of a squeak. She was pleasantly surprised at how great a kisser he was, until she remembered he was *quite* a bit older than her, and must've had a lot of practice. Angelina tried to push the jealous thoughts out of her head. It wasn't like she could change the fact that there were double-digit centuries between them.

"Starting tonight and every night until the

Society Convention next week. Then we can go from there. Is that all right?"

"Sure, I'm fine with that." She quickly rerouted her scheduled in her head. She'd have to rearrange her grading of the mid-terms, get more done on her lunch break. It was a little pushy of him to assume she'd reschedule everything at the drop of a hat, but he'd been correct in his assumption somehow, because she was more than willing to let it slide for a man who tasted like Jolly Ranchers.

"I don't mean to be forceful," he said softly, like he was reading her thoughts. "The meeting is sort of a big deal and I just don't want you to be overwhelmed with, well, all of it really. It can be kind of a lot rather quickly. Are you hungry?"

"Famished, actually. I haven't eaten since this morning and I didn't realize how late it already was."

"Let our official second date be tonight then. I know a great place. They'll fit us in with no problems. It's not so far from your apartment, but quite far from all the chaos here."

Her stomach growled in response, and Jude grinned. He pulled out his cellphone and made a quick call, and then his arm was around her waist and guiding her towards the front door.

All eyes were on them as they strolled back through the palatial venue. Harold pulled up at the front door as if on cue, and hopped out to hold open the door for the pair. *This poor man, does he ever get to sleep?* He always seemed to be wide awake, at Jude's beck and call. "Dr. Arbonne! A pleasure seeing you again!"

"You, too, Harold! I hope you're doing well!" She leaned in to kiss his cheek. Harold glowed and beamed at her while Jude took the opportunity to open her car door. By the time Jude had followed her into the back seat, Harold had already repositioned himself in the driver's seat. "Where to, Mr. Jude?"

"Antoine's."

Her jaw dropped before she could catch it. *Antoine's?* In all her years, Angelina had never stepped foot inside the immortal restaurant's walls. That was a place you go to for wedding receptions, conferences, fancy dinners, and events. Quite a bit more upscale than just a place that could "fit us in." She'd assumed he was talking about Chinese takeout or a nice drive-thru on the way, certainly not something so … *elegant,* at the drop of a hat.

"Antoine's! What a splendid choice on this romantic night!" Good ol' Harold, trying to set the mood. The mood which was already quite obviously set from Jude fanning kisses all down her neck. She turned to him and their lips found each other again. A full make out session ensued and before she realized it, they were turning onto St. Louis St.

Full of old-world charm, New Orleans was just about the most romantic place for new, or old, lovers. The windows were rolled down in the classic car, and the sound of the tires gently sloshing through the puddles could be heard as they neared their destination. By now, it was about 10 p.m., and though not as bustling as the daytime or on the weekends, there was still a good smattering of people on the sidewalks. Somewhere around the corner, the classic jazz music synonymous with the French Quarter floated through the menagerie of neon lights, adding to the atmosphere. Green, wrought iron pillars and decor greeted them as the car creeped to a still, reminding Angelina of the French conservatory foyer at the palatial venue.

Harold slowed to a stop in front of Antoine's. Watching him come around to open her door,

Angelina was keenly aware of her shirt clinging to her. Frankly, at this point, she couldn't distinguish between if it was the humidity or Jude that had her all hot and bothered. She suspected it was equal parts both. A single waiter was waiting for them at the door, wearing black suit and bow tie, white towel draped over his arm. "Welcome to Antoine's!"

The dining room was beautiful, white and gold, and like what Angelina imagined a riverboat to look like on the inside. White columns, crown molding, and gold chandeliers crested a sea of tables adorned with white cloths and champagne glasses with perfectly folded linens inside. It felt very clean and regal, like the dining hall of the *Titanic*. The waiter led them through the opulent main dining room to a little corner that had been cleared away of all but one table with two chairs and a small candelabra. There were a few waiters and busboys doing some detail cleaning on the other side, but in their corner, they were largely undisturbed.

"Are they closed?" she asked, worried. Angelina really tried to not be a nuisance to anyone or make anyone's day harder.

"To the general public, but I've known the family for quite a while now." *Of course he has.* The lighting conveniently dimmed, making the candles appear brighter and more flickering.

The waiter approached. "My name is Henry and I'll be taking care of you on this fine evening! May I start you out with a glass of our finest wine?"

"No, thank you, I'll just have water."

Jude ordered water also, before Henry walked away. Angelina met Jude's eyes through the candlelight. The darkness in the room only made the flames mirrored in his eyes that much more prominent. He was staring at her, only now his gray diamond eyes were full of emotions, like dark tide pools beside a raging fire. Angelina wanted this man badly; she'd already made her mind up. Suddenly self-conscious, she stuttered, "So ... what's good here?"

He gazed at her like he was watching his prey. "Everything."

When Henry returned, Angelina ordered the Poulet Rochambeau. It sounded mouth-watering on paper. *How could it not be delectable on a plate?* To her surprise, Jude also ordered oysters Rockefeller and some escargot dish she wasn't even going to try to pronounce. *He eats out on special occasions?*

Albeit both dishes he ordered were baked, it was still more than filet mignons and coffee, and she was proud of him for being adventurous. Angelina was even more excited that she wouldn't have to eat alone in front of him. Somehow, she felt he could sense that.

Jude stood up after they ordered, offering his hand to her. The music from the street carried through the walls, permeating the room with soulful rhythm. It has that effect, here in New Orleans. With her hand in his, Jude pulled her into his body, and they danced slowly in a French-infused bliss for what felt like hours. Angelina was nervous, though, more now than she had been at any other time since meeting him. They barely talked as he held her close and swayed to the jazz.

She'd all but forgotten that she still hadn't eaten for the better part of twelve hours when buttery, garlicky richness engulfed her nostrils. Her stomach roared back to life when she turned around to see Henry loading up the table with beautifully crafted plates.

Thank goodness Jude had decided to eat with her, or she would've looked like a starved wolf devouring a fresh, juicy kill. The dish she had ordered was to die for, in all of its rich, creamy, saucy goodness. Oysters or escargot were never her thing, but Jude looked like he was enjoying himself as well. Angelina devoured her meal in record time, throwing grace to the wind. The whole time Jude was watching her, amused expressions flecking across his face.

"I thought you only ate filet mignon?"

"You have to enjoy life a little *sometimes*. And when I do, I don't eat fried foods." *This man and the way he says the word* 'sometimes.' It was nothing sexy at all, but it came out in a low, lustful growl.

Ordering dessert crossed her mind for a split second, but two things stopped her. Number one, Angelina had casually noticed the prices on everything when she was ordering and it was a good thing Jude was rich or she would've felt really bad. She'd always been more of a ramen and hot dog type of girl, no fancy frills to be found. Number two, nothing, absolutely *nothing*, would taste as good as kissing Jude again. *So, what's the point?*

When Henry came back to enquire about dessert, Angelina ordered a cup of gumbo to go and let that be that.

"A midnight snack?"

"No, I thought I'd get Harold something, and he seems like a gumbo sort of man to me."

"That's incredibly thoughtful. But you should know, Harold's not waiting on us. He went home after he dropped us off."

"Oh." *Ooohhh. We're … unchaperoned. Am I ready for that step? That's really fast, that's too fast. That's way too presumptive. What am I going to do? I mean, obviously I've thought about it a lot today, especially with how good of a kisser he is. I bet he's great at everything. Other things … ooohh. Ooooh my, no I'm not ready yet. Not today. Maybe tomorrow. No! Not tomorrow, either! Angelina! Get ahold of yourself, what's wrong with you? You're not a slut and don't start acting like one on the second date!*

Jude was reading the panic on her face while her mind raced a thousand miles a minute. "Relax, Angelina. We're not going to sleep together tonight. I'm just going to walk you home. Remember, I can walk a lot faster than Harold can drive. There was no point in having him wait for me, if you're not the one being driven."

"Oh."

Jude smirked. "Is 'Oh' all you can say now?"

"Oh. I, um … I … Are you ready to go? I'm ready to go." She tried to change the subject and save face, but she was a lost cause at this point. Her cheeks had already turned bright red, and her clothing was starting to feel sticky again. Jude just grinned, like he knew every thought before it entered her mind.

By the time they were ready to leave the restaurant, it was well around midnight. Prime time for all sorts of debauchery to happen, but she felt completely safe with Jude. Completely safe with *him*, that is. Feeling safe from her own stupid statements was another thing entirely. Angelina decided she wasn't going to talk again until she had something brilliant and earth-shattering to say. Which should've been easy, being a doctor and all. She was supposed to be spilling over with brilliant thoughts and confident answers. *Except this man makes me a pile of goo with no effort whatsoever.*

Midnight in the French Quarter is a character all its own. Jude walked alongside her, taking care to keep between her and the street, a chivalrous romantic gesture. On the way to her apartment on Dauphine St., Angelina couldn't help but notice how the sidewalks were syrupy with various spilled drinks and alcoholic beverages. A few bars were still open this late, with a handful of overly intoxicated patrons hanging out in front of them.

No one even seemed to notice them, however. Everyone was too preoccupied with their own personal demons to notice Angelina's awkward demeanor next to the most handsome man she'd ever seen.

"Are you OK?" Jude asked, when she still hadn't said anything for at least a good block. She was determined to win this silent round of wits and regain her footing.

"Mm-hmmm." *Score one for the home team.*

"Are you sure? You haven't said anything since we left the restaurant."

"Mm-hmm, I'm good." *Me 2, Jude 0.*

"OK ... are you, though? I'd be happy to drop that off at Harold's on my way home if that's what's upset you."

She handed the bag to him. "That'd be really sweet of you." *Yes, keep it up, girl! You're rocking this conversation right now, keep him intrigued.*

Arriving at her apartment, Jude took her hand in his free one.

"Listen, are you sure you're OK?"

"Yes, Jude, I'm perfectly fine. I had a lovely time tonight, thank you for everything."

"Can I see you again tomorrow night? Well, I guess it would be later tonight technically. I was serious about wanting to date you every night until the Convention."

"Yes, that sounds good. Will Harold be picking me up later?"

"No … I was thinking we could stay in, and I'll make you dinner? Like a normal couple?" The tone in his voice suggested he was unsure, which made Angelina's heart twinge to reach for him. She had won, levelling the playing field once again with her semi-silent protest.

Her eyes lit up at the thought. She strongly, very strongly, preferred dates that were more personal vs. pomp and circumstance. "Yes, that'll be perfect!"

He kissed her lightly. "Then we have a date. Goodnight, Dr. Arbonne."

"Good—oh! Wait, there's one thing I've been thinking about a lot."

"Only one?"

"I, well, do I have to turn? I mean, with the university and everything, wouldn't that be hard for me to still work there?"

"No, you don't have to turn," he said, as he wrapped his arm around her waist and pulled her into him. His breath was on her cheek as he said, "I'd love you until you grew old and died in my arms." Her knees went weak, and she wrapped her arms around his neck for support. His voice softened into a primal, possessive whisper.

"But we'd have to move every few years if you didn't."

"Why?" Her question squeaked out, and she was excited and allured at what he would say next.

"Because people would talk. People always talk. They'd start asking questions, whispering about you. *Why is her husband ten, twenty, thirty years younger than her?'* Eventually, we'd have to start saying I was your grandson."

Then, his lips were beside her ear, whispering seductively. "Plus, I'd have to make gentle love to you, careful that I didn't break your hips. And I am *not* a gentle lover. I'm ravenous and passionate like a starving wolf." By now, he was kissing her, working his way down her neck in the process.

"So, that would be a problem for you. I will make you happy, I will make you strong. And I will make you weak," he growled, as he kissed the nape of her neck.

Chapter

Twelve

Angelina kicked her shoes off beneath her desk before continuing. They were starting to pinch her toes, and she wanted to be fully comfortable to prepare for her fourth date with Jude.

The previous night he'd come over, bringing with him a grocery cart full of supplies. He'd bought enough to feed an army, giving her the choice of several dishes. Angelina had opted for pasta, and had helped Jude around the kitchen with whatever he needed assistance with.

They danced and twirled around each other in the kitchen, hyper aware of each other's movements while they worked. She'd chopped up romaine lettuce for a homemade Caesar salad, and he'd unflinchingly diced onions and garlic beside her. He created the Caesar dressing, fresh from parmesan, anchovies, and a few other ingredients, while she tenderized and seasoned the filet mignons. She used her charcoal patio grill to lightly sear his, and charred hers to perfection outside. Inside, he watched over the pasta, assuring it was perfectly al dente.

Together they made the sauce, accidentally adding too much parmesan. It still tasted phenomenal, and when assembled, their masterpiece was nothing short of restaurant quality. Jude left the pasta for her, but he did drizzle some of the sauce onto his steak out of respect for the evening.

Afterwards, they'd snuggled onto the couch to watch one of her favorite movies, *The Mirror Has Two Faces*.

"It's practically a classic, what do you mean you've never heard of it?"

"I must've skipped that day in Chick Lit 101," Jude teased.

"He's got jokes, this one. It's Barbara, she's an

iconic legend. Ask me why I don't wear make-up."

"I don't need to ask you why. You're stunning without it. To cover up your natural beauty would be an unforgivable sin." He feathered kisses into her hair as she rolled her eyes.

"That's not what you say. You're supposed to ask why I don't wear make-up, and then I answer like this." She proceeded to do her best Barbara impression, horribly butchering the line. "I'd still look the same, only in color!" She burst out in giggles as he kissed the hollow of her neck.

By the time the movie was over, Angelina was lightly snoring. Her head was nestled underneath Jude's chin, her hair tickling his nose. He gently supported her body as he stood up, carefully laying her back down on the couch in the void he'd created.

Jude pulled a blanket up over her shivering body, and moved to the counter to write her a note.

Until our next night, my Queen.

Devotedly, Jude

Angelina had woken up the next morning to the sound of her cellphone alarm going off. She sat up on the couch, glancing around the room for her vampire man. Somehow, she'd fallen fast asleep. And somehow, during that time, he'd managed to completely clean up the mess they'd left in the kitchen without her hearing so much as a *ting* from a dish being moved.

She journeyed over to the counter to make herself coffee before she left for class. Jude's note was propped against the coffee maker, along with one single white rose.

She thought about him all day, which was terribly distracting when teaching a class of one hundred students. Beneath her desk, she rubbed her toes together, each foot massaging the other before she stood up again.

"Sorry, class, new shoes. You understand." A few of the female students giggled in solidarity with her. Angelina padded back across the darkened stage, the screen bright behind her shadowing her face. She clicked to the next slide.

"As I was saying, Atlantis. Does anyone have any theories on the subject?"

A student with black curly hair and rimmed glasses raised her hand. "Some people speculate that it's really a place called Lemuria."

"Ah yes. Excellent. I was hoping someone would mention Lemuria. The thing about legends is that they're often rooted in truth, right? Some event that the people of the time sought to understand, which in turn made them create fascinating stories. I am of the firm belief that if you dig deep enough into a myth, you'll find proof of it to be true. It's the whole reason I became an archaeologist in the first place.

"Let's take the city of Troy, for example. For centuries, it was just a story. Until archaeologists accidentally blew it up, that is." A shockwave of gasps shot across the room.

"Bet you didn't know that, did you? I'm happy to say I wasn't part of that dig, but the tragedy of loss is no less apparent. And we still haven't found the fabled horse, or evidence of it. The things we will never know are immeasurable now, because of human error."

As she talked, she thought about Ludwig. He'd mentioned how easy it was to change history. At first, she hadn't understood what he'd meant, but the more she mulled it over in her mind, the more she realized she did.

The Library of Alexandria, the Pyramids, Troy, Atlantis, Camelot. These were all the reasons she'd become an archaeologist, to immerse and lose herself in the myths and legends of history. Her mind drifted off as her students talked amongst themselves, until her eyes settled on a shadow watching her from the top row of the auditorium.

To become Jude's wife, or queen, or whatever, in exchange to learn the secrets that he knew? To be privileged to know the things that he'd seen? That allure was even more seductive than his perfect, cherry red lips.

Angelina snapped back to her current situation. "OK, archaeologists, I think that's enough for today. Write me a five-page essay on your favorite legendary tale and where you think it might be located, if it were to exist." Groans filled the huge room as papers shuffled and books clapped shut. "Due in by Thanksgiving break. I'm not a horrible person," she called out to them.

A resounding hiss of yeses responded to her previous comment right before the students raced out the door.

Angelina padded across the stage to turn the lights back on for the few remaining students. Jude rose from his seat and casually strolled down the long stairway between chairs. A small duffel bag was hanging off his shoulder. Fully aware of his oozing sex appeal, a few lingering students' heads turned to watch him as he approached her. She couldn't have been prouder of him in that moment.

Her reputation for being an old spinster, even though she was only thirty-five, hadn't been something she'd been able to shake. Despite her best efforts, even her fellow faculty had tried to set her up on horribly awkward dates over the years when she was in town. Of course, they never worked out. Being single wasn't the only qualification to be in a relationship. You also had to have things in common, share similar goals, and be somewhat—even if only mildly—attracted to the person initially.

The first guy she'd gone on a blind date with had still lived at home in his mother's basement, which wasn't a deal breaker in and of itself. The deal breaker was that he was forty-five, an engineer that well could afford ten houses, but had never bothered to move out at all. And he had mentioned several times that his mom still did his laundry and grocery shopping.

In fact, his mom had texted him several times while they were at dinner to let him know if dinner didn't go 'favorably,' there was meatloaf waiting for him in the refrigerator when he got home. Angelina still cringed when she thought about it.

Even worse still was the man who'd snorted with every word he spoke. He vaguely smelled of wet cat food, and his beady little eyes had watched her hungrily from across the table. Angelina had made a mental note to cut out of her life those so-called friends who'd set them up. They'd had nothing in common except a love for crab Rangoon, which was not enough to build a relationship on, no matter who you were. He was pleasant and polite, but Angelina felt creeped out the whole night and had faked being sick to get out of dessert and call an Uber.

There was no comparison to Jude. This man was the whole package indeed: foreign, mysterious, intelligent, humble, and compassionate, all wrapped up in a tall, dark, and handsome box with a shiny immortal bow. He sauntered across the stage to her while her students looked on with dumbstruck expressions. Dropping the duffel bag on the stairs, all six-foot-whatever-inches of him languidly walked up and wrapped his arms around her waist, pulling her into a romantic embrace for all to see. Behind him, her students gasped in shock and awe.

"I missed you," he said, his gray diamond eyes sparkling into her soul.

Angelina felt like hotter-than-room-temperature butter in his presence. A solid form, but if touched, it would collapse. "I missed you, too. Thank you for doing the dishes. What's that?" She gestured to the bag behind him.

"Tools," he said, matter-of-factly.

"Tools?"

"Every man should have tools. I noticed your sink was leaking this morning."

"Yes, but you're much more than just a man." She ran her hands down his broad, firm chest before clasping them behind his waist. "And you have employees to do the medial things. Like fixing sinks."

"Thank you, my Queen. However, I'm not above fixing your sink."

Angelina giggled. "And you thought you'd bring your tools and fix it for me?"

Jude puffed his chest out, standing up straight. "That's what normal men do."

"I'm not doubting you, I'm just pleasantly surprised is all."

He reached behind and took her hands in his. "Then prepare to be amazed. I believe tonight was Chinese takeout night?"

Angelina ran back to her desk to get her shoes and purse before joining Jude on the stairs.

"Atlantis, huh?" he said, as he slung his arm over her shoulders.

Angelina's eyes went wide. "Were you there? Do you know where it's really at? DO YOU HAVE ANYTHING FROM THERE?" Her voice was growing hysterically squeaky.

Jude laughed an uncharacteristically hearty belly laugh. "I'm not *that* old, Angelina."

She liked the way her name circled his mouth before rolling off his tongue, like raindrops collecting on a leaf.

Back at her apartment, she scrolled through her phone to find the closest Chinese restaurant. Jude positioned himself directly in the cabinet, beneath the kitchen sink. She couldn't see his face, but she wasn't exactly disappointed with the rest of the view, either. His caramel-colored, tanned arms reached out from beneath the sink, feeling for whatever tool it was that he needed. His shirt rode up slightly with his movements, revealing just a glimpse of his taut treasures beneath.

Angelina heard a voice in the distance, and realized she was still on the phone with the Chinese restaurant. "Hello? Hello?"

"Oh my gosh, I'm so sorry. Yes, that's correct. One order of orange chicken, one order of Mongolian beef, two orders of crab Rangoon to be delivered." She hung up, feeling slightly flustered at the effect Jude repeatedly had on her.

"I won't eat the Rangoon, you know," the voice from beneath the sink said.

"Oh, I know. That's all for me." If she only got one food to eat for the rest of her life, it would be crab Rangoon. Or chips and queso. Hands down.

He continued clanging around beneath the sink for the next several minutes, and Angelina fought hard not to stare. Finally, he snapped her out of her trance. "Can you hand me the monkey wrench?" Jude asked, feeling around blindly in the duffel bag and coming up short.

"Which one is that? Is that the crab claw?" For all her strengths, home repairs were not high on the list. Jude laughed, his shirt riding a fraction further up his toned abs. Before Angelina could get lost in the sight of him, the doorbell rang. Her stomach had been growling since noon, and that had cemented her decision to order from the closest-possible restaurant.

At the sound of the doorbell, Jude climbed up from the floor, brushing himself off in the process. His hair was wildly disheveled, giving him the just-woke-up appearance. Angelina bit her lip as she sat the cartons on the counter and began opening them.

"I didn't know vampires ate Mongolian beef."

"There's going to be quite a lot you didn't

know," he said with a grin, as he slurped the sauce off the beef. Which reminded her of something which had been nagging at the back of her mind since their first date.

"Why don't you refer to yourselves as vampires? You told me that's what you were in the beginning, yet ever since, you haven't used the 'v' word. I've heard you say 'immortals' several times, or refer to 'your line' or 'your kind.' Even Ludwig didn't refer to you as vampires."

Jude sat his carton down on the coffee table, and turned his body towards her. "We view the word as derogatory slang. We use the term 'immortal' amongst ourselves, but it was easier to tell you we were vampires. It's the closest thing in the modern world that you would've understood. Traditionally, vampires are seen as fierce creatures of the night. Bloodlust and carnal lust control them, according to the rumor. Would you say that I am that? That that description defines me?"

Angelina thought for a moment. "Certainly not. You're kind, loyal, sincere, caring. I haven't seen you harm one thing outside of a rare filet mignon." She smiled before biting into a crab Rangoon. The cream cheesy, crabby goodness squashed into her mouth.

"But are you truly immortal? Can you die? Would a wooden stake through your heart kill you?"

Jude picked up his beef again and settled back against the couch, smirking. "I'd imagine that would kill anyone, don't you think?"

Angelina felt like the biggest idiot. "Well, yeah … but, I mean, you know. Garlic and silver and stuff, too." She had no idea what to say to him or how to continue this conversation without sounding like a moron.

"The answer to your question is that I think we're like everyone else. Our blood is a bit more powerful, we don't damage quite as quickly, and we heal more easily. However, my line has never been in a war, or gotten seriously injured from more than they could recover from in a decent amount of time, even if they weren't immortal. All that to say, I assume we can die in the same serious ways that regular humans can. A bullet to the wrong area, a stake through the heart, a bomb. I don't think that we're necessarily fully immortal.

"On the contrary, if someone receives my blood right before they die, they can be brought back within the day. This has happened only once so far."

His posture went rigid, and his face frowned. Angelina sensed this was a subject he was sore about. Edgar had mentioned it briefly before, when he'd told her his story. She made a mental note to ask either him or Ludwig what the deal was later, and decided to change the subject.

"Where are you from, originally? Do you remember? How old are you?" She word vomited more questions out at him. Jude sat there, quietly chewing and gathering his thoughts.

"I think you're of Macedonian descent," he said, contemplating. "You're stunningly beautiful. Your vibrant green eyes, olive skin, exotic features, and dark chestnut hair remind me of the fisherman's daughter. I used to have a terrible crush on her. I would buy a fish from her and pay double, just to see her smile."

"You're from Greece?"

"I'm from Spain. A lot of my mortal life is distant in memory, but that much I know for sure. I don't know how I got from Spain to Greece, or how I got separated from my parents. I don't know if I had other family, brothers or sisters. I'd like to think if I'd had a wife, I would've gone back for her. But I can't remember more than that."

His voice was wavering, as if trying to remember his past was almost unbearable. "I don't know who I was, other than a soldier. Was I on the right side, or did I strike terror in the hearts of women and children for no reason? I've tried to atone for my sins for as long as I've roamed this earth, but I don't even know what they were."

Tears were rolling freely down his face, and Angelina quickly closed the distance between them on the couch. She wrapped her arms around him, cradling his head on her shoulder as he cried into her. Her heart ached for him, and she imagined her energy reaching out to soothe him. He hugged her body furiously, grabbing a handful of her shirt in the process. She kissed his temple, seemingly calming him into soft sobs.

"When I saw you that first time, everything was clear to me. Everything I'd done in my life was for you, to make you proud. I've been searching for you for centuries. The first time I saw you, Angelina, was the first time I'd seen home since I've been immortal."

Her heart broke and rejoiced at the same time. If she hadn't been sure before, she was certain now.

Angelina had, indeed, and beyond all reasonable doubt, fallen in love with Jude over the past two weeks. Whatever demons he'd faced, whatever pain he'd endured in his lifetime, she wanted to erase it, or at the very least make it her own so he would know he never had to be alone again.

Her mind was made up.

She was going to be his queen.

Chapter

Thirteen

Later that night, the next to last night before the Convention, Angelina told Jude she didn't want to see him the following day. This would cancel their final date, their final night of normalcy before she embarked upon the new world beside him. This was also the final buffer he would have to ease her into his world before this mysterious assemblage of his entire family line officially started. Jude had not yet formally proposed, and Angelina had not yet formally accepted his offer. However, the unspoken bond that had constructed between them, of the things not seen in this world but only felt, replaced any words they ever need speak.

Despite that, his ugly insecurities emerged again that night—vile, putrid saliva seething between teeth. When she cancelled their last date, he immediately started apologizing for rushing her and opening up too soon.

"I can give you more time. Don't leave me, Angelina," Jude pleaded desperately.

She cradled his face in her hands, and kissed his cherry lips. This marked the first time that she had initiated a kiss, and it did not go unnoticed. He gasped into her kiss, and pulled her closer, the tension in his body easing. "Be confident, Jude. I need a day to go see my aunt and handle some personal business. That's all this is."

A worried expression still marred his handsome face. He seemed defeated, but he trusted her even more than she trusted him. "OK." His conquered response made her angry. Whoever had wounded him in the past, if they were alive, they were about to have hell to pay in the form of Dr. Angelina Arbonne. And she suspected she was going to have to start with his first two wives.

"Jude, seriously, stop." She rubbed her nose against his before kissing him again. "You're easily the best man I've ever met, life-extended or otherwise. I like you confident, sexy, and slaying the world."

The following day, Angelina went to visit Aunt Emmaline. She had done her best to try and make weekly trips at the very least. Now, with all things considered, Angelina figured it might be the only chance she'd get for the next several weeks. Her aunt was in a senior living facility, and had been for a while. She'd been diagnosed with Alzheimer's disease when she was only fifty years young, around the time Angelina was applying for graduate schools.

Over the last several years, Emmaline had gotten progressively worse. That didn't stop her from always being thrilled to have the company, no matter who she thought her niece was in that present moment. On most occasions she barely recognized Angelina, but every so often her mind would be as clear as day.

Angelina walked through the front doors of the care facility. A foyer full of palm trees, along with abundant racks of brochures with overly happy people on their covers, greeted her immediately inside the doors. The egg blue walls reflecting off of the speckled linoleum floors always made her feel like she was stuck inside a bird's nest. But despite the facility's best efforts to make it look more like a five-star resort than a nursing home, the subtlest trace of urine and bleach always wafted out to greet the guests immediately upon entry.

Emmaline was the only surviving blood relative she had left. Angelina's parents had died in a car crash when she was twelve, and Emmaline had graciously taken her in and raised her as her own daughter. Ever since then, it had been the two of them against the world.

Emmaline had been a Renaissance woman in her prime, an activist, a feminist, an environmentalist, and a historian. She worked at the local library during the day, educating anyone who was willing to listen on the knowledge she possessed. In the evenings, she was a tour guide, working for tips by charming the locals and tourists alike with her storytelling abilities.

Emmaline was a master storyteller, a craftsperson of words. Angelina always thought she should've used her talents to be an actress, on stage or screen. Her overdramatic nature drew people in, hanging on every word she spoke and still begging for more. The library had paid for their everyday bills. The tour guide gig had paid for Angelina's undergrad courses.

She turned the corner to go down the long hallway to Emmaline's room. Mr. Vernon, the resident cad, was seated just on the other side of the hallway in his wheelchair. He still had most of his hair, which judging from the conversations Angelina had overheard in the cafeteria from some of the female residents, was all a man his age needed in order to be considered a catch. He shuffled slowly by, the wheels on his chair barely turning with his movements as he stepped his feet along the floor.

"Good morning, Mr. Vernon," Angelina said cheerily. He glanced up briefly to look at her before mumbling to himself and carrying on with his business. She continued down the hallway, dodging residents with walkers and wheelchairs leisurely zooming towards her.

Emmaline's door was at the very end of the hallway, one of the more expensive rooms in one of the corners with four windows, instead of the customary two. It was unmistakable, as bright as a Mardi Gras float. A giant black, orange, purple, and lime green glittery, gaudy wreath beckoned to anyone in the hallway. Emmaline had been fussed at for putting such eyesores up for everyone to see, but she did it anyway. Now the staff had just accepted her as the eccentric old lady in 301.

Angelina reached through the middle of the wreath to rap the lion door knocker Emmaline had sweet-talked maintenance into installing.

"Come in!"

Angelina gently pushed the door open, knowing full well what was waiting for her on the other side. She pushed too far, and the clacking sound of the beads slammed against the door. Emmaline had ordered an arbor on-line, and coerced Angelina to put it together for her when she moved into the residence. Since then, she had procured no less than six curtains of beads, all of which now hung from the arbor, which was precariously close to Emmaline's one and only door in her mini-suite.

"Why do you need an arbor in your kitchen?" Angelina had asked.

"Because, my dear, you're never too old to be presented. I want to walk in like a queen to my humble abode." There was also a red-carpet memory foam bathmat beneath the arbor for added effect.

Angelina sidestepped the arbor, not wanting to get her chestnut hair tangled in the beads like she'd done the last time she visited. She walked into the bright purple kitchenette, and set the box of donuts down on the counter. Looking around, Angelina laughed to herself. Emmaline's cabinets were lemon yellow, and all of her appliances and utensils were apple green. Everything Emmaline owned was so brightly colored or lit up, and Angelina always half-expected a crew to walk in and start filming a children's show.

Emmaline was over beside the full-paned glass wall, watering her plants and quietly humming to herself. The pothos vine that Angelina had given her on Mother's Day ten years ago was now so long that it had to be pinned along the length of her open floor plan room, making a border of leaves around the ceiling.

Emmaline's bright red hair stuck out in ringlets beneath her fuchsia headscarf, her neon pink and blue muumuu swaying with her movements as she danced to the music in her head.

"Emmaline?" Angelina walked towards her

quietly, trying not to startle her. "Emmaline, it's me, Angelina."

"Oh, hello, dear! It's time for my medicine, isn't it? You can just leave it on the counter. My sister is visiting me today, she'll make sure I get it."

Angelina looked like the spitting image of her mother. Since Emmaline had been diagnosed, referring to Angelina as her sister instead of niece had become a common occurrence. Emmaline continued watering her plants, moving to the bookshelf that housed all of her succulent terrariums. She raised her water bottle towards them, misting the leaves to create a humid environment.

Behind her, the coffee table was covered in knick-knacks, various snow globes and statues. All of them were subsequently covered in paper towels. Emmaline said it was to keep the dust off, but the treasures beneath were barely visible. Angelina didn't see the point of having a coffee table that looks like a paper towel factory had sneezed all over it, but to each their own.

There was a goldfish in an aquarium beside her bed, barely visible through the aquatic plant forest he inhabited. Angelina watched as a googly eye and a flash of gold occasionally made an appearance, checking to see if she was going to drop some fish flakes on top of the water.

Emmaline turned around. "Hello! I wasn't expecting company today. Please make yourself at home. Would you like a grilled cheese? My niece brought me some muenster when she was here last week."

"No, thank you, maybe next time. I brought you some donuts from that double decker donut place."

"Bavarian filled?" Emmaline sat her spray bottle down on the table.

"Yep." Angelina walked over and picked the box back up, fanning the lid to push the scent towards Emmaline. *Like a cat to catnip.*

"Chocolate-covered?" Emmaline's tongue peeped out of the side of her mouth, pondering how many she could eat without spiking her sugar too high.

"Of course!" Angelina grinned as a cloud of neon pink silk sped towards her outstretched hands. Emmaline's blue eyes glowed, dreams of sugar

153

spinning behind them. She looked up at Angelina, focusing on her face more clearly for the first time today.

"You look just like Amelia, my sweet girl." Emmaline and Amelia had been the talk of the town, the hottest girls on the block, back in their heyday. Angelina could see her mom's features, save the hair, mirrored on Emmaline's face more clearly than her own. "I miss her every day, you know."

"I know, me too." Angelina teared up, thinking about her mom and how many years it'd been since her parents had passed. Emmaline shoved half of a donut into her mouth, a mustache of chocolate coating her top lip. Bavarian crème oozed out of the remaining half, stopping short in Emmaline's outstretched palm. She closed her eyes and licked the chocolate from her lips, a devilish grin replacing the chocolate.

"How've you been, Angie?" Angelina set down the grocery bag she'd forgotten was hanging from her shoulder. She emptied the contents onto the kitchen counter. The loaf of bread rolled out of the bag, knocking over a toothpick holder. Salt poured out of it, and Angelina righted it with a questioning look.

"That's to multipurpose, dear. Toothpick

holder and salt shaker in one," Emmaline said, reading her face.

Angelina nodded, accepting yet another of her aunt's eccentricities. "I've been pretty good. I brought you some of that chicken salad you like. A whole pint, so you can have a couple of sandwiches." She pulled out a loaf of orange-speckled bread, and Emmaline clapped her hands in joy.

"Oh! Is that what I think it is?!" Emmaline grabbed the bread, unknotting the twist tie that held the bag closed.

"Yep, cheddar bread. Don't forgot to freeze it until you need it, or it'll start to mold."

Emmaline moved to the refrigerator and grabbed her notepad. In her clearer moments, she knew what was going on. She had the foresight to write herself notes, which were stuck all over her refrigerator. Whether or not she actually read them later on when she really needed them, Angelina had no clue.

Emmaline's old, twisted hands, like grapevines in winter, scribbled down on her notepad. She'd had the most beautiful handwriting Angelina had ever seen.

Now, combined with her condition and several mini strokes over the years, her penmanship was jittery as she scrolled down the important information.

"OK, now, let's see. 'Freeze bread until needed. Might mold.' Is that right?" Before Angelina could stop her, she grabbed a roll of Scotch tape and wound it around the note and the bag tightly, making any future retrieval of bread slices complicated.

She patted Angelina's hand, squeezing it tenderly. "Do you want a grilled cheese?"

Angelina fought back the tears and tried to smile. "No, thank you, I'm good right now."

"How about some sweet tea? Or I have milk. Do you want milk?" Emmaline shuffled over to the refrigerator. Several sticky notes fell off the door as she opened it, and Angelina made a mental note to buy her several packs of magnets for next time.

"How're things going here? Have they been having good meals in the cafeteria lately?" Angelina took a sip of the syrupy sweet tea Emmaline had made.

"Sometimes. Do you know the other day they

had salad on the menu, and they didn't even buy enough lettuce for everyone? I had to eat macaroni salad, like that's even a substitute for leafy green vegetables."

"It wasn't good? I thought you loved macaroni salad."

"I love *my* macaroni salad. They made theirs with Italian dressing and nothing else. They can't even make their own dressing, for heaven's sake! And they put pickle relish in it. It's like they don't even have a recipe, they just throw together whatever they can find in the kitchen. Disgusting. The Jell-O is good, though."

"It's pretty hard to mess up Jell-O, I would think."

"You would think that, wouldn't you? Since the directions are right there on the box. The old cook used to never put enough water in it, so it ended up being like jiggly rubber instead of a pleasant sliding feeling in your mouth. Utter nonsense."

Angelina stifled a laugh. She tried her best to keep Emmaline in good supply of groceries. She'd been the best cook she'd ever known, and Angelina didn't want to deprive her of that joy. "And that bitch Betty always steals my crackers. I get extra for my soup on Soup Day, and as soon as I turn my head, my Saltines are gone."

Emmaline never would've said a cross word about anyone before. As her disease progressed, her thoughts readily bubbled to the surface more frequently. Angelina was in a full-out giggle now, holding her hand over her mouth to try and contain her donut. She didn't think anyone had really stolen Emmaline's crackers, but, then again, she wouldn't have put Mr. Vernon on her most eligible bachelor's list, either. *Priorities.*

"You know what we really need? A good quiche. The right quiche can solve the world's problems. Or chicken spaghetti. You know they had to rename it chicken casserole just to get all these yakking biddies around here to eat it? They wouldn't touch chicken spaghetti, because they thought it would be too spicy. Then, the cooks renamed it chicken casserole and those dumbasses sucked it right off their plates.

"But don't listen to me blabber on all day, what's new with you, my sweet girl? Who's the man in your life?" Emmaline stared at her, her eyes glimmering as she started in on her second donut.

"How do you know I have a man?" Angelina was thoroughly stunned.

"Because I practically raised you, Angie. Your pheromones are acting up and you smell different."

Angelina's mouth hung open for a second, until she sniffed the air around herself. "How can you smell me? Do I stink?"

"No, goodness no, girl. You smell sweaty, like you just mowed the yard. Fresh sweat, fresh grass, and fresh air. You know I've always had excellent senses. The last time you smelled like that was in college, when that boy on the SGA asked you to be his study partner. That blond kid, what was his name?"

Angelina blushed. She'd tried hard to make him notice her. Finally, after two semesters of giving campus tours to the new freshmen, they'd ended up as tour buddies. "His name was Shane. That was just because giving tours in the sun was hot."

"No, sweet girl, that was your hormones acting up. Hormones and biology. Oh yes, he was the one that was the accountant's kid, right? That guy with the beaky nose who overcharged me that one year. I'm glad you didn't end up in *that* family. So, who's the man? He has to be a man and not a boy, otherwise he wouldn't have caught your attention. Ooooh, I bet he's hot. He's hot, isn't he?" She got up and shuffled over to her bookshelf, rifling through her trashy romance novels.

Finally, she selected one, the delight spreading across her face. "Does he look like this? Please tell me this is him." The cover she'd chosen had an obviously-on-steroids raven-haired man in a kilt, holding a hammer, and a scantily clad woman thrown across his thigh.

Angelina nearly snorted Bavarian crème up her nose. Emmaline was full of surprises, and her type in fantasy men was another new one for the books. "No, Em, he does *not* look like that. I can't even tell if that's a Viking or a Scottish highlander. Jude is foreign, though. But definitely, certainly, way hotter."

"Can I meet him? Will you bring him around for Christmas?" Angelina's heart broke into a billion jagged pieces, because for once in her life, she didn't actually know what the next few months were going to hold.

"That's the thing. He's asked me to go away with him, and I don't know how long I'll be gone, Em. I'm going to make sure that everything is taken care of for you, but it may be a few months. I'm just really not sure."

"Where are you going away to?" Emmaline's gaze was set hard on a third donut. Her eyes looked up and met Angelina's disapproving ones. "Push off, now, I took my meds today. Talk about your man and don't pay me any mind." She snatched the donut up and shoved a bite into her mouth quickly, as if she had to fight off a pack of ravenous wolves for it.

"He's got properties all over the world, he said. He's … a realtor … and he's wealthy and well connected."

Emmaline stopped chewing and watched Angelina carefully. "But? What is it?"

"Well … in not so many words, he sort of proposed. I haven't officially accepted yet, but I feel like I will. We haven't been dating that long, not long at all actually, but I know he's a great man. He's kind and gentle, and when we're together everything just feels … It feels. I feel more, I experience more, I believe in more possibilities with him." Her voice fell silent as her thoughts continued on.

She checked her watch, realizing she hadn't been keeping up with the time. It was 4:30 p.m. Angelina didn't have much longer before sundown, and she knew she couldn't stay. She had, once or twice, and it had nearly killed her. Emmaline's personality would turn ugly, the disease would take over and her beloved aunt would be gone for the rest of the day and night. Emmaline followed her gaze to her wrist.

"Sounds like your mind's made up. I forgot what the problem was. Do you want a grilled cheese?"

"No grilled cheese. The problem is that I might not see you for a while. I don't want you to be left alone."

Emmaline gulped down a glass of milk loudly. "Angie, don't live your life for others. Live the life you want to lead. Don't wait around for me and miss out on your own adventures. I'm not even here most days." Angelina's tears started flowing freely as her aunt moved to sit beside her.

"But you'll be lonely. I don't want to leave you alone," she sobbed. Leaving her aunt to die in a nursing home was unfathomable. Emmaline wrapped her arms around Angelina.

"I'm going to rot away, I've already started. You're young and vibrant and eternal. You're simply wonderful. Go and be that with your man." Angelina leaned into Emmaline's embrace, their arms around each other and their heads on each other's shoulders. Emmaline was the only person who'd ever had the power to make Angelina ugly-girl cry, and the snot was now pouring profusely from her nose.

Emmaline kissed her temple. "You can come see me when you have the time. I may remember you, and I may not. But I won't be lonely. I'm never lonely. People come to visit me now. Friends from the past, lovers who got away. I'm never wanting for company. Just don't cancel my Starz subscription. I need my *Outlander*."

Angelina burst out laughing between her rivers of tears and mucous.

On the way home, Angelina decided to stop and talk to her parents. Their oven crypt was beneath a live oak tree in Metairie Cemetery. Emmaline had made burial arrangements for their family there instead of other cemeteries, because there were less tourists and less restrictions on visiting. Even if she had secretly wanted to be Marie Laveau's neighbor.

Angelina thought about Ludwig's words again, about how easy it was to change history. The words had been rolling around in her mind, popping up in every thought she'd had since meeting these immortal men. The way people are remembered now isn't necessarily how they actually were in their lifetimes. Marie Laveau was a prime example of history reimagined.

In her life, Marie had been a healer, an herbalist, and a near saint of aiding the sick and injured. She traveled around with the monks to hospitals, helping the sick and injured. Yet, that's not what she's remembered for or thought of in modern times. Often associated with voodoo and magical mysticism, no one recalls the true Marie, who devoted her life to helping people.

Angelina strolled through the cemetery, running her hand along the front of each of the crypts until she came upon her parents'. She didn't much believe in spirits, but then, she hadn't believed in vampires until a few days ago, either. Chatting with her dead parents seemed like a good place to get a crash course.

"I don't know how to do this, but I need some help," she said out loud, barely above a whisper in case anyone could hear her. The sun was setting now, and the rush of a cool breeze blew past her as she waited for an answer.

A swirl of leaves and twigs rolled behind her, twisting and weaving its way between the mausoleums. She still had heard no response, but she now felt that she wasn't alone. Angelina turned around and came face to face with a woman in brightly colored clothes. The woman had a purple and golden head wrap, much like the one Emmaline had worn earlier, and a long dress that dragged the ground. The woman's skin was as dark as an obsidian river on a moonless night. Angelina swore she could see her reflection glistening off the old woman's ethereal shimmer.

Even in the shadows of the sunset, the ancient lines that carved her face were visible, each one a different story from a different century. Whether she was a ghost, an angel, or Marie Laveau herself out sightseeing, Angelina couldn't be certain. Bangles chimed on the woman's wrists as she swirled her gnarled fingers at Angelina's face.

"You not be here long, Child." The woman's voice was from a different era, of times long past.

"What does that—wait!" Angelina replied, as the woman turned from her and began walking away. She was faster than she looked and Angelina had to jog to keep up with her. The woman stopped suddenly and turned back slowly, the irritation radiating from her stooped-over body. She stared at Angelina as if she were a cockroach.

"Please just tell me what to do. I don't know—" Angelina stuttered, feeling that she should tell this woman, this stranger, everything.

"You already know, Child. Your aunt be all right." Then, as quickly as she had appeared, the woman was gone. Nothing of her remained, except a few leaves swirling on the ground.

Chapter

Fourteen

Angelina's doorbell rang Saturday morning at 8 a.m. sharp. Rolling out of bed and padding barefoot to the door, Angelina tried and failed to scrub the sleep from her eyes. She tiptoed to the door quietly, peering through the peephole. The top of Harold's chauffeur's hat was barely visible and, if she hadn't seen the sun glowing through his white hair, she probably wouldn't have answered.

Angelina unhooked the chain and unlatched the bolt, then slowly opened the door with a wide yawn.

"Good morning, ma'am!"

"Harold, it's 8 a.m. Why are you here this early?" She shut her eyes, willing herself to go back to sleep standing up.

"Mr. Jude sent me. Ms. Anne scheduled you fittings for your gowns. Plus, Mr. Jude said there's all sorts of things you should be in attendance for, and that you should get to know the Society better. It's a big day, Dr. Arbonne! I've been an onlooker for quite a few Conventions now, and they never cease to amaze me! Ms. Anne puts details into everything." Harold's smile was beaming. His round, wrinkled face reminded Angelina of a patterned Christmas ornament—bright, glittery, and full of cheer.

"I have a dress, Harold. I wasn't planning on getting a new one." She propped her head against the door.

Harold teeter-tottered on his little feet, not intimidated by her at all. He huffed politely. "Bring it along then, and you and Ms. Anne can compare and contrast." He smiled at her, almost sympathetically. "I'll warn you, though. Not many people make a habit to cross her. I'll expect you in the car in thirty minutes, unless you need help packing!"

"Wait, need help? I thought this was a one-day

thing?" *Coffee. Coffee is what I need.*

"It's really more like three, if we arrive on time. Tonight is a ball, and meet and greets. Tomorrow night is formal announcements. Monday is farewells and send-offs." *He would've made an excellent customer service representative in a retail store, friendly yet enforcing of policies.*

"Right, naturally. You win, Harold. Give me thirty minutes and I'll meet you down there."

Satisfied with her answer, Harold clicked his heels together and spun around to go back to the car. Angelina closed the door behind her, leaning against it and sighing. She'd cried herself to sleep last night, overanalyzing and obsessing about what the future held if she made this leap of faith. She didn't not trust Jude, but the closer the Convention drew, the more the whole immortal thing was starting to feel a little bit overwhelming, to say the least.

Angelina got up and walked into the bathroom to take a fast shower and wash her hair. She got out, scrubbing excess water off her head with a towel, and quickly combed through her hair. Haircare wasn't something Angelina dedicated a lot of time to. She'd been blessed with a thick head of luscious chestnut hair that refused to hold any shape beyond its natural waves, no matter what she did with it. In college, she'd finally come to accept that fact and had since then not stressed herself out about it whatsoever.

Before throwing her basic make-up kit into a travel bag, Angelina slid into a pair of blue jean shorts and a yellow blouse. She threw her little black dress and strappy heels into a small duffle bag, along with two extra changes of clothes and various necessities. She slid on her black sandals, threw her canvas messenger bag over her shoulder, and ran down to meet Harold, not wanting to get him flustered from waiting too long. In the New Orleans heat, her hair was already halfway dry in the fifteen minutes since she'd been out of the shower.

When the car stopped underneath the awning of the palatial venue, Harold quickly hopped out and opened Angelina's door. He removed her bag from the trunk and handed it to her. "Ms. Anne is inside; she'll see to you!" Then he hopped back into the car and sped away just as fast.

Angelina walked through the glass doors, into the beautiful antique conservatory. This was by far her favorite room in the palatial venue, that she'd seen anyway. No one was there to greet her, though. No one except Jude's white cat, Neville, who was customarily perched on the edge of the water fountain. He watched her as she walked in, his eyes slightly squinted and sizing her up the way that cat greetings do.

"Meow," he said with no emotion, in his short cat greeting. *I don't have time for this, I'm busy doing cat things.*

"Hello, Neville. Lovely to see you again." She scratched his forehead, which seemed to do the trick. He muttered at her underneath his breath, then hopped down and started walking towards the doors. He stopped and glanced back at her, mumbling to himself yet again. *Come on, already.*

"I guess you're the official doorcat, huh? You do an excellent job of it. Thank you," Angelina cooed at him, not sure why she was desperately trying to win the affection of a vampire cat.

He arched his back as he stood waiting for her, his front paws starting to knead invisible biscuits. "Meow."

The glass doors slipped open *(were they automatic last time?)*, and Neville moved to brush against

Angelina's legs as an acceptance gesture, before turning to go back and sit on the fountain. No actual person was here to greet her, either, yet there were tons of people inside.

Twelve-foot-long tables were set up on either side of the foyer between the ballrooms. Welcome banners and flags draped every surface of the walls, and the table cloths had elaborate neon patterns stretching out for the entirety of their length. Each table was covered in all the swag a person could imagine: T-shirts, brochures, buttons, pens, mugs, baseball caps, sticky notes, water bottles. And they all had the same logo on them in brightly colored letters in some form or fashion.

M.O.E.

Has Jude told me what M.O.E. is? She couldn't remember right off hand.

Angelina walked closer to one of the tables, where a couple was chatting intently about something. The man's back was to her, but from his mop of burnt auburn curls, Angelina recognized him immediately as Keats, decked in acid washed jeans and black Vans. Their banter subsided as Angelina grew closer. Keats quit talking and turned towards her, stepping aside.

Crap.

The person he'd been talking to was a short girl. They hadn't officially met, but Angelina recognized the girl's outline as the one who had been less than friendly to her previously. She was wearing a puffy white blouse, with red polka dots on it, black skinny jeans ripped at the knees, and lime green Converse sneakers. Angelina tentatively approached them, noticing that their body language was rigid and guarded. She was intruding upon something private between them.

The girl slowly peered up at Angelina from underneath her neon yellow baseball cap. M.O.E. was stitched in swirly tangerine letters across the middle. Her frosty glare and personality still had not subsided in the least. Upon seeing her face fully for the first time, Angelina recognized the girl immediately. Her gaze shot to the girl's dark, frosted mocha eyes, then glanced away equally as fast. She'd give anything if Jude was here, even Ludwig or Edgar, to act as a buffer between them.

Angelina felt awkward, knowing what she knew and not knowing what she didn't. *Should she say something?* The elephant in the room that was currently unspoken was the socially uncomfortable equivalent of deciding whether or not to tell someone on national television that they had spinach in their teeth.

Angelina shifted her weight, running her hand up and down the strap of her messenger bag. Harold certainly had not taken extra time to introduce them, and though she'd secretly willed them to in the last several seconds, none of her other newly acquired friends had showed up to save her from this predicament of a child completely upending her.

She decided to take the first step and assert the confidence she seemed to have left back at her apartment. Cautiously, Angelina held out her hand.

"Hi, I'm Angelina." The girl looked down at Angelina's extended hand. Her eyes crawled inch by inch back up Angelina's arm to resume their stare down. She didn't bother to introduce herself. She didn't have to.

The girl spoke, her tone biting. "I know perfectly well who you are. We've got work to do."

Chapter Fifteen

Bergen-Belsen. Poland. February 1945.

The soldiers knew what they were doing, yet they continued to follow orders. An ominous, insidious shadow hung over every camp. Ludwig and Jude had already infiltrated quite a few, and Bergen-Belsen was no different.

The pair had started at Janowska. Then Majdanek, Auschwitz-Birkenau, Mauthausen, Dachau, Buchenwald, Natzweiler-Struthof, Flossenbürg, Theresienstadt, Mittelbau-Dora. Next on the list was Westerbork. As soon as they found out what was happening, they did not hesitate to do as much as they could to stop it. The plan was to counter-blitzkrieg, hit them all to save hundreds.

At first it was sad, shocking. Jude and Ludwig only allowed themselves to mourn the first night. Then they became numb, hardening their hearts to the atrocities around them. It was necessary to survive, or they wouldn't have been able to face it, let alone help anyone.

Dark and foreboding, they couldn't quite believe it even after witnessing firsthand all that had been done. Anguish lay everywhere. The stench of rot, decay, death, leeching from unimaginable places. The bricks, the wires, the ground, all oozed putrescence.

The death camps were searing, unendurable nightmares. Cinders lingered in Jude's eyes, in his mouth, down his throat, and on his tongue. From camp to camp, broken hearts and lost dreams landed on his arms and fell on his conscience. It was hard to tell where the dust stopped and the concrete began.

The only bright color Jude could remember at any of them was a single blade of green grass that had popped through, underneath the barbed wire fence. Too young to have yet learned its lesson in this barren wasteland.

Edgar did not accompany them. He was too recognizable, and his German was elementary at best. Only Ludwig and Jude took on this task. They never stayed more than a few months, slipping in and out through the night, like inconspicuous soldiers passing through. They didn't save more than twenty apiece or thereabouts each time they visited. Blowing their cover would bring attention to their kind, to the cause.

At each camp, they would split up. Ludwig would take the men; Jude would take the women. It was easier like that. Ludwig's broad shoulders, impeccable German speech, and sandy hair disguised him properly. Jude's German wasn't as pristine, but he had charm in spades to smooth over the rough bits. It was easy to distract the female guards. A quick joke or a sly grin could get him through any door he saw fit. The guards were under the assumption Jude was secretly an alcoholic, and that was why his accent was occasionally slurred.

The men made sure to take care of the details, to cover their tracks. The souls they saved were marked as deceased, their departures unnoticeable to anyone monitoring the papers. Just more dead bodies in the piles of dead bodies. And who would notice the absence of two German soldiers with no official documents? Paperwork could've easily gotten lost, and the soldiers could've just simply been transferred without anyone questioning otherwise. For all that had become acceptable, no one assumed immortals were also in the mix.

At Auschwitz, they had nearly gotten too comfortable and almost blown their cover. The guards noticed, and more specifically, Mengele noticed. The Angel of Death.

Ludwig and Jude had had no contact with one another since arriving at Auschwitz. They had their plans mapped out and memorized by heart. At half past midnight, after the last rounds, they would sneak into the bunkers. But they were not discreet enough.

Not long after their arrival, rumors spread of the German soldiers that were feeding the Jews blood. Their uniforms shouldn't have brought them into question, but their elusive answers and behavior as compared to the other soldiers made them the obvious suspects.

One dreary afternoon, Jude and Ludwig were summoned to Mengele's office.

A plain, drab room with two chairs greeted the men. Mengele gestured for them to have a seat.

"There are rumors about the two of you, questionable rumors which make me very curious."

The duo sat in silence.

"Is it true? Is it true that you have been feeding the workers drops of blood?"

Ludwig spoke in perfect German, "Das ist richtig." *It is true.*

"And is it true that you have been encouraging them?"

"It is true."

"May I ask why?"

Jude's face was hard as stone as Ludwig replied. "For the good of the camps, Doctor. We select only the strongest workers, and we give them a bit of blood, just a drop, from our noble genes. The iron helps them to stay strong. We then ensure that they are on the list for one of the working camps. Now, more and more strong and able-bodied workers are available for the arduous labors required of them."

"Do you agree with your comrade?" Mengele asked, looking Jude square in the eyes. Perhaps in another life, Mengele could've been a better person. Not in this one. He was already damned, no matter how nice he was to the children. Jude saw humanity behind his eyes for a fraction of a millisecond, and then it was gone as fast as it had arrived.

"I do. The more we can prepare for the future now, the less we will have to worry later." Jude's eyes stayed purposefully blank, hoping Mengele couldn't hear his thoughts cringing inside.

"Prepare indeed! I should recommend your names to the Führer for outstanding comradeship and leadership! Would you like to be transferred to my labs, to assist me?"

Tension settled on Jude's and Ludwig's shoulders. It was Ludwig's turn to speak and get them out of this one. "Perhaps later. At this moment, we are quite dedicated and fulfilled with making the labor camps more productive, Doctor. You will be the first to know, as soon as we feel our duties have been met."

Mengele grinned, stood, and saluted, approving of Ludwig's answer. "Heil Hitler!"

"Heil Hitler!" the men said, and saluted in unison before exiting his office. Speaking no words as they left, Jude and Ludwig only briefly glanced at each other's telling eyes. They had come too close. That night was their last at Auschwitz.

Typhus was rampant among the prisoners at Bergen, as was starvation. To distract Jude's mind, he counted how many he had turned, how many might make it out. By his count, he was up to at least two hundred total.

Not nearly enough. Not even close.

Jude hoped Ludwig had done better overall. The usual selection process was null; the only qualification required was a willing participant.

Many of the people thought they were practicing witchcraft. Most didn't believe them. The people were weary, as well they should be, of a friendly German officer offering to help. Jude promised them the world if only they would trust him. More often than not, they shunned him. Most of the ones that took the blood did so out of starvation, the last option for food that they had.

Bullets could wound the immortal, and a bullet to the head is fatal for any creature. Jude tried to explain to them, if they could just drink his blood, and try not to get shot or burned, then they might make it out alive. There was a good chance they could survive if they'd only trust him.

Jude was patrolling the barracks early one morning. It was his and Ludwig's last day at Bergen-Belsen. That night, Ludwig and Jude would depart, waking all the undead bodies from the mass graves to take them to safety. They had kept count of the souls and used only one section of one grave so as to collect everyone. The plan was in motion.

The sun was just coming up, and there was a gray glow over the camp. Jude turned the corner, coming face to face with a young girl. She wasn't supposed to be up yet. The workers still had another hour before they had to be at roll call.

She didn't see Jude at first, and he watched her patiently. She was tiny, delicate, and starved. While Jude looked on, her hands flowed up in the air, as if she were a dancing ballerina in a music box. She was smiling and whispering softly to something. Then she brought her hand down to eye level, and Jude noticed a little gray moth sitting atop her pale skin. The girl was comforting it, giving it encouraging words. Until she saw Jude. Her happy eyes immediately turned dark as she looked down. "I'm sorry."

"What were you saying to that moth, Little One?"

She slowly looked up at Jude and whispered, "I was giving him hope."

Hope. Not a word spoken much in this hellhole. Now that Jude was closer, he could see she had the unmistakable spots of the sickness. What strength she had mustered, in her present condition, to even be out at all. She was a compassionate fighter.

She made eye contact, and something inside her was fierce, almost as if she were daring Jude to hurt her. What did she have to lose, after all?

Jude knew easily. She only had a few days left in her, maybe a week.

"Little One, how would you like to make it out of here?"

Her eyes twinkled, but just barely. She was so

devoid of any nutrients. Jude had a potato peel wrapped in his pocket, a large one which he had saved from his soup the night before for just such an occasion. He gave it entirely to her. She took it gratefully, unafraid of him for only a moment. Then she was sad again.

"You can't get me out of here. You wouldn't if you could."

"How wrong you are, Little One. I can and I will, only you must help me help you."

Jude explained to her the situation, the consequences, what she would have to give up in return and how she must do her best not to be shot or burned.

"I'll agree, but only if you save my sister, too. She is here with me. I have already lost my mother and my father." She bargained with him, believing he was the devil.

She told Jude where her sister was located, and he promised. How could he refuse her under these circumstances? Jude gave her his blood, right then and there, and instructed her on what to do next. She immediately went limp from the change, and he carried her body to one of the mass graves. Jude gently laid her on top, with a blanket. He then placed a body over her, to shield her from any others who might be thrown on top of her tiny frame. He would place her sister beside her, and come to collect them early in the morning, free from watchful eyes.

Jude then went to find her sister, inquiring with the other guards only to discover that she had died in the night. His heart broke into a thousand shards for the little one, for all she'd lost. If only he'd been a day earlier, maybe even just a few hours, Jude could've saved her sister as well. Right then, he decided that he would keep her with him, adopt her into his family as he had Ludwig and Edgar.

It was raining that night; not a cleansing rain, but a heavy, thick pouring from the sky, collecting the particles as it slammed down. Ludwig had managed to make a hole in the fence, in a hidden corner that would give them enough time. He and Jude met up in the early hours of the morning and began digging out their treasures.

One, two, three … they helped each of their souls crawl out of their graves. One by one, the people slowly smiled, understanding that Jude and Ludwig were indeed on their side. These two SS officers before them were only disguised as their enemies. Finally, the little one came out. She saw Jude and her face lit up. Then she looked around for her sister.

"Margot! Where's Margot?" Jude was crying for her, though the rain cloaked his tears from her. And then she understood. She screamed and ran into him, beating her weak fists against his chest for a moment before Jude held her pinned against him. She fell to the ground, and he fell with her, holding her tight as she sobbed.

"But I saved her my peel! She needed it!" she screamed. The potato peel fell from her tiny, clenched fist.

"Jude, we have to go now. We've taken too long," Ludwig said, approaching from behind him, delicately shaking his shoulder.

With her fragile body clinging to Jude for dear life and her head sobbing on his rain-soaked shoulder, he lifted her into his arms and carried her into the woods to safety.

Ludwig and Jude took the souls to one of Jude's properties, a safehouse north of Bergen. Thirty-five people they saved from there that night. Thirty-five people they saved from being pointlessly murdered in the coming days.

The group stayed at the safehouse for several days, the two men accompanying them the entire time. Ludwig had noticed a while back that that was best for the souls' well-being. "They're afraid. They're not ready to be on their own yet. This is a whole new world to them that they've come out on top of. They need a few days to find their feet, to learn how to live again."

The men, though they tried to sympathize, had never themselves experienced the kind of atrocities actually being done to these people.

The people were fed, more than potato peels and rolls. Jude fed them whatever meats he and Ludwig were able to acquire, cooked in with a vegetable stew. For the first few days, whenever the souls tried to sleep, they'd end up crying for the lives and loved ones they'd lost. The men evenly distributed clothing, money, and beds in the underground bunker they'd built, just in case of emergency. The souls felt safer down there anyway, locked away from harm.

Such a little thing, she wouldn't let go of Jude. He sat with his arm around her, her face snuggled into his chest. After the first few days, she started opening up to him.

"You are the Angel of Life. You are not the devil. You are the most beautiful man I've ever seen. What's your name?" she cooed, as Jude looked into her darkened, shadowed eyes.

Until then, they hadn't even formally introduced themselves. The times they were in transcended simple formalities. "My name's Jude. What's yours, Little One?"

"Annalies Marie Frank."

Chapter

Sixteen

"We are not friends," Anne stated, as she braided Angelina's hair. She'd led Angelina upstairs to a room that was full of bright colors and happiness. Exactly how Anne Frank was supposed to have been, an innocent girl with hopes and dreams. "I drew the short straw and had to babysit you today. I'll tolerate you to make Jude happy, but don't think it makes me all warm and fuzzy to see you here."

Angelina thought for a moment. Before today, she'd considered getting out of awkward conversations one of her superpowers. Nothing could've prepared her for what she was currently facing. *Anne Frank hates me.*

"I'd like to be friends." Angelina picked at her cuticles nervously. *I can't let Anne Frank hate me.*

"Why? Because you're here? You think you're one of us now? You don't even know me." Anne tugged at the braid she was working on, purposefully making Angelina wince in discomfort.

"I do know you. I read your diary." Angelina watched Anne's expressions in the mirror.

A cloud crossed her face before she shook it away. "I am not the same person. That was a different time." She pinned the long chestnut braid around the back of Angelina's head, making a rather fashionable braided chignon.

"You lost your optimism?" Angelina continued watching her as she darted around the room. Anne disappeared behind a closet door, huffing loudly. A lot of rustling ensued, before she finally emerged with several elegantly stitched gowns draped over her arms, much too long for herself.

"No, but I gained caution. People are not good. Try these on and pick one for later. You need to look," she glared at Angelina from head to toe as she stood up from the vanity chair, "somewhat presentable, at least."

Anne crossed over to the table beside her window, lifting the silver lid of the small buffet server Angelina hadn't previously noticed.

"Do you want an egg roll or not?" Anne said exasperatedly, as if she had already asked the question twenty times before. She shoved one into her mouth, the crunch loud enough for Angelina to hear from where she was dressing in the bathroom.

"I asked for an air fryer for Christmas. Jude gave it to me early," Anne stated smugly, winning a secret battle in her head against Angelina.

Just then, there was a knock on the door, and not a moment too soon. Ludwig pushed the door open widely, and strolled through without waiting to be invited. He looked like he'd just wandered in from the beach in his brown Teva sandals, khaki Bahama shorts, and light green polo shirt that matched his jade eyes.

"I'm here to rescue you from Anne's overbearing intenseness," he announced. His eyes roamed Angelina's body as she exited the bathroom in a black and emerald green gown. "You look exquisite, my Queen." Angelina felt herself blush as their eyes met.

Anne's eye roll and subsequent fake gagging sound echoed around the room. "Shut up, Wig. Go count your coffee beans and leave me alone," Anne shot back.

Ludwig tore his gaze from Angelina's, a devious sparkle in his eyes. "Don't knock the perfect bean-to-water ratio, kid. You have no idea what sipping earth's nectar can do for the soul." He winked at Angelina, before she turned to go into the bathroom and change back into her regular clothes.

"Don't call me 'kid.' I am a woman. I'm over eighty-five years old."

"Those neon stickers all over your mirrors suggest otherwise. I trust you've been your usual, cheerful self to Angelina?"

"Positively delightful," Anne said through clenched teeth.

Angelina exited out of the bathroom in her regular clothes and practically ran to Ludwig, her expression silently thanking him for saving her from Anne's wrath. He ran a hand through his sandy brown locks and closed his eyes in exasperation as soon as the door shut behind them.

"Yeah, Anne can be kind of a lot sometimes. I didn't know you were here already, or I would've met you at the door." He shoved his hands in his pockets as they walked.

"She said you all fought over who had to babysit me. Is that true?" Angelina wasn't short on confidence, but she didn't appreciate being somewhere she wasn't wanted, either.

Ludwig growled in frustration. "She's such a pest, sometimes. That's the furthest thing from the truth. We're all thrilled to have you here, cross my heart. Anne was quiet before the war, but then a few years later, after Nadine, she got even more vocal and protective of Jude. The fact that she's even going out of her way to talk to you is a good sign.

"And the fact that she offered you an egg roll means she's just giving you a hard time to amuse herself. She hoards egg rolls and *never* shares, not even with John most days. I wouldn't worry about it if I were you. Anne's extremely mature for her age, but at the same time she's also eternally fifteen years old. She still has spells of teenage angst and drama and hormones from time to time, and all that comes with those."

Angelina's mood immediately lightened at his explanation. They descended the stairs and headed towards the ballroom where his grand piano was. Only instead of a wide-open floor plan, the ballroom had been turned into a conference center. Gold Chiavari chairs lined the expanse of the room in rows, all angled towards the stage.

On the stage, a band was rehearsing. The drum set had "XXVII" in gothic letters on the front.

Ludwig made his way to the middle of the room, three rows back from the stage. He plopped down on one of the chairs, propping his feet up on the back of the chair in front of him. Angelina sat down beside him, blinking twice at the singer in front of her. *Was seeing celebrities who weren't really dead ever going to get easier?*

Ludwig had that sort of lackadaisical, devil-may-care attitude and wicked charm that drew people in. Particularly women. He would've been the kind of guy that ended up being fraternity brother and baby daddy to three different women. This also made him easy to talk to and be around. The current singer on the stage winked at him, her raven black hair cascading down her shoulders. He blew her a kiss, before focusing his attention back onto Angelina.

"Single and ready to mingle," Angelina countered him first. "Are the two of you dating?"

"Nope. Know anyone?" He grinned, amused by her.

"Nobody your age." Angelina sat back in her chair, pleased at her joke.

"Ah, she's witty *and* gorgeous. Deadly combination in a queen." Ludwig nodded approvingly.

"Are you hitting on me?"

"Yes," Ludwig said bluntly. "I will always hit on a Queen when the opportunity offers itself. Even though you're far out of my league, and off limits. Not all queens are worthy of my advancements, however." His voice lowered as he leaned in a little closer to her. "But for *you*? I promise I'll be loyal to you until the day I die."

"And that's not a line in itself?"

"Merely a statement of truth. Have you decided your official answer? To the queendom?" Ludwig changed the subject, focusing the conversation back onto her.

"He hasn't officially asked." Angelina pressed her lips together. She didn't want to give away her eagerness for the question to be delivered.

"But he will. I've known Jude a long time. You should know, he's been different since he found you. I don't mean just since Café du Monde, either. The first time he saw you on television, he was changed. He became more focused and determined, driven to be someone you would say 'yes' to. I've never seen him act like that for anyone."

The band members changed places again while they sat there. The raven-haired woman picked up a tambourine while a man in bell-bottoms positioned himself at the microphone. Angelina's mouth dropped for the millionth time since meeting Jude. Ludwig chuckled beside her, watching her reactions as she recognized each one of the musicians.

"Anne wanted him." He motioned at the shirtless man on stage. "She made me change him. I had to make a whole trip to Paris to set it up. But if you think that's a lot, wait till you see Nadine. She'll expect you to fawn and faint over her. The newbies always do. She'll only be here tonight and then she'll go back to Hollywood."

"Who's Nadine again?" Angelina made a mental note to draw herself a family tree. It was seriously starting to get overwhelming. "Is there a phone tree or something I can have to help keep up?"

"She's the second queen."

"Right. Is it normal for …" she didn't want to offend him, but she'd recalled him saying that both he and Jude had been married to the first queen, "for your people to marry several times?"

"Well, my people will soon be your people, too." He winked at her. The band changed sets and singers yet again. "The patchouli is strong with this one," Ludwig said, jutting his thumb towards the stage in reference to the new vocalist at the mic. "I like to watch him rehearse, though."

The guitarist, who was wearing tie-dyed pants and a bright orange, Shakespearian-type ruffled shirt, began slow, melodramatic guitar riffs. His eyes closed as the chords filled the ballroom, the acoustic haunt settling into Angelina's bones.

"So anyway, as I was saying. Nadine. She doesn't go by her former name anymore. Try not to stare at her too much or she'll get all overdramatic. She loves the attention, and the more recent Society members eat it up whenever they see her. She works on Hollywood Blvd., as a lookalike, much to Jude's dismay.

"If anyone ever ran a DNA test on her, they'd know she was the real deal and not some medically enhanced doppelgänger. She's out in the open and her picture is plastered everywhere with tourists from all over the world, who are none the wiser to know they're standing next to an immortal queen. They think she's just a player in the comedy. The sad part is she is, only it's a tragedy." He rolled his eyes, scrubbing away the irritation from his face with his hands.

"Why doesn't Jude put a stop to it?"

"Have you ever tried to tell a woman no? Much less a queen who was formerly a siren of the silver screen? He'd be more productive if he created an army of alley cats." As he spoke those words, Neville strolled in nonchalantly and hopped up on the chair opposite Angelina. He positioned his body facing forward, strutting his chest out in a regal pose, as though he expected everyone to admonish him for gracing them with his presence.

Ludwig ignored him. "She used him hard, and nearly broke him. She had plans to turn her lover, but then he was murdered. In broad daylight, no less. Jude had no clue until it happened. When she found out what had happened, she started screaming, throwing things, breaking dishes, slapping Jude as hard as she could and yelling that she hated him. She confessed her plans right then and there, because now she had nothing left but an eternity with a man she didn't even like, let alone love.

"Her grief was unbearable, and for a while she locked herself away from everyone and everything. Jude and Nadine were only married two years. Two years, in a lifespan so far over 2,300 years. So no, to answer your previous question. Three wives isn't too much, I don't believe. Not when time is limitless."

Angelina sat quietly, not sure if she should cry or not. Ludwig was harsh, but soft and to the point at the same time. "I say all this not to make you pity Jude, but to impress upon you the gravity of the situation. I like you, I really do, but if you do not want eternity, then you should walk away right now. He thinks you're a goddess, and learning anything to the contrary would completely, savagely, ruthlessly destroy him."

The band changed sets again, and a woman with daisies in her hair wrapped her hands around the base of the microphone and began wailing out her melodies.

"Have you ever changed normal people?"

"No. Not everyone's famous, but everyone is accomplished at something. We don't change sheep. Jude doesn't see it like that, but that doesn't make it any less true. We're wolves, each and every one of us. Nice wolves, but wolves, nonetheless. We attack, we prosper, we're aggressive, and we change the world.

"Normal people focus only on their problems and their tiny lives. They accept things around them as they are, instead of seeing potential and possibilities. There's no space for passive personalities in a room full of immortals. Now, was everyone who was changed deserving? Probably not. My personal opinion is that Nadine was a waste of a turn and of a queen, but that wasn't my decision. Jude did it, and he's got to live with that. I try to stick to musicians, hence the band. How old are you?"

"I'm thirty-five."

"Ah, well, that's a shame. You missed Woodstock. It was epic." He slapped his knee. "'Ludwig went to Woodstock.' I dare you to sat that fast five times and try not to say Wigstock."

"I missed the whole Sixties and Seventies all together, I'm afraid. Who changed you?"

"Technically Jude. But it was more of a command than a request from Marie. He owed her, and she wanted me. At the time, I wanted her just as much."

"And Marie was your wife?"

"And Jude's before that. But that's a story for a different book," he said, winking at her. "She was another waste of the queen status. I think you'll be much better than the two of them combined."

Anne walked through the entrance to the ballroom, her arms loaded with notebook and files. She spotted the two of them, her face dropping at the sight of Ludwig.

He beamed a million-dollar smile at her, further ruffling her feathers. "Anne's a wolf, too. Bet you didn't see that one coming, did you? Did she tell you about Argentina yet? Damn good story."

Chapter

Seventeen

Buenos Aires, Argentina. January 1953

"He'll be there. We'll have to find him, but he will be there. I hesitate to say this, but we actually need you. He's a sucker for beautiful women, and if you don't talk much, you can pull it off." Ludwig fake-gagged into his fist, ruffling the feathers of the tiny blonde standing in front of him. Her lavender eyes narrowed at him, striking him down with her expression. He ignored her and continued, "Are you going to help or not? Be a decent person and do something good, for once in your miserable life."

"You know what the heat does to my hair. This

better be worth it, me coming all the way down here. I'm about to get married, and to a better man than the two of you combined." She looked Jude and Ludwig up and down, disapprovingly.

"You're helping me and my people. Once we have him, you can go on trolloping your way around the world." Anne moved to stand in front of Jude and Ludwig, not backing down. She'd become exceptionally protective of Ludwig, each adopting the other like a sibling. Ludwig snickered. "And you might want to wear something more reasonable than your stupid stockings. Do some research. Argentina is hot in January."

"Fine, fine. Whatever you little peons need, I suppose it's *my* duty as *Queen* to fulfill the whims of *my* people," Marie said overdramatically, with a flick of her wrist towards the group, as if she were swatting away a fly.

"Ex-queen, lest you not forget, dearest," Ludwig said, reminding her of her position.

"A former queen is always a queen, lest you forget, dearest Wiggy." She sighed, rather exasperatedly, and rolled her eyes. "When is it that we are to leave?"

Jude had remained silent up until then. Marie always drained the life and his emotions right out of him, and he preferred not to interact with her until absolutely necessary. "In three hours. The others will meet us at the secondary location."

"This reminds me of old times, Wiggy," Marie said, as she clung to his arm. "The two of us, strolling through Bonn, falling in love on the Rhine. Do you ever miss us, Wiggy?"

She was dressed in black high heels, black elbow-length gloves, and a knee-length pink afternoon dress, concealed by a ridiculous mink coat. When Anne had protested, Marie had countered her class. "Mink is for millionaires. You wouldn't understand, darling, but mink can open doors just by being present." Her blonde hair was conformed to a chignon bun and topped with a pink pillbox hat with a birdcage. Her usual heavy make-up was toned down, revealing the true and youthful beauty underneath her usually theatrical appearance. Ludwig was dressed in a casual suit of equally high caliber that mirrored his partner, portraying the couple's assumed obvious wealth and status.

"Can't say that I ever do, *mein Schatz.*"

"Oh, Wiggy," Marie feigned admonishment. "I think a part of you does still care about me somewhere deep inside."

He stopped and kissed her temple as he opened the gate for them. To anyone watching, they appeared an adoring, loving couple. "Only for appearances, *mein Schatz.* Never forget that. You are to be married, and I am to live blissfully without you."

A single tear formed in her eye, before she shook it away. Marie was not a fan of showing her true feelings.

"Keep a lookout. He won't make it easy, but he will make it obvious. He's too arrogant to stay in the shadows and be a nobody, particularly around his wealthy friends."

Her hand ran along his forearm, toying with him playfully. "I know my way around a man, Wiggy. I'll send my salon bill when this is all over."

The couple climbed the stairs, disappearing into the rows of boxes at the Autódromo Gálvez that were only reserved for the elitist ticket holders. The Argentine Grand Prix was scheduled to start in the next hour, and they knew they had to move fast in the crowd. With the amount of people who were here, thanks to President Perón's decision to allow the public to freely line the track, it would be easy to slip in and out undetected, but not after the audience was settled.

Particularly, not after Hitler was settled. The M.O.E. had been tailing him for weeks, bugging his phone, watching his house, following his associates. Their intel had all led to the same conclusion: Hitler would be there, and other than being accompanied by a few of his fellow officers, he would otherwise be incognito and largely unprotected. Sometimes, the only disguise a dead man uses is death itself.

Additionally, they had also been fortunate enough to get a seat directly in front of him.

Ludwig and Marie split up; he took the top and she took the bottom, casually and nonchalantly surfing the crowds of faces to assess the risks around them. Marie gazed up through the observers, as if searching for her seat. The eyes of every man in the crowd focused back in lust of the little blonde thing who was obviously lost and helpless.

They began to drool and rearrange in their chairs as her mink coat casually dropped off of the shoulder facing them, revealing the slender body beneath. Marie continued to glance down at her ticket, rereading it and laughing nervously as she looked around.

Several of the men approached her, offering to assist her in whatever she needed assisting in. She caught Ludwig's eye as he nodded at her, giving the go-ahead. Marie brushed each of their chests in a light pat. She giggled lightly and flirtatiously, her eyes lingering on the man she'd been putting the show on for. "Thank you, my loves, but my husband has since arrived and can save me from this embarrassment!"

Ludwig moved down the stairs to claim her, and together they ascended halfway back up the stairs. The pair made their way down their designated row and took their places, directly positioned in front of their target.

Ludwig proceeded to run his hand up her thigh and beneath her skirt, as if they were a honeymooning couple in love. Marie turned sideways, positioning herself so that she could easily look back at their mark and assure his interest. She had no trouble identifying if he, in fact, was interested. A wicked gleam sparkled in his eyes as he leaned slightly forward in his seat. Marie grinned at him and wrapped her arms around Ludwig's neck.

Now shaved, the old man stared back at Marie with a gleam in his eye. Ludwig kissed her neck, and then fanned kisses across her collarbone as she teased Hitler's gaze flirtingly, her eyes focused on him as Ludwig's mouth met hers. She watched the bob of Hitler's neck as he swallowed.

To draw him in further, Ludwig started whispering sweet nothings in perfect German, with each kiss he layered on. *"Mein Schatz ... Liebe meines Lebens ... Göttin ..."*

Marie met their onlooker's gaze once again, and grinned at him. "Wir haben Gesellschaft, meine Liebe." *We have company, my Love.*

Ludwig turned, facing their target head-on for the first time, and deadpanned in his pristine German accent, "Möchte er später zu uns kommen?" *Would he like to join later?*

Hitler nodded ever so slightly, silently agreeing to the unspoken, illicit rendezvous that would take place later. "You are both German?"

Marie spoke breathlessly, as if she were in the throes of passion, nibbling on Ludwig's earlobe for added effect. "He's from Bonn and I'm from Vienna. We're here … on vacation before we get married. Are you married, sir?"

"I was. She died in the war." He looked away, seemingly hurt. Allegedly, they had committed suicide together. This confirmed what Ludwig and Jude had suspected, that she had gone through with it, and he had played the coward's hand.

"Oh my! You poor, sweet man. That must've been painfully difficult for you. You must be so lonely and want for a woman's company after that. After the race, my fiancé and I are going to a club. Please, won't you join us? It's exclusive. There won't be any *unsavory* characters." She wrinkled her nose for added effect.

"She despises the lower class," Ludwig added, playfully chucking his finger beneath her chin. She grinned and leaned in to rub her nose against his, before he kissed her again.

"Why, yes, I would love to. And might I just state, you are positively stunning. The both of you, a radiant portrait of young romance."

"Tell you what, darling. How's about we meet you at the gate after the race, and give you all the information? You simply must see the car that my fiancé bought for me! Top of the line!" Wealth always drew wealth.

Ever wanting to be the head of his class, Hitler nodded furiously. "Ja!"

As the crowds filtered out, Hitler followed Ludwig and Marie to their car, a 1953 silver Hudson Hornet.

"You simply must drive it! Ludwig can sit in the back, he doesn't mind. I'd love for you to feel the power of the motor!"

Hitler excitedly strolled to the driver's side, while Ludwig climbed in behind him. Marie opened her purse, and ruffled around until she found her lip gloss. Hitler side-eyed her for just a second, before dismissing his uneasy feeling and starting the motor.

As the Hornet roared to life, Ludwig bounded over the seat and wrapped his arms around Hitler's throat in a sleeper hold, until Hitler's portly body was rendered unconscious. Marie reached back into her purse, moving her lip gloss and compact aside to pull out a tiny glass vial. She scooted over to their victim, pulled down his jaw—exposing his vulnerable opening to her—and tipped the bottle's contents down his throat. She poked his cheek for good measure, to see if he would respond.

"What did you decide to go with?" Ludwig asked. He got out and circled the car to open her door for her.

"Strychnine. Ugly little poison. Don't worry, it's not enough to kill him, just to make him quite uncomfortable. Do you require my assistance any further?"

"No. I think I've had enough of your company for another few centuries. Thank you for going out of your way to right the wrongs in the world."

"It's my utmost pleasure, Wiggy. Will you be attending my wedding next month?"

He ignored her, and slammed the car door closed before rounding to the driver's seat. Ludwig pushed Hitler's lifeless body over to the passenger's side before taking his place behind the wheel. He bound Hitler's hands and feet with ropes, making sure they were tight enough to hold him. Then the car roared to life and headed towards the Argentine jungle, leaving Marie standing in the dust.

The roads wound and snaked through the landscape, growing further and further from any signs of humanity. The buildings became trees, and the trees became a blur. Finally, after several hours, the Hornet rolled to a stop outside of a long-forgotten, ramshackle stone hut in the intersection between somewhere and nowhere.

The dilapidated house was crawling, twisting with jungle vines and moss. It would better have served as the location for a treasure hunt, instead of what was about to happen. Jude and Anne exited as the car's engine died. A group of people that Ludwig fondly recognized trickled out behind them. They looked well, healthier. Some wore pleasant expressions, some wore sad. Some looked like they were going to vomit, and some looked like they were ready for destruction. Beside him, Hitler's body twitched. Strychnine or consciousness, Ludwig couldn't be sure.

Jude came around to the passenger door and opened it. Hitler's chubby body rolled to the side, jostling him awake enough to be panicked. His eyes darted furiously as Jude and Ludwig rolled him out of the car, his mass making a large *oomph* as it landed on the jungle floor.

Ludwig glanced at Anne. Her body was unmoving, but her eyes shone of tears and rage. A few of the other men from the group came over to assist Jude and Ludwig in hoisting up Hitler's body, as he started to groan in the awareness of his situation.

They lugged him into the hut, dark with the shadows of the decayed walls. There was no roof present, except that of the jungle's canopy. A beautiful place to die. Almost too beautiful, Anne had thought, if it wasn't for the fact that no one would ever find him there.

The men hoisted him up, laying him in a small boat, just large enough for a grown man. It sat supported with rocks to keep it from tipping, and was positioned on top of a makeshift stone slab table not far off the ground. Hitler's eyes darted furiously to each face of his onlookers, no recognition crossing him until he landed on Ludwig.

"Du Verräter!" he shouted when their eyes met. *You traitor!*

Ludwig smiled broadly at the insult and shook his head to the contrary. "Nicht ict, sondern du." *Not I, but you.*

"You are a traitor to the human race," Anne said, stepping forward. She clasped her hands together, trying to contain her violent shaking. "You are a traitor to the human spirit. You are a traitor to the world." Jude walked up behind her and wrapped his arms around her fragile shoulders.

The men, women, and children who had accompanied them out to the fortress of solitude stepped forward, each one of them clutching photographs of their loved ones. One by one, they moved to form a circle around Hitler, and held their photographs up for him to see. Jude and Anne broke through the circle, moving to stand directly over Hitler.

Jude motioned at the souls surrounding them, his face a cold glare. "You thought you silenced them. You thought you had the power, the control, the influence, to destroy an entire people. But there was a force you were ignorant of. A group working entirely against you in the darkness. We rescued just over five hundred souls from you. Five hundred people you thought you had killed. There were countless more that we weren't able to get to in time.

"You didn't succeed. You didn't exterminate. You didn't even fake an honorable death in battle. You let your wife commit suicide, and then you fled like the roach you are. But we found you. Now, you'll certainly not die with honor. You'll die pained, miserable, and screaming, like all those you sentenced. Maybe history won't know. But we, and you, will know how defeated you were in the end."

Hitler's body continued in miniscule spasms, his eyes twitching from the strychnine subduing him between worlds. One by one, members of the group tiptoed forward, afraid to truly be seen by their enemy. Out of each of their pockets, they produced small bottles of honey, and proceeded to start pouring them onto Hitler's bound body.

"Flöhe! Keime!" Hitler shouted insults at the souls as the steady streams of honey rained down on him.

Anne was the last in line. She held a picture up of her sister and her mother, and for the father she would never again be able to see.

"Dumme Schlampe," Hitler muttered, ignoring

her sorrowful look. Ludwig, close enough to be in earshot of the conversation, walked straight up to Hitler and punched him square in the nose. Hitler gurgled and flinched, as trickles of blood rolled down his face and pooled into the corners of his mouth. Anne poured her bottle of honey directly onto his face. The sticky sweet drops coated his eyes and ran off them like tears. The last drops she poured over his mouth. They chased the blood, swirling citrine and crimson together in the final tango.

"Here's what's going to happen," Jude said calmly, his voice lowered and steady. "There are creatures in this jungle you can't even fathom. Slowly, deliberately, they will smell you. Smell your fear, your piss, your blood, and your shit. And they'll be drawn to it. They'll surround you, nibble on you, lick you, bite you, gnaw on you.

"You'll allow this, because you'll have no choice. We're going to feed you curare, enough to render you immobile. On the off chance that, say, a jaguar snips through your bindings and frees your limbs, your body will still fail you. These people, your audience, if they so choose, will stay until your final breath. The people you tried to erase will erase you, and watch as your body is degraded into nothing but a pile of bones. Even if they leave—because they're not heartless, soulless beings such as yourself—Ludwig and I will stay.

"You will not escape. This is the end. We will watch you take your last breath. The last eyes you see will be those of your enemies who conquered you."

Jude poured the final vile straight down Hitler's throat, a mixture of several poisons used by the locals. Hitler gagged and spurted his fate, before Jude shoved a wad of banana leaves into his mouth as a makeshift gag.

While the hours tolled away and the creatures came, the only other witnesses to the vigilante crime taking place were the family of capuchin monkeys watching from the tree limbs directly over the hut. While Adolph took his last breath, the capuchins' cries resounded out over the jungle in triumph of a new day.

Basel, Switzerland. October 1953

Otto Frank sat at a café on the Rhine, watching the passersby. In the background, the Easter egg roof on the Basler Münster framed the most scenic of landscapes. Its two cloisters stretched and reached up to the sky, as his daughters should have been able to do.

As he sipped his caffè crema, he wiped away several rogue tears before they formed an icicle trail down his cheek. Bach's third Sarabande floated through the buildings and out across the water from somewhere unknown, casting a somber and haunting mood over the scene.

With the shelter of the building to disguise them, Anne and Ludwig watched him as he sat and pondered.

"Can't I walk by? Can't he see my face, just once? To know that I made it out?"

"No, Anne. You can't get closer than this. If he were to see you, it would ruin our missions. If you were to turn him, he would surely die. This moment has to be enough."

Her breath caught in the air, her sobs freezing in her throat. Anne turned and pressed her face into Ludwig's chest to disguise herself from the curious spectators who were starting to notice her tears.

By the time Otto felt two pairs of eyes upon him, the shadow of her green peacoat disappeared from sight.

Chapter Eighteen

Angelina was in complete and utter shock and awe. She had a completely newfound appreciation and admiration for Anne. At the same time, Angelina was completely confused, and was having a lot of trouble grasping the concept of these alternate realities she was learning. Ludwig chucked his fist underneath Angelina's chin, prompting her to close her mouth as Anne started towards them.

"That's who we are. We make things better, and we change the world. Under the guise of being anonymous immortals."

"Her family, though. I just can't help but think how lonely she's been since the war. How much rage and isolation she must've felt."

Ludwig giggled. "I wouldn't put Anne and the word lonely in the same sentence. She's built a vast network of friends and allies all across Europe, and she and the others from the war have a whole pen-pal thing happening. Plus, I'm pretty sure," he pinched the air between his thumb and index finger, annunciating the 'e' into a high-pitched syllable in and of itself, "that she and Keats are together again. Or maybe they broke up again. I can't keep up with them anymore, but I think that's why she's been so hostile lately. Every time they break up, she gets crabby and he gets wimpy. They've been on and off since the Eighties, ever since he helped her tear down the Berlin Wall.

"The Society in-house emails between them are all, 'Per my email five emails ago,' and, 'Per last year, when I was wearing the red shirt, you said exactly, and I quote.' Oh yeah, we walk on the wild side here in Immortal World," he stated loud enough for Anne to hear.

Angelina burst out laughing as Anne approached them, slapping Ludwig's Teva-sandaled feet off of the back of the chair.

"I'd like to get my deposit back," Anne said, sitting directly in front of Ludwig, preventing him from propping his feet back up on that specific chair. He winked at Angelina, discreetly nudging her ribs.

"Hey, news flash, it's cheaper just to buy chairs. Why don't you ask John his opinion on accounting?" Anne turned around and shot him yet another death glare. "See, I'm right. Lovers quarrel." She whipped her head back towards the stage, her short hair flying out sideways from beneath her baseball cap.

"Say, Anne, why don't you explain to Angelina what the Society of M.O.E. is? It's on all of the flair. She ordered *all* of the flair. Did you give Angelina a welcome bag? Anne's got reusable bags, beach towels, you name it, M.O.E. is emblazoned on it."

He chided her until she finally pulled her phone out and furiously started texting. Ludwig tried desperately but failed to keep himself from laughing at her expense. She turned back around once more, her body sideways against the chair and her knee propped into the chair on her left. Ludwig stretched back, clasping his hands behind his head.

"Fine, *Wig.*"

"My dearest, darling Anne, please call me Lu. I positively despise the name Wig, or Wiggy. You know the reasons."

"Fun fact, did you know that 'loo' is another term for toilet? Surely you don't want to be called toilet." Anne smiled smugly, but Ludwig was quicker.

"My sweetest Anne, if that is indeed the case, then you should have no trouble using it." He grinned back at her, flashing his million-dollar smile, their battle of wits seemingly over for the time being.

Anne launched into an artificial tone that reminded Angelina more of an airplane stewardess than a hospitable hostess.

"The M.O.E. have existed in some form or fashion for well over two-thousand years. The Society of Messengers on Earth, as we are formally called, seek to perform actions for the justice and betterment of the world and its inhabitants. We stand for what is right. We stand for what is good."

"Geesh, that was so … *boring*, Annie Bananie." Ludwig fake yawned. "Tell her how you really feel."

Anne loosened up, just slightly. "I've had a lot of time to think about it over the years. Why we're here, why we exist at all. A lot of people pray and wish and cast spells or what have you, without actually taking action to fix the problem. I think Jude was created as a weapon to help someone, some group, or maybe the world. Who knows? Instead of being selfish, though, he paid it forward.

"Not many people would've done that. So, in a sense, whoever picked Jude out of every living person at that time knew exactly what they were doing. Then through the years, Jude saved the world by creating us, essentially. We're not angels, but we're not demons, either. We're messengers. Messengers on Earth."

"And what's the message?" Angelina leaned forward in her seat slightly.

Anne's eyes narrowed into slits, as she held her index and middle finger up level to her vision in a V, then turned them towards Angelina. "We're coming for you, so you'd better watch your six. We don't tolerate bullies or injustice." *Anne is a wolf, all right.*

"There she is. That's the Anne I know and love." Ludwig reached up and mussed her baseball cap around on her head. "And also, by being the Society, our ultimate mission is to influence history for the better, no matter what form that takes on. History is a funny thing. For example, had you known me in my human years, you'd probably say I was arrogant and conceited.

"But now, if someone were to write an account of me, and paint me in a better light, they could say I was intelligent and charming. Which I obviously am." Ludwig held his hand to his chest dramatically before he continued.

"Tweaking facts, if you will. Now, say that person A dies, killing the negative memory of me, and person B dies, killing the positive memory. But person B wrote down their account of me. So now, in memories I'm carried on as intelligent and charming, and no one is any the wiser that I was actually a complete asshole. That's what we've done, and that's what you'll see before you in this room tonight. Influencers, changers, wolves, and messengers. All different words, to describe the same ideology."

Someone ran towards them down the row of Chiavari chairs, breaking up the conversation. Keats nearly tripped over his own feet trying to balance everything he was carrying.

"I brought one of everything, like you said." He handed Angelina an umbrella, three beach towels in different colors, and a miniature sculpture of Neville that was tucked beneath one of his arms, before unloading the four different styles of reusable shopping bags, all filled to the brim with various items. Ludwig snickered beside Angelina as the mountain of stuff piled up around her and at her feet. Neville hopped down in disgust, offering his chair for Keats to also fill with items.

Anne beamed at Angelina, thoroughly proud of the store she'd set up for the Society.

"Oh my, Anne. This is … this is really something." Angelina was trying hard to find a compliment between all the clutter, since Anne had seemingly slightly unthawed towards her in the last several minutes.

"Told ya, she ordered *everything*."

"It's for the Society. Everyone can take home whatever they chose to. It's very classy to have your logo on things," Anne said cheerily.

"I just … I'm not sure where I'm going to put all of this. I only brought a *very* small suitcase."

"Oh, you can put it in Jude's room. John, take this stuff for her." Anne snapped her fingers, and Keats quickly regathered all of the merchandise and scuttled away. Angelina looked from Ludwig to Anne. She hadn't even so much as thought of the sleeping arrangements yet.

"Where is Jude, anyway?" Angelina hadn't seen him for nearly two full days now, which was the longest amount of time they'd gone without seeing each other in … in a week. Somehow it felt like more; they felt like more. She was enjoying her present company immensely, but missed him terribly.

"He's at the airport," Anne replied. "He drives the shuttle bus back and forth to pick everyone up, and Harold makes round trips in the car. They have a whole system."

"Wait, what? Jude, the king, is driving a shuttle bus? Why doesn't he have someone else do it?"

"Well, that wouldn't show very good leadership, now, would it? Wouldn't you be thrilled to be picked up at the airport by none other than your president, knowing that he put driving his people ahead of doing paperwork? He and Harold take turns; one is here while one is there, to keep a constant flow of arrivals." Anne said this matter-of-factly, as if the President of the United States *should* be at the airport picking up Americans flying in from out of town. Like there wouldn't be millions of tax dollars being spent and security risks happening at the same time.

"Right, obviously."

"He'll be through later this afternoon, well before the Society Convention officially starts. You'll need to be in one of the dresses I picked out for you by 5 p.m. I think the emerald one looked the best, but it's your choice. Whatever. And don't mess your hair up." Anne stood to leave. "Wig, I think the food is ready now if you'd like to escort Angelina to the banquet hall."

Ludwig took a deep whiff of the air. "Mmmm, smell that? Mud bugs and macaroni, the noodle WITH CHEESE, not the fashion. Let's be clear about that."

Angelina giggled. "You seem to have offended yourself."

"I said that around my ex-wife once and she dressed me in the worst outfit imaginable. Bright purple, striped, horrendous calf-length pants, with a frilly collar, a wig two-feet tall AND pickle wickers."

"Winkle pickers?"

"Whatever. It doesn't matter. I had flat feet and curled toes for a year after that."

Chapter

Nineteen

Ludwig and Angelina slowly ambled through the rows of Chiavari chairs, making their way to the exit. There were noticeably more people mingling about since Angelina had arrived that morning. Except for Keats and Anne, who were once again working the welcome tables, Angelina was relieved to see that she didn't immediately recognize any other famous historical figures. She wasn't sure how much more sensory overload she could handle.

The crowd did recognize her and Ludwig, however. Upon seeing him enter the foyer, they all stopped and stared. He was quite handsome, Angelina thought, even if they had seen him before. Add in a dash of famously talented composer, and Ludwig was enough to turn heads completely around. Their eyes didn't stay on him long, however. Everyone's gaze quickly shifted to Angelina, and her breath was taken aback. Slowly, as she and Ludwig passed, everyone watching her slowly lowered their heads, as if she were the Queen herself. *As if I am the Queen already.*

Angelina smiled awkwardly at them, and paced faster, trying to shield herself with Ludwig's shadow. "Ludwig, what's going on?" she whispered loudly.

"Call it respect, or call it destiny. Either way, you're already the Queen to our people, whether you like it or not."

"But how do they recognize me? I just got here."

"Everyone got an email last week," he said nonchalantly, as if Anne had included it in as a P.S. to an email reminding everyone to put out their recycling.

The banquet hall turned out to be the opposite ballroom, with buffet servers, cold bars and tables lined around every edge Angelina could see. Ludwig followed her gaze.

"Jude splurges on everyone with the banquet. Everyone, absolutely everyone gets to pick a dish, whatever it is. They send it in two months beforehand, and the kitchen staff make up everything. It can be anything you want, from anywhere, at any time and place. You may or may not be required to provide a recipe, if it's something, say, from 83 BC and not in current cookbooks. Otherwise, the utmost accommodation will be provided to fulfill the request. This way, we all get to try something new from around the world. And I don't know about you, but I get cranky when the food's not good at a big event."

Angelina's eyes were growing fashionably larger than her stomach. "But I thought you couldn't eat all these kinds of things?"

"I can assure you, my Queen, a vast majority of us do not share Jude's dietary sentiments."

Angelina's eyes grew wider, but not from hunger. "So, you ..."

"Oh, heaven's no, that's disgusting." He wrinkled his nose. "That part was real, only a few drops from a glass." He wandered along the wall until he found what he was looking for. "I save my appetite for *these*."

The table he stopped at had large dishes of extra-cheesy-looking macaroni, and a pile of what looked like little fried chicken nuggets. On the other side of the table, extravagant, colorful sushi rolls drizzled with multiple sauces and topped with red and black roe ran in patterns. Ludwig popped several of the nuggets into his mouth, savoring the fried flavors. "Muuuud buuuugggsssss, mmmmm," he hummed to himself.

"What is a mud bug? Those aren't chicken nuggets?" Angelina picked up a sushi and popped it into her mouth. The salty roe squirted against her teeth, battling against the avocado and cream cheese to be her favorite flavor.

"Crawfish, crawdads, mountain lobsters, mud bugs, whatever name you call them, they're a fresh-water delicacy. There's nothing quite like a fresh, fried mud bug. Do you like the sushi?" Ludwig asked, grabbing a plate and piling it high with macaroni before topping that with crawfish, too.

"I love fresh sushi. I didn't used to, but now I crave it."

"Be sure to tell Edgar. That's his side of the table. His sushi is Jude's filet mignon." Who knew

Edgar Allan Poe would become devoutly addicted to sushi?

"Ludwig, there's still something I'm confused about."

"Yes, my Queen? Fire away; I'm your open book of knowledge."

"Hitler died in the bunker. Everybody knows that."

Ludwig laughed. He'd been asked this question before, it seemed. "Did he? Haven't you been paying attention? Hitler most certainly did *not* die in that bunker. He fled to Argentina. Argentinians saw him. I saw him. Jude saw him. Anne saw him. There are books, newspapers, documentaries, *actual buildings and locations*, all proving that he was in Argentina after the war was supposedly over.

"He tried to create the Fourth Reich, stupidly and unsuccessfully. The popular narrative tried to rewrite history to make you think the war had ended. They epically failed. The war wasn't officially over until *we*, the Society, ended it."

"OK, but one more question."

"If only one, you'd better make it count," he said teasingly.

Angelina smiled. "One for now. Why didn't you or Jude stop him? You could've prevented everything if you'd just killed him beforehand."

"Human error is the fallacy, the fatal flaw in the design. Jude and I were around during baby Hitler's time. We could've destroyed him if we'd had the chance, but that would've been pointless and we would've been forever branded, even to ourselves, as baby killers. You can't ever know what a child will grow up to become, what events and decisions will shape them. Think about it. Humans only reward success, no matter what that looks like.

"You only know Edgar for what he ended up accomplishing. But what if he'd come to you as a boy and said, 'I'm going to be the greatest writer who ever lived.' Would you get his autograph? His daguerreotype? Interview him for the local newspaper? No. You'd laugh and say, 'Sure, sure, run along now, child. Dream your dreams and let me be.'

"Celebrities are depressed and isolated because they can't trust people after they've achieved fame for just this reason. 'You bullied me before, and now you want a front row seat because I achieved greater accomplishments than you? I outdid you in some capacity, so you reward that *now*, instead of treating me like an equal *all along?*

"Killing the man wouldn't have killed the idea. Hitler didn't create the Nazi Party, he only brought it more publicity. You can't kill an idea any more than you can travel back in time. You'd be a wise queen to question everything. Never take anything at face value because there are multiple sides to every story. Try and see the world from multiple views, because nothing is ever as simple as it seems."

Ludwig paused, looking slightly perplexed at himself. "I went off on a tangent, didn't I? All that to say humans are stupid. His ideas were too widespread, are still widespread today. Killing him publicly back then would've made him a martyr to his followers and given even more voice to his cause. Instead, he died a nameless death at the hands of his enemies. That's the answer you were looking for."

"That was … really deep." Angelina popped another sushi roll into her mouth.

"Deep as the ocean, my Queen."

Excitement crackled through the air, and a hush fell over the ballroom. Angelina turned around instinctively, knowing exactly who'd caused that sort of reaction from his people. Jude was at the door, dressed all in black from head to toe. Plain, but regal. His beard was slightly scruffy, Angelina's favorite look on him.

Her heart burst into a million pieces at the sight of him, her emotions overwhelming her. His gray diamond eyes darted along the faces before him, searching for the one who would make him stop. He didn't have to search far, because Angelina was already moving towards him. The chemistry between them drew them together. As their eyes met, his cherry lips curled up into a grin. Before he could even smile fully, she was in his arms kissing him, her hands tangled in his hair.

"I missed you," she whispered, as she hugged him tight. He breathed in her scent, her hair, her full presence in his arms.

"I missed you, too." They embraced again, and the room resumed their movements, trying to give the couple some privacy.

"Two days was too long. Let's not do that again, OK?"

"You'll get no arguments from me." He swept her hair behind her ears, and kissed her forehead. Angelina ran her hands down his hard, firm chest, before wrapping them back around him and pulling him in towards her. He kissed her again, right before someone cleared their throat rudely beside them.

"You both need to get ready, it's almost time," Anne stated matter-of-factly towards Angelina. She turned her attention to Jude. "Can I have a word please?"

"Not now, Anne. We can talk later."

She tapped her foot on the marble floor. "It's really kind of important, you'll want to know."

Jude looked at her. "I trust you to handle it. You trusted me with your life, and I trust you with mine. Send me an email and I'll look over it when I have time." His eyes reverted to Angelina.

"That's not fair. You're the king, Ju—" Anne began to protest, before one look from him shut her down. She threw her hands up and stormed out of the ballroom.

"Anne Frank hates me," Angelina whispered, so no one would hear her but Jude.

"I already told her, she really doesn't," Ludwig said, strolling by, his mouth full of macaroni. "She's just pissy at Keats, and therefore, at everyone who comes into contact with her."

Jude led Angelina out of the ballroom and

down the long hallway to his room. "All of your dresses and belongings are in my room, for safe keeping. Not that anything bad would ever happen, but I figured you were more comfortable staying with me than Anne."

"Absolutely," she said, wrapping her arm through his as they walked, simultaneously wondering when he *was* going to ask her officially. "Did you have a good day driving the shuttle bus?"

Jude looked down shyly towards the ground, smiling to himself. Her heart lurched out of her chest and reached for him. "Yeah, I did."

"I love that you like being there for your people. It's adorable."

"Adorable wasn't what I was going for, but I'll take it." He pushed open the door to his room. It was the room at the very end of the hall, the one with the unique balcony that she'd seen from the back patio.

"What were you going for?" Her eyes lit up at the interior. The walls were aligned with beautiful, vibrantly colored mosaics, various images of old-world Moroccan influences. Each window was a pointed arch, with accompanying mosaics lining the insides.

She expected a genie's magic lamp sitting beside the bed, which was a four-poster canopy with purple netting draped over the top. Glancing at the side table, Angelina was not disappointed. There, a tiny bronze genie lamp was sitting, with a candle wick poking out of the top of it. She walked forward to the double doors that led to the balcony she was so curious to explore.

"Manly and sexy," Jude said behind her, fully aware that Angelina didn't hear him. She was too far gone, mesmerized with the colors and the culture around her. His room looked exactly like walking through an archaeologist's dream.

"This is what heaven looks like," she said, as she twirled around. "I'm sure of it. I think we get to pick out our own heaven when we get there. Mine looks like this, and smells like new books on a rainy day. I'm sorry, did you say something?"

"You'll appreciate what comes next," Jude said, watching her intently. With her hands on the knobs, Angelina pushed the balcony doors open, walked out, and gasped. Jude was close behind her, his arms wrapped around her waist as her eyes roamed the columns. Each column supporting the round portico that was his balcony was shaped like a stack of books.

Each spine held the name of a different classic novel or influential book, each book elaborately colored and carved with gold or silver leaf inlaid into each pattern. *Now. Now is the perfect moment*, Angelina thought to herself.

He kissed her neck, sending shivers up and down her body. "I designed this room for you, in case you said 'yes.' I thought you'd appreciate being gone and abroad at the same instance."

"But you have places all over the world?"

"I do, but you only have one aunt. I don't want you to have to leave her and regret being with me." Angelina squeezed her eyes shut, and fell one step deeper into a love she could never recover from.

"We should get ready soon," he whispered. Angelina turned to meet his gray diamond eyes, silently pleading with him to make this the moment he officially asked her. It was perfect. The sun was setting, the columns of books were around them, the cicadas were singing a symphony in the background, and a few random, off-season fireflies were creating a paper lantern and tealight effect in the air around them.

"Jude …" was all she could think to say. She

wanted him, more than she had realized until this point. She knew she'd say yes, but she hadn't been fully aware of how much she was in love with him.

Not really. Not until they'd spent two days apart and it had devastated her. Not until she had seen him walk into the ballroom, his eyes searching only for hers.

She was about to say it, about to say those three words that would rip her heart open and forever bind their souls together. He kissed her nose, knowing what was on the tip of her tongue and being, if only temporarily, afraid to touch it.

"Save that thought until after you've experienced the Conference, my Queen. Then we'll talk." But there was nothing else she needed to know. Of that, she was certain.

Chapter

Twenty

Angelina emerged from the bathroom in her emerald green, sweeping, off-the-shoulder, A-line gown with black sash and heels. Paired with her olive skin and chestnut braided chignon, she looked like Hollywood royalty.

Jude was standing in the middle of the bedroom floor waiting for her. He, in turn, looked like a dream, in a black, well-tailored Brioni suit, with a black tie and dark gray shirt and pocket square that deviously highlighted his gray eyes. They gaped at each other, each doing nothing to hide their approval. Angelina wiped the corner of her mouth, consciously afraid that she'd outright drooled in front of him. *Again.*

He walked around her slowly, admiring the view. Her head turned with his movements until he was out of her sight. Jude came up behind her and placed a solitaire emerald necklace around her neck and fastened it for her. Then, he turned and offered her his arm.

"There are no words to describe your beauty, Angelina." He kissed her cheek lightly, and her heart scattered into a million palpitations. Angelina smiled quietly to herself as they walked out of the room, and tried to focus on breathing steadily.

She was extremely nervous, even though Jude had promised to not leave her side. "Tonight is really just meet and greets. There will be an opening song, a reading, and dancing. And you've already seen the food. We have tons of food. Tonight is about being relaxed and having fun. Tomorrow is a little more formal and put together."

When they got to the end of the long hallway, Ludwig was waiting for them. He was also dressed in a

Brioni suit, though the opposite style to Jude's. His was dark charcoal gray with a gray tie and black shirt. He smiled at the pair as they approached. Edgar was nowhere in sight, and Angelina realized that she hadn't seen him the entire day.

"Where's Edgar?"

"He'll be joining us a little bit later. He's been up in his room working on his top-secret poem all weekend. Nobody's seen him except for the kitchen staff when he sneaks down to steal a plate of sushi and then runs back upstairs," Ludwig answered.

In the hour or so that Angelina and Jude had been absent, the entire immortal population had somehow managed to transform into evening wear. The entire ballroom looked like a glitzy awards show afterparty, with gowns, jewels, and elaborate fashion as far as the eye could see. Jude led Angelina to the seats in the middle of the room, with Ludwig close behind them. The trio sat down, and Ludwig produced a seat holder from his suit pocket and placed it in the chair next to him for Edgar. The lights flashed three times, and the excited chatter in the ballroom quickly died as everyone scattered around to find seats.

Angelina and Jude were holding hands tightly,

his thumb casually stroking hers as the lights darkened completely for a few moments. More movement in the dark alerted them that the seats in the back were almost completely filled now, and the ruffling of fabric and footsteps died to a quiet calm.

A soft blue glow came from behind the stage, and a spotlight found a curvaceous brunette, concealed by the shadows with her back to the audience. She was wearing a deep navy sparkling dress that shimmered like a disco ball in the spotlight, giving her an ethereal appearance.

This was clearly part of the show, because as soon as the light brightened on her, she spun around on her heel, bit her glove off with her teeth, and sauntered catlike towards the stage, her hips swaying seductively like a pendulum. Angelina half-expected her to lick her hand and rub it behind her ears.

Angelina's eyes went wide in recognition. Finally, she understood who Nadine was and her entire back story. She looked at Ludwig for clarification on what she was seeing. He whispered, "Don't gawk at her, it only makes her more dramatic. Pretend like she's just another leaf blowing in the wind."

She continued to stare, completely confused at what was happening. It dawned on Ludwig what she was shocked about. "Oh, right. Her hair. So, in addition to curing some ailments, the blood makes our hair sort of like plastic, so we can never dye it. Her signature locks are eternally brown now, her natural color. Let me tell you from experience, do *not* mention that or she will flip to psycho mode real fast."

The woman took the stage, and Jude's grip on her hand tightened. Angelina hated Nadine immediately for how she'd wasted the heart of this perfect man beside her. Nadine started singing a welcome song in her slow and breathy voice, and Angelina felt a groan rise up inside her throat. She glanced over at Ludwig, who was more amused with examining his cuticles. "How long does this go on for?"

"Yeah, she has that effect on people. She's not a bad person, she's just a *lot* to handle. When her song is over, her part at the Convention is over. Each Queen is required to have some sort of program participation." He glanced at Angelina right as the look of dread settled on her face. "Don't worry, you'll start next year." He winked at her, and she turned her eyes back towards the stage to watch the once and former queen.

Nadine threw her arms up and popped her hip out to the side. "Welcome to the 78th Annual Convention for the Society of Messengers on Earth!" The room roared back to life, and deafening applause rattled the crystal chandeliers. Nadine waited for the crowd to settle down, her arms still stretched out to embrace her audience. "And now the moment you've all been waiting for." She enunciated each word in a dramatic breath, "The. Edgar. Allan. Poe!"

More uproarious applause filled the room, and Angelina clenched her ears to stifle the noise. The trio erupted in clapping along with everyone else, joining the room's standing ovation. An awful clambering racket came from behind the same darkened curtain that Nadine had emerged from. Edgar's unmistakably tall and lanky figure walked awkwardly out from the darkened shadows, wearing none other than a full knight's armor.

A red feather sprouted from the top of the helmet, bobbing with Edgar's movements as he clanged up onto the stage. His visor flapped up and down with each step. Finally, he made it to the microphone, and gestured for everyone to be seated. Ludwig was snickering loudly, completely amused at his friend's bumbling appearance.

"Ladies and gentlemen, queens of the ages, and my King, welcome to the 78th Annual Convention." The visor slammed back down over his face, and he struggled with his metal-covered fingers to unjam it and lift it back. "If you'll kindly allow me, I'd like to read you a poem I've been working on. It is titled *Sir Bilbert*, hence the armor."

Everyone clapped, encouraging him to continue. Edgar smiled appreciatively, and held up the paper he'd been carrying. A pauldron fell off and clanged to the stage loudly. Edgar looked down at it with a sad expression. Beside her, Ludwig was shielding his eyes with his hand as he stared at the ground. He was laughing so hard there were tears in his eyes. Angelina looked at Jude, who was suppressing a grin, but trying desperately not to laugh at his friend.

"And now, Society, *Sir Bilbert.*

"Once there was a knight,

Sir Bilbert he was called.

Many thought him quite funny,

many thought him quite odd.

His hair was blond,

his eyes were hawky.

His body tall,

and quite gawky.

The spectacles of which he wore,

were wire-rimmed glasses.

And he always fought dragons,

with the staggering speed of molasses.

His limbs were quite long,

his armor rather dull and quite phony.

His horse was crotchety and quite gray,

her name was Ginerva,

and she hated hay."

Angelina looked at Ludwig, searching for answers to

all of the questions racing through her mind. He leaned over and whispered, "'Twas the laudanum that slayed the beast. He's never quite regained his way with words since he turned. My fault, I'm afraid, but still terribly amusing. Remind me to tell you about the time he tried to court Emily Dickinson." Edgar continued on the stage.

"Yes, what Ginerva only drank,

was the milk from the cows.

She was very worried about her bone structure,

when she walked, her joints made horrid sounds.

Yes, quite a pair they made,

defenders of the kingdom.

I heard the town whispering,

when they had first seen them.

My precious knight, Sir Bilbert,

he can do no wrong.

For once I was sitting in my garden,

and I heard the sweetest song.

Yes my darling Bilbert,

had come to call for me.

My darling Bilbert had proposed,

so ever after we could live happily.

He asked for my hand in marriage,

and my father did agree.

Bilbert then took my hand and we danced under the sun,

then we frolicked through fields of barley."

Edgar took an awkward bow, and more pieces of his armor fell to his feet. The room gave him a standing ovation once again, loudly cheering and praising him. Edgar bowed again, before searching the crowd for his friends. When he spotted Jude, he hopped down and jangled loudly towards them, the pieces of his armor now hanging by threads. He squashed between the people, side-walking like a crab until he got to his seat by Ludwig.

"How was it? Was it entertaining?" he asked

eagerly.

"It was all that and more, Old Chap. You never cease to put on a show," Ludwig said, patting him on the back, the chainmail beneath Edgar's armor rattling in response.

"Nadine didn't help me with my costume. She always tries to upstage everybody. Do I have helmet hair?" He lifted his helmet up and over his head. His black hair was matted down, conforming to his bulbous crown.

"Yeah, buddy. You might want to fluff it out a bit and let it dry."

"Confounded rodents!" Edgar yelled loud enough for their group to hear, pumping his metal-clad fist in the air.

"That's all right, Edgar." Angelina leaned forward, reaching across Ludwig to take Edgar's metal gauntlet-covered hand in hers. "I'll help you put it back together. You were far better than she was, and the audience loved you more."

Edgar smiled appreciatively, and leaned back in his chair.

"You have such a tender heart," Jude whispered.

Next, Anne took the stage. Angelina couldn't help but smiling at her, even if Anne did or did not harbor negative feelings towards their friendship. She was radiant in a simple black dress with black elbow-length gloves, and she reminded Angelina of Audrey Hepburn in *Breakfast at Tiffany's*. No doubt that's what Anne had been going for, because the only other adornments she was wearing were a simple strand of white pearls around her neck, and pearl earrings to match.

Keats was off to the side, watching Anne adoringly. From what Angelina could tell, he was dressed in a brown striped suit, but nothing nearly as fancy as Jude and Ludwig. It reminded Angelina of Henry Higgins in *My Fair Lady*, and she now strongly suspected that anything and everything relating to Audrey Hepburn was high on Anne's list of favorite things.

"Thank you, Nadine and Edgar, for that charming welcome! Everyone, meet back here tomorrow, same time, same place for the official program. Oh, and I'll kindly ask you to please move your chair to the edge of the room when you get up, to clear the dance floor." She did a mini drumroll on her thighs. "And now, the reason we all *really* came here tonight. It's time to PARTY!"

Chapter

Twenty-One

Angelina and her trio of men stayed seated while the crowd filtered past them. Some stopped by to shake their hands and welcome Angelina, and some just waved. Edgar finally stood up after numerous people asked for selfies. Angelina quickly helped him reassemble his suit, to make him picture perfect. A steady line of people trailed along behind him as he made his way over to one of the picturesque windows to use as a background.

A large group had gathered around Anne on stage, and Angelina noticed most of them were wearing lapel pins in the shape of the Star of David on their evening wear. Her heart warmed at the sight of them together, that their legacies had been able to continue because of the man she loved.

"Are you having a good time so far?" Jude asked nervously, when most of the people had cleared out and headed over to eat. The DJ was setting up the stage for the dancing that was about to start, and a few rogue attendees rushed around to rearrange the chairs to allow maximum floor space. He hesitated. "I'm sorry, I should've warned you about Nadine."

Angelina took his face in her hands. "Quit apologizing to me about everything. I'm here. I'm with you."

The lights dropped, and waltz music crept out from the surround sound speakers. By now, they were nearly the only people left in the ballroom, besides Edgar and Anne's respective fan clubs. Angelina supposed being in their company never got old, no matter how long you'd lived.

From the darkened ballroom, Angelina peered through the large front windows and saw that the entire front lawn and fountain were illuminated. People were starting to file outside to socialize, their plates piled high with elaborate recipes from the banquet hall.

Jude led Angelina to the middle of the ballroom and took her in his arms. "Tomorrow will be a lot more business-related. When we first started, everyone got so caught up in seeing each other that they couldn't concentrate. That was when we realized we'd have to extend it to a whole weekend and make the first night a party."

She twirled a strand of his hair around her finger as they swayed to the music. "And a feast. All of the feasting. Seems not everyone keeps as strict a diet as you." Jude closed his eyes and chuckled.

"It's just something I like to do for them. I like everybody to feel excited that there's going to be more available than cold coffee and continental breakfasts."

"Oh, gosh yes. Powdered eggs are the absolute worst. And plastic gravy with cardboard biscuits!"

"Yes! And those little muffins that taste like glue! Where do these people even come up with such recipes? They *know* that's not healthy for anybody." They quit dancing, their laughter filling the space between them.

Angelina's stomach growled. "I am kind of hungry, though, now that we're talking about food. I didn't eat quite enough of Edgar's sushi because I wanted to save room for everything else, and then I got swept away in the moment when you walked in."

"And what a dazzling moment you were, my Queen. Shall we?" He took her hand in his, and they headed towards the banquet hall.

The lighting in the hall was darkly dimmed to give the crystal chandeliers full opportunity to radiate brightly over the whole room. Candelabras lined the walls between each of the windows and reflecting mirrors on the opposite side, enhancing the candlelit glow of the crystal. Each table was piled high with delectable foods and desserts, and what appeared to be a larger-than-life punch fountain made up the centerpiece of the floor. Angelina couldn't make out many details from it because of the people hovering around it and refilling their glasses repeatedly, but she added it to her mental list of things to check out.

"I took the liberty of ordering chicken alfredo and tiramisu for you. I hope you don't mind. Those seemed to be high on your list of favorites," Jude said, while Angelina scouted out the endless row of silver buffet servers.

"I don't mind eating myself into a carb coma. I

don't mind at all, as a matter of fact." She kissed his cheek and went to grab a plate. The stack of dinner plates, she noticed, weren't really plates but platters. The actual, regular-sized dinner plates were labelled as dessert plates. "I like the way you do things here. I like it a lot."

"Next year, if you're still here, you can order whatever you want."

Angelina paused in mid-air, chicken alfredo dangling from the serving spatula. "I'll be here, Jude." If he didn't hurry up and ask her, she was going to have to go into contemporary woman mode and ask him herself. The urging pull she had for him was nothing like she'd ever experienced before. *Surely he must know that? Be able to sense how I react to him, mentally and physically?*

He watched her pile her plate with alfredo, then more of Edgar's sushi, and a few of Ludwig's crawfish just to try. The next table was piled high with egg rolls, crab Rangoon, beer-battered fish, and small ramekins of homemade sticky toffee pudding.

"This is Anne and John's table. He likes food that reminds him of home, and she likes any fried Asian food. These are her favorites. Last year she had chicken feet and cream cheese wontons."

"Chicken feet?" Angelina was intrigued.

"Yep. I was on the fence at first, but they were surprisingly delightful. Can I get you some champagne or punch?"

"Actually, I think I'll just have bottled water right now. Where is that?" Angelina shoved a piece of dragon roll into her mouth.

"I'll go get you one." Jude disappeared into the crowd before Angelina could protest. A few yards away she saw the fountain again, spewing purple liquids. It was calling her name. She weaved through the crowd, artfully keeping her Rangoons balanced around her plate as she moved. Her eyes traveled upwards to the top, counting each tier of punch. Ten tiers. Ten tiers of punch on the floor. *I think there's a song in there somewhere*, she giggled to herself.

Mesmerized in the flowing amethyst falls, Ludwig walked up beside her and refilled his cup. "My Queen, I see you decided to try the crawfish after all. What do you think?"

"I think they're absolutely divine. Like little,

fried, meaty bites of the Earth's ecosystem. I can practically taste the river flowing through their veins."

Ludwig grinned widely, pleased with her approval of the Southern delicacy. As they stood there chatting, Ludwig continually refilling his drink from the punchbowl, a parted hush fell between conversations, long enough for one distinct voice to rise above all other conversations taking place.

"And then I said, 'So let them eat cake!'" The crowd around her roared into wild laughter.

Ludwig heard her the same time Angelina did, his posture stiffening straight up into discomfort. A detached look crossed his face as the banshee squealed from across the room.

"WIGGY!!!!Is that you, Wiggy?!" His eyes shifted to Angelina desperately, pleading for her to somehow save him, even though he'd been spotted and his fate was already sealed.

The woman's voice was wavering and old-fashioned, like Katharine Hepburn, but a few tones lighter. Angelina remembered her voice. It was the voice that belonged to the ex-wife who'd showed up, furious that Angelina had slept in her jewelry-box reject room that night.

"I thought that was you, Wiggy!" The woman parted the crowd, arriving at Ludwig's side. The petite woman, dressed in gold glitter heels, stockings, and a lavender and gold beaded flapper dress draped her arms around his shoulders and kissed his cheek.

Her blonde hair was shorter than Angelina remembered, cut now into a cropped bob style of the 1920s with a lavender headband surrounding her crown. A faint lavender choker was around her neck, barely bright enough to be visible against her snowy skin.

The man accompanying her was someone Angelina recognized not only from the previous encounter, but also from the silver screen.

Flynn Tremaine had been a prominent star in the 1920s and '30s. He had mysteriously died in a car accident, though his body had never been recovered. It finally dawned on Angelina in that moment. Everyone who was now immortal had had some sort of mysterious death or suicide, some conspiracy theory or scandal associated with their name to cover up their turning.

She had not thought that far ahead as to how she'd like to go out, but she supposed she'd prefer to fade away into obscurity.

Flynn's expression was that of utter boredom and indifference to his melodramatic thespian of a wife. From her antics currently on display, accompanied by the stories Angelina had heard thus far, she imagined she was an extremely exhausting person to be around for any amount of time, let alone eternity.

"Wiggy here likes to pretend that his hearing goes in and out just to spite me," the woman squealed in the loudest, shrillest voice imaginable, directly into his ear. She was immediately obnoxious and rude, and Angelina hated her already. Ludwig's placid face flinched ever so slightly, like he had had plenty of practice at ignoring her.

Flynn, his expression still blank and removed from his current situation, turned and walked away without notifying his wife. "Did you ever hear of his *Immortal Beloved?* That's me! Wiggy here made our love legendary!"

"And don't think I don't regret it every time I watch a documentary about myself. You never even said the cake line. Why do you keep lying to people?" Ludwig barked at her.

"Oh, *meine Schatz*, I simply give the audience the entertainment they demand!"

Her chuckle sounded like a chipmunk while she patted his stomach degradingly, as if he weren't a walking Adonis.

"Piggy Wiggy, I saw your table of macaroni and cheese in there." She proceeded to rub her hand around what Angelina assumed was his flat and obviously toned stomach, judging from the way his sinewy muscles had highlighted him in shorts and polo shirt earlier in the day.

"And I saw your table full of bonbons, you pugnacious glitter wench," he said, not missing a chance to strike a blow. "You should drink more water. You're starting to bloat like a decomposing whale."

Jude raced up beside and slightly in front of Angelina, partly shielding her body from the oncoming blows. Marie casually glanced at him, waving her hand to brush him to the side. Her iced lavender eyes, like violets covered in the morning frost, refocused on Angelina.

A rush of air to Angelina's right signaled Anne's arrival to the situation. She faced off Marie between Angelina and Ludwig, her posture defiantly challenging the woman. Angelina realized that maybe Anne didn't hate her, or at least hated her less than this queen.

The blonde, her eyes bouncing bored between the four, finally enlightened the fact that Angelina was indeed someone of importance to them.

"Well, well, *well.* If it isn't Broody Judy and his Band of Immortal Misfits. You must be the new flavor of the decade."

Her lavender snake eyes sized Angelina up and down with menacing glare, as if trying to determine where her biggest weakness was. Edgar, sensing the tension, rushed up to the situation in his knight's armor, positioning himself in front of both Jude and Angelina.

"You will not talk to her that way! She is our queen!"

She held her pointer finger up directly to his visor, which slammed down once again. "Silence, Egg. You forget to whom you speak."

"I know exactly to whom I speak."

"She may be the future queen, but I was the first queen. You'd be wise not to forget that, Eggy Poo." Her violet eyes were back on Angelina.

"Look, toots, ain't nothin' personal, but all Jude here's ever lookin' for is two tits, a hole, and a heartbeat." She said the words with a wicked glimmer in her eye.

"You're such a vile, wretched woman. That's never been true and you know it. I'm sorry I ever made you my queen." A pained expression crossed the woman's face at Jude's words, and then it was gone just as quickly.

Angelina had already known who the woman was the minute she saw her face in clear view. Of course she knew her. Her aunt had commemorative china with the woman's portrait on them, passed down through the generations of their French ancestry. Her radiant beauty, stunning porcelain skin, and picturesque profile was unmistakable, even in this modern world.

"Aren't you going to introduce us, Broody Judy?" The tiny woman laughed a ladylike cackle, further dismissing Jude. A dainty white hand, as fragile as bone china, raised itself up towards Angelina, as if she were supposed to kiss it. "Marie Antoinette, darling. Simply charmed."

Angelina didn't shake her hand. She merely practiced the same mannerism that Anne had pulled on her when Angelina had introduced herself. Her eyes slowly climbed inch by inch up Marie's arm, in mock disgust until she matched her, penetrating stare for penetrating stare.

One eyebrow cocked in feigned amusement. "Oh, *Judy*, you've got a feisty one here," Marie said, amused. "Wiggy and Jude seem to have the same taste in women. They're starting to form a habit. I can practically smell Wiggy heating up from a mile away, like pure masculine sex on a stick."

Marie licked Ludwig's ear, and his nostrils flared cringingly as he closed his eyes slowly, trying to will her to disappear.

Marie cupped her hand over her mouth and whispered loudly, "But I'll let you in on a little secret, if you don't want to waste your time with both." She grinned at Angelina deviously. "Our Wiggy here is a *much* better roll in the hay, and more, shall we say, *well endowed*, than our beloved king." Her violent violet eyes glared an evil sparkle. She let out a heinous cackle as Ludwig's face turned bright red.

"Don't let him fool you with his selective deafness. He can *certainly* hear screams!"

Angelina watched Flynn Tremaine shamelessly flirt with Nadine from across the room. He leaned in and whispered into her ear, and she in turn placed her hand on his chest, lingering far too long for any woman to give more than one obvious impression, and threw her head back in laughter.

By now, Angelina had had enough of this show. "I wouldn't throw insults, babe. Seems to me like you're the saddest woman in the room. You threw away the two most eligible bachelors here for a man who can't even stand to be seen with you." Angelina destroyed Marie, unknowingly hitting her in her weakest point. Ludwig bit his fist, trying to keep from laughing.

Marie's eyes narrowed yet again, as she sliced Angelina apart with her gaze. "Don't worry, *babe*, Judy will be done with you faster than you can say, 'Bite me.'"

"I am curious as to why your husband is openly and blatantly flirting with Nadine?" Marie paled, if that were even more possible. She turned and spun on her heel, marching to find her husband.

Angelina would've felt bad, had Marie not put down her entire group of friends and the love of her life.

Anne turned to Angelina, an apparent and approving smile across her face. "If you get hungry later, you can reheat anything in my air fryer to make it crunchy again."

"Thank you so much, Anne. I just might take you up on that. No, I'll definitely take you up on that." Anne nodded before turning and leaving.

"See, that was her version of BFFs. You're BFFs now. She'll probably want to paint your toenails or something, too," Ludwig said. "I really love how you levelled Marie out, by the way. Top notch classic moment, right there."

Edgar bowed, his tall body stooped lower than Angelina's waist. "My Queen, you are the true queen. You are royalty, you are dignified, you are sent from the heavens. Please allow me to serve in the presence of your magnificence. I am not worthy, but I will make you proud to call me your loyal subject."

"Dude, seriously, get up," Ludwig said, tapping him on the head. "You're freaking her out. Look at her eyes, she's completely freaked out. I think she gets the point."

Angelina and Jude laughed at their exchange, though Angelina noticed a sadness in his eyes.

"I'm going to go get some fresh air, OK?" Jude said, before kissing her cheek and leaving her alone with Edgar and Ludwig.

Angelina watched him leave, wanting to follow him but not sure if she should.

"He gets mopey like that sometimes around her. It's not personal," Ludwig answered the questions painted all over her confused expression. "She's the true definition of a vampire. She'll suck you dry and leave you for dead."

"Why does she affect him like that? Is he still in love with her?"

"Absolutely not. But he was for a long time, and before her, he was alone for even longer. They had a tumultuous relationship. I meant what I said before, Angelina. He's changed for the better since he found you. Give him a minute, and then go to him."

Loud music began pulsing and echoing through the building. The chandeliers began to jiggle, the light reflected in them glittering across the room. "Ah, the party's officially started. Come on, Edgar, now's our time to shine!" Ludwig winked at Angelina before slapping Edgar's armored shoulder.

Edgar shook his head. "See you on the floor, Ed." Ludwig left the two of them alone. Angelina looked down stoically at the last bits of her food, which had grown cold since the confrontation.

"He's right, my Queen. Never has there been a more wonderous, a more beautiful, a more dazzling woman to catch Jude's heart. The first two had only visuals and nothing more. You, as the children are saying contemporaneously, are the whole package. Shall I escort you somewhere?"

"No, thank you, Edgar. I'm going to finish my toffee pudding and then go and find Jude. You should go and have a good time out on the dance floor with Ludwig."

Edgar awkwardly wrapped his armored arm around Angelina's shoulders in a side hug. "We're overjoyed to have you with us. Do not doubt that for a trice."

Chapter

Twenty-Two

Angelina headed out the front door, where only a handful of people were still mingling about. She did not see Jude anywhere, though several people did stop her to take selfies.

Instinctively, she knew he wasn't in the ballroom where the majority of the group was. The floors were slightly shaking as she trotted back through the foyers, making her feel dizzy. Angelina walked to the entrance of the ballroom anyway, to see what was going on.

The room was blacked out, except for the menagerie-colored lights that were washing over the dance floor. The crowd was dancing to the music, jumping up and down in time with the beat. Somewhere in the center of the room, loud chants were urging Ludwig and Edgar on. From where Angelina stood in the door, she could only catch a glimpse as Edgar did the worm in the middle of the dance floor, his armor falling in heavy clunks by his side. Ludwig, in turn, was doing the sprinkler. Angelina laughed at the entertaining pair, and then turned and headed out to the back patio.

It was quieter out in the back. Tiki torches lined the walkway down to the river, creating a romantic atmosphere for the couples who were scattered out over the grounds. The full moon reflected on the river below, streams of black and silver peeking through the live oaks along the riverbank.

Angelina glanced over at the swing she and Jude had previously visited, and smiled to herself. A couple, who very much appeared to be Anne and John, were furiously making out in the guise of nightfall. Her eyes followed the stone patio further, until they reached Jude's balcony. A dark shadow fell over the columns, and Angelina's heart beckoned her to follow.

Moonlight cast a darkened silver haze over the room, making the mosaics appear almost underwater.

Angelina stepped further in, and the breeze from the river met and surrounded her, pulling her closer to the outside. She walked towards the balcony.

Jude's back was to her, his hands shoved into his pockets. Angelina walked up behind him and wrapped her hands around his chest, pulling his body against hers. Her cheek rested against his back. "I missed you."

His body shivered under her touch, as emotion caught in his throat. "Those things she said, how I felt about you, they're not true. Nothing she said was true."

Angelina moved around to face him. His hands stayed in his pockets, his body still guarded from her. "I know they're not true. I've never doubted you for a second, Jude."

"I don't know why. I'm a mess. You shouldn't be here, Angelina. You're better than all of this. You deserve better than me." He looked away from her, his emotions threatening to spill from his eyes.

Angelina was furious at the situation. She forcefully removed his hands from his pockets and wrapped them around her waist. "Are you serious right now?" His expression roamed hers, searching for a truth.

"You pursued me for three years, Jude. You followed me around the world for three years, confessed your undying love to me, and now you're just going to give me up because your trollop of an ex-wife said you were just a horndog? You think I'm going to let some tiny little witch I can dropkick into the next millennium intimidate me? Scare me away from quite literally the best man I've ever met? I don't think so, Buster."

"What if this life is a curse? You're better than this. You deserve to live a normal life, have children, grow old with your husband. I can't give you any of those things, Angelina. You're the most intelligent woman I've ever met, and," he sighed, defeatedly, "I've done nothing to deserve you."

"That's not what I heard. Plus, you saved the world and killed Hitler. That already puts you pretty high on my list of good men. And you're not a curse, you're a blessing on all humanity. Jude, I don't even know what to say around you. I love you, but it's me. I'm the one who feels so … so stupid, really." Her hands flew up around her head in frustration.

"You're otherworldly, knowledgeable and experienced, and you've seen so much. I'm an archaeologist, but I can only pretend to know and understand history. You've *actually lived* everything I've ever wanted to know. That's mind-blowing to me. Don't you get that? I can't even describe to you how baffled you make me feel. I've never had a confidence problem before but I just have to say I feel like a toddler around your whole … family. There are celebrities, artists, and world-famous people that I could never hold a candle to."

She huffed, agitated at her mortal-ness and lack of knowledge and experience. Without knowing, their roles had shifted. Angelina had managed to restore Jude's confidence and lose her footing at the same time.

"Let me stop you right there," he said, and brushed his finger against her lips to calm her down. "I am positively captivated by everything you do, and I haven't even gotten you into my bed yet." A mischievous grin spread across his face for a fleeting second, and Angelina's knees went weak.

"I want you for my wife, for my queen, for all of my life. We'll make more memories together, and live longer than history itself. My life so far has been just a day compared to the life that awaits me with you. And as for saying things to keep me engaged," he hovered over her lips, their breaths intertwining wisps, "I believe that's the first time you've said you love me. That, my Queen, is all you ever need to say to hold my attention."

Angelina raced to fill the short distance between their lips and kissed him hard. He had such a way of making everything seem easy, making problems rush away like leaves falling into a rushing stream.

"I love you," she said, as his lips crashed onto hers again. Finally, after what seemed like hours of making out but which was really only about twenty minutes, their lips parted.

"I love you, too, Angelina." Jude rubbed his nose on hers, before resting his forehead against hers.

"I have to ask, and I hate to ruin the moment, but was that the official proposal?"

Jude laughed into her hair. "What do you think?"

"I think I just gave you a whole speech about how stupid you make me feel, and I still don't know if you've proposed yet, which makes me feel even more stupid. You've said multiple times that you want me as your queen and as your wife, but you have yet to *ask* me if I accept. I'm a scientist. I need facts."

Jude was clearly tickled, and could barely contain his snickering as he watched her mental breakdown with an amused expression.

"I said I need facts, Jude." She slapped the back of her hand to her palm, reiterating her point. "Cold, hard, documented evidence on the circumstances surrounding the event."

"I understand. Please enlighten me, what evidence do you have so far?" He was clearly egging her on just to watch her get flustered.

"What I just said. You want me for your queen and your wife. You've spent adequate time, albeit over three-ish weeks, to get to know me. You've introduced me to your family, which I know is not something men do if they're not serious about you. OH! And I know you sent out a newsletter prematurely announcing me as queen. So there." She swatted his chest.

Jude nodded, stroking his beard as if in deep thought. "Well, Dr. Arbonne, that is some pretty good evidence. But do you have any solid proof? Like a ring, per chance?"

Her eyes narrowed at him. "I do not have a ring and I do not appreciate you playing with my emotions. Do you want me to ask you instead? Because I will. I wasn't born two-thousand years ago and nowadays the woman can ask the man. It's totally a thing."

"I would decline if you asked," Jude said matter-of-factly.

Angelina gasped. "Wh-what? What do you mean?"

"Because you can't propose without a ring. Everybody knows that, it's totally a thing," Jude said, playfully mocking her. "And I know for a fact that since you're making this up as you go along, that you have no ring. Therefore, I cannot and will not accept your fake proposal." He spun on his heels and walked into the bedroom.

Angelina stood there, stunned. Her mind was racing in a million directions. She knew he was just teasing her, but her emotions were taking over the logical portion of her brain. Had she been wrong? Did he not love her? Did he have a ring? Did she need to leave and go cry over a pint of Chocolate Therapy? Her eyes stung as the tears threatened to come out and destroy the composure she was desperately clinging to.

Jude returned a moment later, a sly grin on his face. "Dr. Arbonne, you didn't think I was serious, did you?"

The tears released their hold and flowed freely down her cheeks as she stood upright, holding her chin higher. "Of course not."

He held her in his arms until her sobs stopped. Instinctively, he knew she wouldn't be able to hear him or concentrate until her mind had settled down.

When she did finally stop crying, he kissed her damp lips softly. "As it happens, I do have a ring. If you don't mind, I'll be the one proposing." Angelina shook her head up and down, sniffing loudly. Jude got down on one knee, and took her hand in his.

"I've made a lot of mistakes, but searching for and following you across the globe was not one of them. From the moment I saw you, my life changed for the better. I wanted to be someone who would make you proud to be with him, and I hope that I've done that, at least enough to trick you into staying with me." Angelina laughed, the tears of fear now replaced with glistening happiness.

"For well over two millenniums, no woman has captured my heart the way that you were able to in a single glance. You are the one true love of my many lifetimes and I would be most honored and humbled to be the man of yours." He opened the box he was holding. Inside was a green moldavite ring, the same color as her eyes and clearly from another time and place all together. "Angelina, will you marry me?"

In his eyes, she saw those of a newborn deer. Gentle, passive in nature. But his presence told a different story, that which was consumed with a raging fire that would destroy all in its path, if not contained.

In that moment, she chose her final fate.

"I thought you'd never ask. Yes, of course I will! I've been dreaming of this moment for three weeks!" They both burst out laughing as he slipped the ring onto her finger.

Chapter

Twenty-Three

Angelina awoke in the four-poster bed, her green dress splayed out like a leaf from a gingko tree. She shifted her leg, feeling that her foot was caught up in the purple netting. Angelina groaned to herself and rubbed the sleep from her eyes.

She paused, noticing something different on her hand, and then smiled broadly when the events of last night came flooding back to her.

"You can take the bed, and I'll take the floor."

"I, we, don't have to, you know," she'd hinted

to him while she pulled the covers back.

"I will not take your virtue until our wedding night." Jude crossed his heart with his hand.

Angelina burst out laughing. "I haven't had that kind of virtue since high school, and you haven't had it for a few years longer. I won't tell if you don't."

"I'm doing things right with you, Angelina. Please, just give me this."

"OK, fine. I won't say another word about it."

She sat upright, leaning forward to untangle her foot. Angelina noticed light snoring, and leaned over to look at her new and perfect fiancé, sleeping on the floor.

He looked peaceful, albeit a little dead, but she figured that was borderline normal, considering. He'd taken his suit off, staying only in his boxers. A light blanket covered his legs, but his torso was completely bare and exposed, revealing his caramel chest, dark hairs, and perfect washboard abs. Angelina's gaze lustfully roamed her fiancé, stopping at the large, silvery caramel scar that ran across his stomach and around to his back.

She hopped down off the bed and moved to sit beside him. Trying carefully not to wake him, her fingers moved to trace over his wound. Jude flinched when she got to his ribs, and she made a mental note to use his ticklishness against him later. He stirred awake as her touch continued, and moved his head into her lap.

"You don't exactly make it easy on a girl, do you? You need to wear a shirt from now on if you don't want me to attack you."

He wrapped his arms around her waist and snuggled into her. "I'll have to remember that."

Jude moved to stand up, pulling Angelina up along with him. He turned her around, and unzipped her dress. Angelina let out a loud sigh of relief.

"I should've asked you to do that last night. This thing was like a corset!"

Jude kissed each of her bare shoulders gently as she held the dress against herself with her arms. "Anne has all your clothes picked out for you, complete with detailed sticky notes. I think we're supposed to wear white and cream this afternoon." He disappeared into the closet momentarily, and re-emerged with two outfits in plastic sleeves.

"I love how much detail she puts into everything." Angelina took the sleeve he offered her. Her eyes lit up as she began to unwrap it. Inside was a white summer dress with a cream sash, chic and vintage like something that would be found in an Anthropologie catalog. Tied in a plastic bag around the hanger's handle was a pair of cream-laced wedge heels.

"Yeah, she says it's better for pictures if everybody just does what she tells them to. Plus, the king and queen need to always look presentable. After it's over, she'll be hard at work on a commemorative slideshow to email everyone documenting their weekend. You can submit pictures to her, if you want. She'll also put together a yearbook, which is really more like a giant family newsletter, and will send out copies for Christmas."

"I haven't taken any pictures this weekend. And if I did, it would've mostly been of the food. I'd hate to get on her bad side again when she got a dozen attachments of foodie pictures." Angelina disappeared into the bathroom to get changed.

Her braided chignon was an unsalvageable disaster. Angelina painstakingly removed all of the pins from her hair, combing her fingers carefully through her tresses as she went. She washed her face, then reapplied her mascara and nude lip gloss for a light afternoon feel to match her designated dress.

She exited the bathroom to see Jude, in coordinated fashion, wearing a white polo shirt and cream pants. "Don't you look positively dashing, my King." She tried to curtsy and nearly fell over in her platform heels. Quickly rebounding, she held her head high and strolled to the door, ignoring Jude's quiet chuckles.

There was nearly no one inside except the kitchen staff. Hand in hand, Jude and Angelina walked through the glass dining room and out onto the back patio, stepping through time, it seemed.

All one-thousand or so of the Society members were stretched out over the backyard, down to the banks of the river. Each and every one of them matched Jude and Angelina's wardrobe in color and style, nearly a Georges Seurat painting come to life.

The women wore afternoon dresses, similar to Angelina's. They donned parasols and various styles of straw and felted hats with flowers lining the brims. Most of the men, who weren't actively participating in the sporting events happening around them, were dressed similarly to Jude. Modern, yet somehow otherworldly at the same time.

"I feel underdressed and in the wrong century all of a sudden," Angelina whispered, noticing Anne making a beeline towards her.

"Where is your hat?! Did you read the instructions? Argh!" She threw her hands up in frustration. Daisy petals showered off her head as she turned and stormed away down towards the river.

"Aaaand we're back on her bad side," Angelina said amusedly. The smell of charred and simmering meats hung in the breeze. Angelina's stomach growled, realizing she had forgotten to take advantage of Anne's peace offering to use her air fryer.

"She's never had a queen that she liked before," Jude tried to comfort her.

"I'm not convinced she does now."

"Just be patient." They walked down the steps towards the riverbank, where lots of shouting and yelling was happening. There appeared to be some sort of makeshift net haphazardly tied to a tree on one side, and strung from a pole on the other side. A group of people, including Ludwig and Edgar, were playing volleyball.

"He's going to burn. Do you burn? Can you burn?" Angelina asked, pointing out Edgar's paleness in his cream shorts and tank top. His bare arms and legs were blindingly like the color of a dead sand dollar in a beach gift shop.

"Not really. He usually gets a little bit blistered, but nothing debilitating. I suppose if he was out here for a couple of days, then we'd have a problem."

Edgar tripped and fell onto the sand, and a very shirtless and glistening Ludwig came over and offered him a helping hand. All of the muscles in his torso flexed as he took on Edgar's weight to counteract the movement. Behind him was a row of strategically placed shaded picnic tables, lined with an audience of about thirty women of varying ages who all sighed heavily.

"I didn't know he had a fan club, too." Angelina's gaze traveled behind the women to a single woman underneath a tree, sitting at a table all to herself. She was painfully gazing on at Ludwig.

"She looks sad. We should go sit with her."

"I'd really rather not, if I have a choice."

"A wise king keeps his friends close and his enemies closer. She looks like her dog just died."

"She doesn't have enough heart to have a dog, or any living creature, in her company."

"She's still a person, Jude." Angelina fussed at his dismissive behavior.

"Of the soul-sucking leech variety. You do what you need to do, but count me out. I'm going to go get us some burgers. Do you want potato wedges?"

"Yes, light on the lettuce and ketchup, *heavy* on the wedges." Jude winked at her before he turned to leave.

Angelina refocused her attention back onto Marie. The woman was sitting in a short summer dress, which Angelina realized was the first time she *hadn't* seen her in a flapper dress. Which meant even Marie was scared to cross Anne's clothing wrath. The dress was mid-calf length, and so consumed with lace it could've doubled as a wedding dress. Or at the very least, an after-wedding reception dress. A thin black ribbon choker hugged her neck, the only contrast to her otherwise muted outfit.

She wore her favorite silver heels, her ankles crossed beneath her. The pale pink peonies in her hair were wilted, like the woman they adorned. Angelina approached her cautiously, expecting her fiery temper to lash out at any moment.

The opposite happened. Marie was melancholically stirring a chalice of green liquid, dropping sugar cubes into it and watching them swirl and dissolve at the bottom.

"Marie? May I sit with you?"

Marie looked up and almost through Angelina blankly. "Oh, it's just you. Whatever."

"It's a beautiful day today, wouldn't you say?" Angelina had no idea how to talk to members of actual blood lineage royalty, she realized.

"Sure," Marie sighed exasperatedly.

"Where is Flynn? Did he go to get you something to eat? I'll gladly leave if I'm taking his place."

Tears rolled down her eyes and bounced into the glass of green liquid. "He left with Nadine last night."

Oh. *Oh.*

Marie looked up at Ludwig out on the court, more tears forming and flowing freely in a rare moment of complete candor. "Don't make the same mistakes I did. You won't, because you're smarter. I can tell by the way Jude looks at you. Don't let him go."

Her gaze traveled down to Angelina's ring, and she smiled faintly. "He puts serious thought into everything he does. Sometimes he gets in his own way, but sometimes he gets it right."

Marie's eyes traveled back to Ludwig, and the tears and unfathomable sadness resumed. Angelina felt helpless at not knowing the actual situation she had walked into, and the history of all who were involved. She turned to follow Marie's eyes, watching the game play out.

Edgar and Ludwig were clearly on the superior team. With Ludwig's brute strength and Edgar's lanky height combined, they were nearly unbeatable. Edgar positioned himself by the net, more often than not, and blocked the opposing team's pass with a lazy swoop of his hand. Any ball that Edgar happened to miss, Ludwig was quick to lunge for, fiercely sending the ball back over the net into the sand, and obliterating the other team.

Angelina could tell the six players on the opposing team were just thrilled to be in their company, while the members on Ludwig and Edgar's team were struggling to be relevant at all. She thought she vaguely recognized a few of them, but then again, she had to remind herself where she was in regard to the realm of newfound possibilities.

The game finished and, spotting Angelina, Ludwig and Edgar headed over to where she was sitting. Ludwig's pace slowed upon realizing who she was sitting with. He toweled the sweat off of his tanned torso as he approached. Marie quickly wiped the tears from her face. Her expression was emotionless and cold, like the version Angelina had known previously. "That was a great game, Wiggy. You did so well. You always were an athlete," Marie said cheerily, shedding her typically snarky tone for a happier one.

"Angelina, I didn't realize you were hanging

with the wrong crowd nowadays. Where's Jude?"

"He went to get us some food. He'll be back soon. Would you like to join us?"

Edgar came around and sat down beside Marie, eyeing her aggressively. Ludwig sat down beside Angelina and across from Edgar, giving himself maximum distance from Marie. Ludwig continued to ignore Marie, though she was making concerted efforts to pretend she wasn't obviously watching the few remaining beads of sweat trace down his rippled chest.

She stirred her green concoction slowly, adding yet another sugar cube. By Angelina's count, she'd added at least twelve in the time she'd been sitting with her.

"That's not how you do it," Edgar fussed. Marie just waved him off with a flick of her spoon.

"Did I ever tell you about the time Toulouse and I drank and drank and drank absinthe until we were dizzy in the head? I must've slept for three days straight. But then, after that I was fine! They say it rots your brain or something," she shot a side-eyed glare at Edgar accusingly, "but I felt just fine after sufficient rest."

"That's because any brain you had left leaked out when your head plopped off." Angelina could feel the tension at the table as Ludwig and Marie stared each other down. Confusion, hurt, and anger crossed Marie's face in a carousel of emotions.

Marie tried to contain her temper, shattering the glass in her hand in the process as she squeezed the life out of it. Green, syrupy absinthe trickled down her wrist, leaving a trail of lime green veins along her skin.

"He left me last night!" she stood up and shouted, shedding the last ounce of control she'd had over herself.

"And what do you want me to do about it? It's about time, I'd say," Ludwig said nonchalantly, as if her life wasn't ending right in front of him.

"Don't you feel anything?!" she screamed, throwing the spoon at him. He caught it in mid-air, and forcefully slammed it down flush on the table. Edgar spread out on his side of the bench, preventing her from reseating herself should she choose to do so.

"What, pray tell, should *I* feel for *you*?" He removed the towel from around his neck, revealing his full, tanned torso just to spite her.

Her mouth fell open temporarily, before she narrowed her eyes at him. "I want you to care. I want you to care about me! My husband left me for another woman!"

Ludwig pounded his fist down aggressively on the table, causing one of the wooden planks to dislodge from its nailing and bounce up. Angelina and Edgar both jumped in shock.

"And *my* wife left *me* for another *man!*" Ludwig shouted so loudly, that everyone within earshot stopped and turned around to listen. "I'd say karma is a damn fine broad I'd like to take out to dinner!" He threw his sweat-soaked towel across the table, hitting Marie squarely in her face and dislodging her wilted peonies from her hair. He spun on his heel and stormed away towards the mansion.

The three remaining watched the peonies fall in slow motion, landing on the wooden picnic table with a thud, the petals bouncing off and scattering around the stem. Marie burst out crying and ran away towards the trees to sob herself into ruin.

Angelina looked at Edgar.

Edgar looked at Angelina.

A beat of silence passed between them before either knew what to say. Edgar drummed his fingertips against the table.

"They were married for quite some time, my Queen."

"You don't say?"

Chapter

Twenty-Four

Later, after Angelina had successfully eaten herself into a carb coma and had a subsequent nap to recover, the second and final night of the Society Convention was about to begin. The outfit theme was "Black & White," and Anne had paired Jude's classic tux with a stunning full-length white Vera Wang gown with black lace accents for Angelina.

Outside the ballroom, Jude and Angelina greeted everyone as they walked in. Ludwig and Edgar soon joined. Angelina's eyes traveled to Ludwig, whose face was slightly puffier than normal, his eyes slightly red. She opened her mouth to speak before noticing Edgar, who subtly shook his head "no," motioning for her to leave it be.

Marie approached them shortly after that. "May I sit with you?" She looked at the four of them hesitantly. Angelina was the only one to make actual eye contact with her. Marie's face was splotchy and puffy, a fact made even more evident by the layers of make-up and concealer she'd caked on. Her skin was coated so heavily, she looked more like a cake frosted in white buttercream icing than an actual person. She and Ludwig seemed to have quite a disastrous effect on each other.

"No. You may sit at the gateway to hell, where you belong." Ludwig, still otherwise not acknowledging her presence, turned and walked into the ballroom, leaving Marie in the dust.

Marie scampered off like a wounded cockroach, trying desperately to keep anyone from seeing her damaged ego.

The lights flickered, signaling everyone to find their seats. Jude left to go behind the stage. Angelina headed in after Edgar, taking their previous places around Ludwig as he sat in silence, staring ahead in front of him with his arms crossed and his expressions turned off.

"I'd like to apologize for earlier," Ludwig leaned in to whisper to Angelina after she'd sat down. Angelina noticed he wasn't particularly looking at anyone or anything as he spoke. "I don't usually let my emotions take control like that. Marie's secret weapon is the ability to bring out the worst in people."

Angelina placed a hand on his arm, and felt his tight muscles slightly relax at her touch. He unfolded his arms and moved his hands down, clasping them together in his lap. "It's all right, Ludwig. I understand. You don't ever have to apologize to me."

He snickered. "But she really is dreadful, though, right?"

"Absolutely horrid. A complete monster." Angelina felt bad for both he and Marie, and suspected that today was the first day that Ludwig had let her glimpse his unabridged side. The loud sound of shattering glass got everyone's attention, as Marie tiptoed out from behind the curtain and onto the stage.

Ludwig's head fell immediately to the floor,

refusing to look at her. A few people cheered her on, but most didn't. Still wearing her silver heels, Marie was now dressed in a black, body-hugging, full-length gown, with a halter top with black elbow-length gloves. The simplest and most elegant thing Angelina had seen her wear so far. The only thing white she'd paired with it were white diamond stud earrings, that more matched her heels than Anne's wardrobe specifications.

"Whoopsie doopsie, can we get a clean-up on Aisle 2?" Marie hiccupped loudly into the microphone. Her usual shrill voice was replaced by a more calm, womanly voice. The voice of someone who'd had a hard life and learned a lot of lessons the unfavorable ways. "Ladies and gentlemen, welcome to the second night of the Society Convention.

"Something happened last night, I know you know what I'm talking about. Word travels fast, and let's face it, the word is usually about me. AmIright?" She slurred the last three words together, wobbling on her heels before grabbing the mic stand for support.

Angelina, Ludwig, and Edgar realized, albeit a moment too late, that maybe Marie had had a little too much absinthe after the fallout that afternoon, and that the shattering glass was the proof of that.

300

Jude noticed, too, and promptly went on stage, waiting in the background to stop her from embarrassing herself if she went off script. Which undoubtedly, she would do.

Marie flung her arms out. "That's all I've got to give you, my people. *My Society.* I don't have a winning on-screen persona, or," she sought Angelina out in the audience, pointing at her dramatically with one finger, "or a charming personality. I've got drama, drama in spades, that I can supply *my Society* with."

Jude moved to approach her, and she raised her palm up to him, stopping him in his tracks. "I rewrote my speech this afternoon. You only want the best from your queens. AmIright? That's a great phase. Pays. What's the word? Ssslogan." Her slurring speech was worsening as the absinthe wound its claws into her. "We'll go with it. I hope you've had a brilliant time here at the 78th Annual Society Convention. I hope you've lived, laughed, and loved. I know I certainly have.

"So, here's my spoke. Speak. Here's my speak, straight from you to me. Ludwig." The audience gasped, and Ludwig's head shot up at her. Jude took another step closer and Marie stared him down. "I said stop it, Jude. Stop it right there on that spot right there." She turned back to the audience.

"Ludwig, I know you don't forgive me. And I don't forgive me, either. I made such a mistake. I stayed with Flynn for so long trying to atone for it, and prove to myself that a mistake I did not make. You don't have to forgive me; I'll never forgive myself. But I can promise you now more than ever, that I know you're the love of my life.

"I'm going to leave here tomorrow. And I'll give you space to not hate me. If by next year, or at a Convention thirty or even fifty years from now, you can find it in your heart to forgive me, well, that's more than I could ever hope to get from you. Even if you don't love me, Ludwig, I simply can't stand that you hate me, too."

Tears rolled down her face as she watched for any sign from Ludwig to react to what she'd said. He did nothing but stare back at her, and gave her not a drop of affection to go on. Marie's face and posture fell at his response, and her voice quieted into barely a whisper.

"Ladies and gentlemen, once again, welcome to the second night of the 78th Society Convention."

Chapter

Twenty-Five

After Jude had helped a sobbing Marie down the stairs safely, John took to the stage. His mop of red hair contrasted sharply against his black and white tux. Angelina laughed, thinking of a joke that no one would ever know was even hilarious. *What's black, white, and red all over? John Keats, of course!*

"Well, that was ... interesting," Keats began. "There's never a dull moment when the family gets together. You can expect this to be the centerfold in the yearbook this year!" The audience roared with laughter, though Angelina, Ludwig, and Edgar stayed silent.

It seemed to Angelina that Marie was frequently the butt of jokes and gossip, whether or not she deserved it. Angelina couldn't help but feel sympathy for the woman, who'd had such a hard life in her human years. To be a mockery, even in death and immortality, must be the loneliest existence anybody could possibly imagine.

She wanted to mention to Ludwig her opinion on the subject, but decided to stay silent for the time being. He and Edgar had been the most supportive and helpful friends she'd ever had in her life. At the very least, she could be on his side right now.

"And now, a word from the one who brought us all here—" John stopped, getting bumped out of the way by his tiny girlfriend. He frowned and descended the stage, his shoulders sagging in a defeated manner.

"Not just yet, not just yet. I'd like to make an announcement first. Several weeks ago, I was approached by someone, a group, who requested to speak tonight. They explained their story, and I humbly accepted. If you'll please give them a moment of your time, they have journeyed far to be with us here tonight. Ladies and gentlemen, Humboldt Wudge!"

A few people clapped, but most people leaned forward in their seats trying to see what was actually happening. Anne motioned to John aggressively to help her, and together, they pushed a small staircase up to the microphone.

Angelina could see Jude's face from where she sat. His body was stiff and rigid, his lips pursed together tightly. He clearly did not like surprises.

She looked at Ludwig and Edgar, who were as shocked as she was. "What's going on?" There was noticeable tension in the room as everyone glanced around questioningly trying to figure out what exactly was happening.

"I'm not sure, but I don't think Jude knew about this, either." Ludwig's eyes were wide as he continued to stare at the events unfolding before them all.

A sea of gasps rippled across the ballroom as three short figures trotted out of the foyer and onto the stage. The tallest one stood no more than a foot high, with pointed ears and a muddy complexion. The female's skin was a pale, almost luminescent green that reminded Angelina of her aunt's green milk glass collection. Their hair was like blades of grass—smooth, straight, and dark green.

They wore shoes made from river birch, the bark itself curled into a frilly lace of decorative adornment. Nature's garland. The two males wore wooden bark armor and weaved moss clothing, and the female wore a small crown of flowers and a vine-woven dress. Their clothing swished slightly as they clopped up the stairs in their wooden shoes.

"What are they?" Angelina whispered to Ludwig. She'd never seen anything like them in real life.

"Uh, they look like forest trolls to me. I have no clue."

The tallest one stood up on his tiptoes to reach the microphone, and Anne quickly scuttled over to help him lower it. In the spotlight, it was visible that he was wearing a M.O.E. pin across his armor, no doubt supplied by Anne.

He curtsied to her for her help before clearing his throat. "Good friends, we are honored to be in your presence. We are the People of Wudge, and we have journeyed far and wide, from the land of the Massachusetts, to seek your alignment. My name is Humboldt. This is my wife, Falena, and my brother, Iksander. Your welcoming nature humbles us so."

Everyone was looking around, trying to decide what was happening. Humboldt pulled a tiny scroll out from underneath his armor, and raised it in the air.

"The Ancient Scrolls foretold of the Warrior for our people. The one who would save all species. 'When hums the ground, the Warrior shall be found.'"

Falena and Iksander, standing to Humboldt's right, both closed their eyes and simultaneously hum-chanted the prophecy in a ritualistic fashion. "Whennnn huuummmms the grounnnnddd ..."

"What the ..." Ludwig murmured to himself. Jude, from beside the stage, was still stoic and stone-faced, betraying no emotion other than the clear shock everyone else was feeling.

"The auguries are aligning now! Millennia ago, there was an epic battle between our people and the Ancient Impieties. Rougarou, Skinwalkers, demons, all different names for the same evils. They were nearly wiped out, but not completely. They spent centuries rebuilding their armies and factions. The Ancient Impieties, the Original Paradigms, want to destroy anything that is not them. Anything that is not pure evil. Their message is clear: arm yourselves, because the war is coming.

"Several months ago, they nearly wiped out my people. They attacked upon us in the night, brandishing a dust over our village that rendered us weak and unable to clear our heads. We are all that's left in America. They kidnapped our son, Wembley. We don't know if he's dead or alive. Please, we beg you, please, help us." Tears rolled down his and Falena's faces. Iksander bowed his head in silent tribute.

Angelina's mouth fell open. She could feel the shift in the air around her, the tenseness coming from Ludwig, Edgar, and the audience.

"There are others like you, other vibrations all over the world. We must build an army against them; we must stand and unite!"

Even though Angelina was new to this world, she knew that this was major, headline news. Jude had thought he was the only one who'd been created, the only original immortal. The crowd's eyes shifted to Jude, who looked just as stunned.

Jude moved to stand beside the Wudge people, and Humboldt offered the microphone back to him.

Jude's voice was unsteady as he spoke. "Thank you for … thank you for that, Mr. Wudge. I think we've got a lot to discuss. If the Society Council would meet me in the conference room, along with the Wudges, I'd like to go ahead and dismiss the rest of you early to enjoy your evening. Can we get the band set back up quickly, please?"

The members of *XXVII* scrambled up on stage with their instruments, eager to take over the show. Jude walked directly towards Anne, who had a look of worry across her face.

"Conference room, now." His tone was harsh and uncharacteristic as Angelina, Edgar, and Ludwig approached them.

"I told her, sir. I told her she needed to tell you, that this sounded like a big deal. You did put her in charge, though, sir," John stammered, trying to smooth over any ripples he could to dismantle Jude's growing temper.

"Shut up, John!" Anne hissed at him, as the group moved down the hallway alongside the ballroom, entering through a new door Angelina had not yet been on the other side of.

Inside, giant LED screens lined the far wall, giving the illusion of a large window. A long black table with at least twelve fancy chairs ran down the middle. Jude, usually calm and collected, lost his patience as soon as the door shut behind Edgar.

"Why didn't you tell me any of this?" he yelled at Anne harshly.

She defiantly stood her ground, raising her chin up to meet him squarely face to face. "I tried. You were otherwise indisposed." She sharply cut her eyes over to Angelina, daring her to further come between her and Jude.

"You should have told me. Or at the very least, you could've told Ludwig. That was a blatant dismissal of my authority, and you know it."

"Wrong." She produced a yellow legal pad containing a list of dates, times, and notes ranging across the last several weeks. Beside each date and time were notes detailing how Jude had shrugged her off or ignored her calls when he was with Angelina.

"I made ample opportunity to include and consult with you. Here is proof." She shoved the notepad into Jude's chest, slicing his argument to shreds and daring him to cross her again. She was wickedly brutal with her note-taking skills.

"Ludwig is not the king," Anne stated matter-of-factly. "You are, lest you forget. You've been … preoccupied with less important matters."

"My queen is not 'less important matters.' You should've told me. You had no right to withhold this information."

"I had every right! I am the Vice President of the Society. You left me in charge! Not Edgar. Not Ludwig. *Me.* You told *me* to handle it, whatever it was, and that you had every ounce of faith in my abilities. I believe that is a direct quote. I did what I felt was necessary. They kidnapped his son. His son, Jude! Voices should be heard! Entire races and species should *not* be wiped out!" John rushed to wrap a sobbing Anne in his arms.

"I tried numerous times! You were preoccupied and you left me in charge."

"She did try quite often," John quietly scolded Jude, narrowing his eyes at him in the process.

A small knock on the door snapped everyone out of the situation at hand. No one had even bothered to notice that their guests of honor hadn't even entered the conference room yet.

Edgar moved to hold the door open, while the

three short beings tromped into the room. Humboldt spun one of the chairs around like a stepstool, holding his arm outstretched for his wife to go first. Falena gracefully hopped up on the chair, and then the table, the other two swiftly behind her. They stood in the middle, surveying their audience.

"We are so grateful to be in your presence, Warrior." Humboldt looked directly at Jude and curtsied so low that he nearly touched his chin to the table. Falena and Iksander followed suit behind him.

"I'm not your 'Warrior,'" Jude stated factually.

"Oh, but you *are*. The Ancient Scrolls say so! "When hums the ground ..."'" Humboldt pulled the scroll out again, and it unrolled in a sweeping motion.

Edgar was completely entranced by the creatures. He scooted a chair up to them and placed his elbows on the table, balancing his head on top of his clasped fingers. A doe-eyed expression came over him. "What else do your scrolls say?" Humboldt held the scroll up, level with his shoulders, and let it flutter with his movements.

"As above and so below,

Protection from the doom foretold.

When hums the ground, the Warrior shall be found."

They all closed their eyes, chanting in a singsong whisper again, "Whennn huummmms the groouuunndd."

Clearly, that was their favorite prophecy. Humboldt continued reading from his scroll.

"Upon the battlefield, the keys shall reveal,

When guardians are one, the olden ways are done.

What has been will not be, in future laid out, a new decree."

"And what does all that mean, exactly, Mr. Wudge?" Edgar asked. He pulled Anne's notepad over from the corner of the table, flipping over her notes in the process so he could write everything down.

Humboldt shook his fist in the air, a triumphant smile playing across his face to reveal his dark green teeth. "The auguries are aligning! The ancient parchments will come to pass!"

"What humming?" Jude asked, interrupting Humboldt's dramatic decrees. "What is even going on right now?"

"The earth's humming."

"Yes, you mentioned that. Can you be more specific?"

"We, the Wudge, are in tune with the sounds of nature. We are from nature, and we will return when we die. Everything gives off a frequency."

Ludwig leaned over to Angelina and quietly whispered. "See? Forest trolls."

"Several years ago, we noticed a steady frequency that grew louder and louder. Then *they* showed up, demanding the keys from us. We are the protectors of the keys to their destruction. We are the only ones who can locate the keys, which is the only way *they* can be permanently destroyed. *They* wiped out our entire village, except the four of us. We hid, but they found my son. They heard his cries, and pulled him from the hollow trunk he was hiding in. There was nothing I could do to save him! Nothing!" They were all three hysterically crying and hugging each other.

"Go on, Mr. Wudge," Edgar encouraged, when Humboldt had calmed down. "We're here for you."

"They think my Wembley knows the secrets of our people, but he doesn't. He's only a child! Just a child!" Falena remorsefully squealed, which sounded more to Angelina like a squirrel having a heart attack.

Anne grabbed a pack of peanut butter crackers from the snack bar and nudged them beneath Edgar's elbow. Edgar unwrapped them and handed one to each of the Wudges to calm their nerves. The trio devoured them through their tears, crumbs flying out in all directions onto the table. "How can we help you, dear people of Wudge?"

"We can find the others, the ones like you. We can feel the vibrations that lead us to them. We know where our ancestors hid the keys, also. The ancestors built charms across the land. There are dead zones, entire areas, that don't give off any vibrations because our ancestors protected them. *They* can't find them, because *they* can only feel when a prophecy is happening. But the people of Wudge know all the time; it's in our blood and it's our sworn destiny!" Humboldt pumped his little green fists into the air. Edgar, charmingly elated with the creatures, pumped his fists in solidarity.

Jude closed his eyes and rubbed his temples, massaging away his unseen migraine.

"Can these beings, or whatever, be stopped?"

"Yes, with the keys."

"Right. And do you know what the keys are? How do you even find them?"

"They're the ancient tools. We follow the earth."

"You follow the non-vibrations of the earth, which will lead you to the magical keys, and to the others like us. OK, so we hum and the keys hum? Everything hums."

"They are not magical. They are legendary. There is a difference."

"Right. And you need our help why?" Angelina moved to stand beside Jude when his tone started to get noticeably short. She rubbed his back to calm him down, and he sighed heavily.

"Because you're the Warrior of prophecy!"

"You keep saying that, but what does that mean? I'm no warrior, and I don't know anything about a prophecy."

Humboldt frowned at Jude, his dark green eyebrows wrinkling in disgust. "Because of the vibrations." He stomped his foot, and Ludwig's hand shot up to his mouth to disguise his snicker.

Angelina piped up, "I think I understand. Mr. Wudge is saying that he'd like us to travel with him and his family to find the others like you, using the Wudges' vibrations like a sonar to track them down. The keys that we need to defeat the beings also give off vibrations. The Wudges know which lands they're in because of the absence of vibrations that the land gives off. They believe you are their Warrior. In return for helping you defeat the beings, they'd like us to help them rescue their son. Is that correct, Mr. Wudge?"

The tiny trio jumped up and down on the table while bits of moss dislodged from their clothing and fell around their feet. "Yes! Yes!"

Anne and John, who had been quietly frowning and standing in the corner after Jude's outburst, started clapping profusely. Jude glanced back at Anne, his expression telling her to quit encouraging these creatures. She clapped louder and more aggressively.

"Mr. Wudge, you stated that some lands gave

off no vibrations. To disguise them, correct? What lands?" Edgar asked. He'd been reading and rereading over the prophecies, trying to decipher them.

"There are no vibrations from China, Mexico, and Egypt. There are also areas in England, Peru, and other countries. Our ancestors constructed the ancient charms to protect them."

Somewhere in the back of her mind, a few puzzle pieces aligned perfectly and clicked into place. Angelina's mind started spinning, her heart racing as her archaeologist training kicked into high gear. She left Jude's side and went to sit down beside Edgar. Her hands were visibly shaking, and Jude pulled up a chair beside her, taking her hands in his. "Are you OK? What's wrong?"

"Let me see that, Edgar." He slid the paper over to her. Angelina read and reread it furiously, her mind connecting at least some of the dots. "It's the Hunter," she quietly whispered.

"What's the Hunter?" Jude asked.

Angelina analyzed and reanalyzed everything she could remember. "I know one of the prophecies! 'As above and so below, protection from the doom foretold.' It's the constellation Orion! Orion's Belt. It's been long speculated that the pyramids in Giza, Xi'an, and Teotihuacan were built to align with Orion's Belt."

She repeated, "'As above and so below, protection from the doom foretold.' The pyramids are shrouded in so much mystery and legend, no one can decipher what's true or what's false. You're telling me that the Wudge people built the pyramids to ward off evil? How? How did they do it?"

"With the vibrations," Humboldt said confidently.

Jude groaned underneath his breath. "How are you even keeping up with this?"

Angelina ignored him. "You're saying that the ancient Wudge people originally constructed all of the pyramids to align with Orion's Belt in order to ward off the evils of the world? That's what you're saying?"

"I thought they were just tombs," Ludwig muttered.

"They weren't *just* tombs, they were *also* tombs. There was far greater symbology and structure behind all of them than *just being a tomb*, that, until today, no human knew." Ludwig raised his eyebrows in defeat.

"What happens if we just ignore this whole

thing?" Jude asked, not making eye contact with the clearly flustered Humboldt Wudge.

"Then they don't find their son. We don't fight evil. Potentially, the world ends. No big deal." Angelina looked at Jude pointedly. His face and shoulders fell simultaneously. Angelina took that as her cue.

"Mr. Wudge, we would be honored to help you find your son."

"And save the world at the same time!" Edgar said cheerily.

Jude stood there, otherwise expressionless except for the perplexity and frustration that kept flashing across his face in waves. "I don't … what is even happening?"

Chapter

Twenty-Six

"I think it's safe to say that this was a disastrous first Convention for you to experience. I am so sorry. It's not usually this dramatic and—" Jude ran his hands through his hair.

"And filled with earth-shattering revelations? I've had more drama this weekend than I've had in my whole life." Angelina laughed, and Jude buried his face in his hands. Angelina grabbed his wrists and pulled them around her waist.

"Hey. It was great. I learned something new, and I met an entire new species of beings. Plus, I got engaged to a majorly sexy guy, which was my favorite part, by the way. How do you feel about a Christmas wedding?"

"How do you feel about turning before the wedding? It would be better to do it sooner rather than later. It could take you a few days to feel normal. If that's what you still want. You can walk away at any time. I won't blame you."

"You better stop putting yourself down right now. I want you, I love you, and I'm here with you. I'll have a week off for Thanksgiving. We can do it then."

"What will you tell the college?" Jude asked, kissing her forehead.

"I was planning on leaving in the summer, but I suppose I'll have to bump that up. I'm going to tell them that a private investor offered to fund my expeditions and that it's too good an opportunity to turn down." She kissed his neck as he nibbled on her earlobe. "Which is incredibly, undeniably true."

His stubble scratched her cheek as his cherry lips moved to find hers. "This is a mistake. There's got to be someone else. It's not me the Wudges want."

"Yes, it is. They're here because of you. I'm here because of you. Everyone is here because of you. I don't think it's a mistake at all. I think you're the bravest, most honorable man I've ever met, and I'm thankful and amazed that I'm going to get to call you my husband.

"We need to go with the Wudges. The others like you, they need to know you exist, that you all exist. What if they thought they were the only ones this whole time? You told me how lonely you were. They should see you, Jude. They need to know you were also made."

"I thought I was the only one this whole time! I don't even know what's happening right now."

"Surely there were bound to be at least a few more like you. Didn't you ever wonder?"

"Of course I wondered. And I wandered. I'm nearly 2,400 years old, and I've never met another immortal outside of my line. I never knew about the grass elves, either."

"Wudges."

"Whatever. So, there's the Wudge people, there are other vampires I've never met, and there are Skinwalkers. What else do I not know? What other species are out there? Is the Midgard Serpent real? He's probably over at the Aquarium gift shop, right? What about Romulus and Remus? I heard they're hanging out in a zoo in Sydney this week."

He ran his hands through his hair and groaned loudly. "Frankly, I'm frustrated and ticked off. This wasn't what I had in mind for us. I thought we could spend eternity sitting beneath the Eiffel Tower, or running through the halls of Neuschwanstein Castle."

"We'll do all of that, too. But first, we'll save the world. It's not eternity without a little rough and tumble, right?"

Three weeks later, four days before Thanksgiving, Angelina's heart was heavy as she set foot into her classroom for the last time. It was a bittersweet, yet necessary, day in the epic history of her short life thus far. She sat behind her desk, watching her students file in. Mindless, unimportant chatter ran rampant, from the previous night's big frat party, to everyone's plans for going home for the holidays.

Angelina watched them get situated, and a thought befell her. This was the same way she'd always viewed ants on their mounds. Tiny, miniscule little creatures going on about their daily lives and completely oblivious to the world around them as they scavenged for their crumbs, cut their leaves, and built their mud pyramids.

If any creature or any human knew immortality was possible, would the world be different? What would change if the impossible was suddenly common knowledge?

She shuddered as she realized the obvious. *There would be more demons of a human variety, and more indestructible evil in the world than we are already dealing with.* If she'd learned anything from her career, it was that it's always entirely possible to have too much of a good thing. Humans always seek to destroy, whether it be from greed, corruption, or both.

Angelina snapped out of her thoughts. The class had grown mostly silent, soft whispers floating between the students concerned for her mental health while she stared off into space.

"I'm sorry, everyone. I was daydreaming there for a moment. I believe your five-page essays were due today? Who would like to go first and present your theory?"

Subsequent groans followed at the thought of anyone having to be involved in public speaking. "Fine, fine. Pass them forward and I'll select one at random to read *to* you."

"All right, Dr. A!"

"You rock, Dr. A!"

A blizzard of stapled clusters of paper snowed down the auditorium and pooled at the only empty desk on the front row. Angelina walked over, assembling them in a nice and tidy pile. She held them up and closed her eyes, fanning through until she found one at random.

"Why the Yonaguni Monument is Atlantis, by Devon Winchester. Excellent! Mr. Winchester, would you like to come down here and talk about it, or do you want to take me up on my offer to read it for you?"

Devon was one of the cockier frat boy students Angelina assumed he was just taking her class for an easy credit, which was why she called him out. She also knew he'd never miss the opportunity to put on a show.

"I'll come down and save you, Dr. A. I'm always one for chivalry." He shot finger guns like he was in a Wild West movie as he clopped down the stairs, his flip-flops smacking loudly against his bare feet. A few of his fellow frat boys laughed, while the A+ bookworm students on the front rows rolled their eyes.

"All right, Dr. A, prepare to have your mind blown." He took his paper from her and cleared his throat as he held it up. Angelina looked him up and down, wondering why and how students ever thought it was cool to wear thick winter hoodies with shorts, flip-flops, and sunglasses that cost as much as her rent. He looked like he was trying to straddle all the seasons in one outfit, and to top it off, his skin looked practically like a glowing tangerine. His whole persona was obviously fake, in more ways than one.

"The floor is yours." She sat on the edge of her desk, bracing for impact.

Devon ruffled his hair and winked at one of the girls in the front row, who fake-yawned in response. "Here goes. The Yunaguni Monument is a wicked, cool place. A diver discovered it, and it has all these, like, jagged rocks that aren't really jagged rocks at all. They are actually cut stones, and therefore Atlantis.

"The Yonaguni Monument has, like, mad straight angles, and a lot of people have tried to say it happened naturally. But, like, do skyscrapers just naturally happen? Nah, they don't."

He proceeded to give a less-than-researched and well-thought-out presentation. Angelina found herself struggling to stay awake while listening to his brainless droning. After what seemed like two hours ended, Devon proudly sauntered over to Angelina and handed back his paper.

"Thank you, Mr. Winchester. That was … unique."

"Yeah! Nailed it!" Devon leapt onto the first stair and started up towards his seat.

"You most definitely did not 'nail it.' You're very publicly failing this class," a student in the front row groaned loudly, which received roaring laughter from the studious section. Devon grumbled and muttered a few snarky remarks that Angelina couldn't make out.

"OK, you guys, settle down. Nobody's failing, because so far nobody's made less than a D."

"Yeah, 'D' for Devon." More laughter from the front row.

"Anyway, I have an announcement to make. Professor Briggs will be finishing out the semester with you, as I've taken on a new role. Several new roles, actually. I'm leaving immediately after class today to start a new job as chief archaeologist for a privately funded mission."

"Where are you going, Dr. A?" Several students nodded their heads in agreement. Angelina had given her answer a lot of thought, and had decided to go out on a myth of legendary proportions.

"I'll be the head of a team that will be searching for Atlantis. It's no secret how many underwater cities have been found throughout the world, and over the course of the next decade, we're charted to examine three of them in closer depth. We'll be starting in Santorini."

Gasps of shock and awe echoed around her. She'd decided she'd like to go out on a mystery of legendary proportions. "So, if you never, ever, see me again, please, I beg of you, assume I've been adopted by the people of Atlantis."

She was met with an audience of wide-eyed students, trying to decide if she was indeed joking or not. "I'm also getting married soon, and my fiancé owns real-estate all over the world. If the people of Atlantis don't get me, it would be safe to assume I'm lounging instead on the beach in Nice, France. Or, you know, something like that."

"Is it that hottie who was here before?" A few of the students who'd seen Jude started whispering excitedly. Angelina nodded. "Way to go, Dr. A!"

"I think you'd be really hot with gills, Dr. A!" Devon shouted from the top row.

"Thank you for that vote of confidence, Mr. Winchester. Everyone, please have a safe and happy Thanksgiving!"

Chapter
Twenty-Seven

Jude was waiting just outside the door, leaning against the building with his arms crossed against his chest and a devilish smirk on his face. "Atlantis, huh? That's what you decided to go with?" he asked, entertained at the thought.

"Don't judge. It's my funeral. Besides, now I'll be immortally cool as the archaeologist who turned into a merperson and was never heard from again. There are worse legends to be associated with."

"Naturally. Are you ready?"

Things seemed like they were moving at rapid speed, and not rapid enough. They had previously discussed Angelina turning before the wedding. A knot formed in her stomach. She hesitantly answered, "I am."

Jude's head snapped back to her, sensing her uneasiness. "But? You don't have to. I don't want you to do anything you're uncomfortable with. I'd rather die than cause you any regrets."

Angelina honestly believed him. Her heart broke at his kindness. "I won't have regrets, Jude. I'm just nervous because I don't know what to expect."

"Well, according to everyone else, it won't hurt. You'll just get sleepy for a couple of days until your body adjusts. If you don't eat anything beforehand, it'll be a shorter recovery time because there will be less to process."

Angelina giggled. "You make it sound like I'm going into surgery. But after I … *recover*, we're spending Thanksgiving with my aunt. Deal?"

"I'd expect nothing less."

"Oh! And I'd like to invite everyone to go with us, too. She'd love nothing more than their company."

"I'm sure that can be arranged."

When the car slowed to a stop beneath the large iron columns, Angelina noticed there were Mardi Gras colored streamers and balloons everywhere.

Jude groaned and ran his hand through his hair. "Oh, I forgot to tell you, Anne went to Celebration Center and got decorations for your turning. She said it was the closest thing to a queen's coronation she's ever witnessed firsthand, and, I'll just tell you, it looks worse inside. There usually isn't an audience. If you don't want an audience, we can do it in private. We'll do whatever you want to do, no pressure."

Angelina's hand went up to her heart. "I'm honestly touched. I didn't think of it like that until now, but if I'm going to be their queen, then whoever wants to attend should be able to."

When they walked through the glass doors of the conservatory, Anne, John, Ludwig, and Edgar were waiting on either side of them with party poppers. Feather boas, beads, and even more streamers were strung from anything in the room even remotely sticking out. While the three men continued shooting confetti towards Jude and Angelina, Anne rushed up and draped Mardi Gras beads around her neck. She then pulled out—from a large plastic bag wound around her arm—a giant, gaudy, purple velvet crown with rhinestones bedazzled into it.

"Oh, um, thank you, Anne." Angelina graciously placed it on her head.

"It was the fanciest they had. All the tiaras were on back order."

Angelina embraced Anne's tiny body and kissed the top of her head. "It was so thoughtful of you to do this for me. I absolutely love it." Anne grinned bashfully, her cheeks slightly blushing.

The Wudges, who had taken up residence in one of the live oak trees in the backyard since the Conference, fluffed flower petals around Angelina's feet as she stood.

Angelina bowed to them partially, forgetting she had a crown on her head. Her hands shot up to catch it right before it slid off. "Thank you, everyone, for being here. It really means a lot to me. I'm honored to be your future queen and I hope I'll make you proud."

A silver glitter heel made itself known from the corner of the conservatory. Marie was sitting in a chair in the corner, bobbing her crossed leg up and down, actively not participating but still trying to be involved. She was filing her nails, and looking rather bored by the whole ordeal. "You call this a coronation? Mine was *far more* extravagant than this gauche debauchery," she mumbled loudly to no one in particular. At some point in the last week, she'd decided to come back to the palatial venue, much to everyone's dismay.

"Because you had no other salvageable traits to celebrate, besides your lust for all things inane, you blighted barnacle," Ludwig stated loudly, causing Marie to wrinkle her nose. He looked back at Angelina, smiling. "*Our new Queen* takes delight in gifts of thoughtfulness." He enunciated the first three words slowly, driving home the fact that Marie was not accepted by her peers.

"Guys, this is Angelina's day," Jude cut into their bickering. "Angelina, where would you like it to take place?" Marie very loudly yawned and obviously rolled her eyes.

Angelina thought back to where the first defining moment in this journey had happened, when her heart had first twinged for the man who would be her husband. The first time she'd really seen a hint of who he was had been on the back patio, after the fight with Marie, when he'd been defeated and unsure of himself. She reached down, taking Jude's hand in hers. "On the back stairs."

Edgar spoke up, holding one finger raised in protest. "My Queen, if I may suggest a table instead of stairs. You may likely pass out upon consumption."

Angelina heard her stomach rumble. She hadn't eaten all day. She looked to Jude, who only shrugged his shoulders as if to say, "It's your call." She removed her pink blazer and tossed it onto the couch, revealing the black lace camisole and gray dress pants that were in league with her usual classroom attire.

On the patio, Edgar and Ludwig carefully lifted and moved one of the wrought iron tables towards the center of the area. Then they, along with Anne and John, moved to stand around the table in a semi-circle. The Wudges hopped up onto the wall, and for all their clothing they might as well have been garden gnomes with how well they blended into their surroundings.

Marie stayed inside, occasionally glancing through the window and complaining about the wind messing up her hair.

Angelina sat upon the table. She removed her crown and handed it to Anne, so it wouldn't get damaged in case something happened. Jude positioned himself between her legs, their bodies intimately close in front of their audience. Her heart skipped a beat at his nearness to her.

Angelina looked up into Jude's gray diamond eyes, which sizzled with excitement and lust. "Are you sure you want to do this? Once it's done, it's done."

Her eyes roamed his cherry lips, her fingertips traced his black stubble that lined his jaw. "Are *you* sure you want to do this? You're going to be stuck with me for an infinite amount of time if you turn me. Are you prepared for that? Have you thought it through?"

The audience faded from her vision, and then it was only she and her love. Jude grinned at her and wrapped his arms around her waist, pulling her against him. His cherry red lips crashed against hers, stealing her breath and her conscious thoughts along with it. Her hands entwined into his hair and pulled him deeper into her.

Ludwig cleared his throat, and suddenly they were reminded of their audience. Jude broke the kiss, his nose lingering on the tip of Angelina's. "I'm sure."

He gently lifted her wrist to his mouth, and Angelina watched in amazement as his ivory fangs slowly extended. This was only the second time she'd seen them, and she had to resist the urge not to stick her hand in his mouth and poke them to see if they were real.

Jude kissed the delicate skin over her veins, his eyes never leaving hers. Warmth flooded throughout her body at the intimacy of the act, before pooling in her belly. She watched as his pointed teeth slowly sank into her skin, and she had to resist the urge to laugh. Edgar had been right—it felt exactly like a mosquito—and she flexed her fist trying to subconsciously scratch beneath the skin.

"You are bound to me, as I shall be bound to you," Jude whispered. Edgar nudged a small chalice into Jude's hand, and he held it up for Angelina to take. "What would you like to mix it with?"

"Lemonade." Jude's eyebrows raised in amusement. Angelina didn't know why she said that, it was just the first thing that popped into her head.

Anne shuffled quickly inside and returned

momentarily with a can of lemonade. She popped the top and handed it to Jude, who poured no more than an cighth of a cup into the small glass chalice. He bit into his wrist, and then held it over the lemonade to allow his ancient lifeforce to fall.

Drop.

Drop.

Drop.

Angelina held her breath as the ruby beads marbled into the citrine, turning it a beautiful sunset pink. Tilting her head back, she downed the contents in one gulp.

She sat there on the table for a minute, looking from face to face of those around her. Each one was excited, eager, and welcoming of her presence and new role in their little group of immortals. Anne's hands were clenched together like a nun, eagerly awaiting Angelina's first words as an immortal. Edgar was crying tears of happiness. John was smiling wide and Ludwig's head was bobbing up and down.

Her eyes returned to Jude, who was intently watching her every movement for any sign of change.

"How're you feeling, Angelina?" He pushed her hair back behind her ears, then placed his hands back around her waist in support. Nothing had changed, not yet anyway.

"I feel fine. I feel normal. I don't think anything's changed. Are you sure—"

Before the final words left her lips, the question of if he'd given her enough of his blood or not, her heart rate plummeted. Everyone around her disappeared out of her peripherals, and she tried desperately to hold onto the image of Jude in front of her. Her vision faded to white, and Jude snowed out of focus as her head lolled to the side in an unconscious state.

The last thing she remembered was her body collapsing against a warm, yet firm, surface.

Chapter Twenty-Eight

Jude caught her as her body rolled forward towards him. He wrapped her arms around his shoulders as he tried to pick her up, which did little good because she was fast turning into an overcooked spaghetti noodle. Edgar and Ludwig rushed to his side to support her head, and Jude hoisted her up into his arms and carried her to his bedroom.

"Do you think she's OK? Does she need anything?" Edgar was fretting over her, fluffing the pillows beneath her as Jude gently placed her onto the California king-sized bed.

"She didn't eat anything today, which is what I advised her to do. I think the blood hit her faster because of that, and hopefully she'll recover faster, too."

"Yeah, dude, I was out for four days. Remember how you fell over straight away, Edgar? You nearly knocked your head off, and then you were out for three," Ludwig said, going over to the other side of the bed to help Jude pull the comforter up over Angelina. "She just needs rest, then she'll be a pristine queen."

Jude sat beside her the entire time, watching her chest slowly rise and fall. He remembered none of this process himself, only the cold, dark emptiness he had awoken into. There had been no one to guide him. No one to teach him. No one to coach him on what he was and was not. The only traces of his former existence he'd had were deep, pink scars, occasional nightmares, and faded, blurry memories that darted out of reach when he tried to focus too hard on them.

The other four members of his family took turns checking in on the couple, offering to take Jude's place in case he wanted to rest awhile. He did not move, he did not even flinch. He stayed statuesque by her side, in silent support of his future bride.

Angelina was different. He'd known it the first

time he'd laid eyes on her. Confident, well-spoken, and highly educated with common sense and intelligence to match. She was nothing like his previous wives, and everything he'd ever wanted in a lover.

Three years ago, Jude first saw Angelina. Three years ago, he fell in love with her instantaneously. Three years ago, he started making changes to try and be the man he knew she deserved. Emotionally, he worked on forgiving himself for his past mistakes and shortcomings, though he still struggled with that a lot if he was being completely honest. Physically, he invested into even more real-estate, and started eating a healthier diet beyond the fried foods and bread that he had consumed himself with.

Anne, John, Ludwig, and Edgar weren't just his Society members, they were his family members. Though he'd turned them all, he felt they were more akin to siblings and best friends rather than his children. They were the only real family he'd ever had, that he could remember. Jude thought the world of them, and knew in his perceived shortcomings that they completed him each in their own way to make a full person. And Angelina deserved every part of his heart.

He laid his head on her chest, listening to the

sound of her lifeforce beating against him.

Thump.

Thump.

Thump.

Her heart rate had slowed to one beat per hour, and Jude knew it wouldn't be much longer. Her breathing had abated, trying to match pace with her heart. He marveled in the curves of her body, the contours of her face as she slept peacefully. Her chestnut brown hair, now golden brown in the sunlight streaming through the windows, lay fanned around her head like a sleeping princess in a fairytale.

Her eyelids fluttered, and her cheeks flushed slightly. Jude looked on as her skin turned to goosebump-covered flesh. He pulled the comforter higher before situating himself along the length of her body. He gently kissed her forehead, and wrapped his arm around her, immersing her into his warmth.

Jude awoke with a jolt, unaware that he'd fallen asleep.

It'd been nearly two days since Angelina had turned, and he'd managed to stay awake for nearly forty straight hours. She stirred beside him, subtly moving beneath the comforter. Jude sat up to give her more space. Her eyes fluttered for the next several minutes, her mouth gently falling open. He laid his head against her chest once again, and heard nothing.

She hummed to herself, a barely audible wisp meandering through the silence. "Angelina?"

A slow smile spread across her face, and her eyelids fluttered open. Her emerald eyes were a deeper, more savory tone, matching closer to her malachite engagement ring, with swirls of chartreuse. She locked onto Jude, her pupils dilating at the recognition of him.

"How are you feeling?" She sat up, her chocolate-colored hair falling down her back. She ran her hands up over her bare arms, only covered by the slim straps of her camisole.

"Cold and hungry. How long was I out?"

"Right at two days." Jude went to get a blanket, and wrapped it around her shoulders.

"OK! That's good, we didn't miss Thanksgiving. We've got to get started immediately. The turkey is going to take a while and we've got to go grocery shopping. Anne and John are coming, too, right? I think they should."

Jude's mouth fell open in stunned fascination. "Thanksgiving? Is there anything else you'd like to talk about first? Maybe how you're feeling now that you're not fully human?"

She pounced on him, pinning him to the bed and grinning widely. "I'm feeling a lot of things. Chatty is not particularly one of them. We've got a lot to do in the next day and I'm not going to miss having Thanksgiving with Emmaline. Do you want to keep talking, or are you going to feed me?" She leaned down and licked his cherry lips, before bounding off the bed and out the door.

Jude hopped up and bolted out of the room, struggling to catch up to her.

Angelina arrived in the kitchen, holding her arms out wide. "Where are my people?" she shouted loudly enough that her voice echoed throughout the palatial venue. Anne and John ran in from the ballroom, at the same time as Ludwig descended the stairs and Edgar walked in from the patio. Marie was nowhere to be seen.

"My Queeeennn!!!" Edgar squealed with delight. "How're you feeling?"

"I feel great! We've got a lot of work to do, though. I'd like to invite you all to participate and attend Thanksgiving with my aunt. I've never had a big Thanksgiving, so it'd really mean a lot to me if this was our first event as a group, or family unit, or whatever we're calling this."

"We're family. One-hundred percent," Anne said, nodding her head. "What do we need to do?"

"Edgar, start a grocery list. We've got to get everything today before the stores run out, so we've got to move fast. We're already ten steps behind." Edgar pulled a tiny notepad from his pocket, noticeably covered with scribblings from an active mind.

Angelina barked orders at the group, as if she'd been planning the entire thing during her slumber. For all Jude knew, she entirely could have been. "Anne, I want you on turkey duty. That's the most important part, and fried turkey is the absolute best. I was thinking you could dress it up and throw it in your air fryer."

Anne jumped up and down, clapping. "With beer! I've always wanted to try beer chicken! I bet we could do it with a turkey instead!"

"Right! Yes! I like it. Beer turkey. Ludwig, I want you to make that fabulous macaroni. Edgar, you're on pie duty. Two or three kinds, minimum, and pumpkin absolutely has to be one of them. John's responsible for dressing and rolls, Jude's responsible for the healthy options, like a vegetable and cranberry sauce. I'll be making Emmaline's favorite dish, triple-cheese mashed potatoes. Oh, and we can't forget to invite Harold. Let's move out! The day's already halfway gone! Go, go, go!"

It took trips to three separate grocery stores to collect all the ingredients on the day before Thanksgiving. Thank goodness the kitchen was built for commercial events, or they would've massacred each other for space. The crew was up until midnight cooking and assembling everything, since cooking Thanksgiving dinner was not on their list of acquired skills thus far.

The next day, Angelina woke up early to reheat

the necessary dishes, and the bedraggled crew climbed into the shuttle bus and headed to the nursing home.

During the ride over, Jude leaned in to whisper to Angelina. "If I may make a suggestion, you might want to eat a light meal until you master how your new system is going to handle everything. You won't be able to process in the same way that you're used to."

"Nonsense. It's not Thanksgiving if you don't stuff yourself silly and take a nap afterwards. Nobody ever started day one of dieting on Thanksgiving Day."

Not wanting to argue, Jude held his hands up in surrender and didn't say another word about it.

One by one, they entered through the forest of beaded curtains. Last in, Edgar's rowdy mane got tangled more than a few times, causing him to nearly drop his pies. He opted to stand still until John could set his dishes down and come free him.

Before Angelina could introduce anyone, Emmaline sprang from her recliner by the window and ran straight towards Ludwig, linking her arm through his. "My oh my, you are simply *delicious.*" Her enunciation lingered heavily on the 's,' like a snake circling its dinner.

"Aunt Emmaline! Ludwig, I am so sorry. She forgets to use her social filter sometimes." Angelina felt bad that she'd forgotten to warn them about Emmaline's forgetfulness. A symptom of the Alzheimer's was that she spoke whatever was on her mind now, more often than not.

Ludwig placed his hand over Emmaline's and grinned widely down at her. "I've had worse compliments."

Emmaline's eyes widened as she puddled in his charm. "If I were forty years younger, I'd make you cry from pleasure!"

"Emmaline!" Angelina stomped her foot, her face noticeably blushing.

"Nonsense, dear, you have to be blunt with men. They can't read between the lines, bless their hearts."

"If I were forty years older, I just might let you," Ludwig teased back, much to Angelina's horror. He wiggled his eyebrows, and Emmaline burst into a fit of giggles.

"Oh, you teaser! You know how to make a girl

blush!" Emmaline reached down swiftly and pinched Ludwig's butt.

Angelina hid her face behind her hands and turned to Jude, who was clearly entertained. "Maybe this was a mistake."

"He's a grown man, he'll be fine. He loves attention." He wrapped his arm around her shoulders while Anne and Harold rushed around them furiously grabbing silverware.

Edgar and John had already rearranged the living room furniture, pushing together as many evenly flat surfaces as they could find to make a long dining room table. They were in the process of moving Emmaline's recliner to the head of the table when Anne and Harold started setting the place settings.

While Jude and Angelina unwrapped the food and created a buffet on the countertop, Emmaline— staying attached to Ludwig—dragged him over to her plants to tell him about all of the varieties and what their temperaments were.

"Does this look correct?" Edgar held up his pumpkin pie to eye level, wiggling it profusely. "I baked it extensively, until it no longer had the jiggle.

That's what the google advised."

Returning to the kitchen with Emmaline still glued to him, Ludwig took two paper plates out of the bag. Dishing out a large helping of the macaroni for each of them, he explained to Emmaline how he was up until all hours of the night making it just for her.

She cooed and pressed herself tighter against him. "I just love a man who knows his way around the kitchen." Her plate could've been piled full of dirt and Emmaline would've been none the wiser. Her doe-eyed gaze was plastered on Ludwig's handsome face the entire time.

Anne and John went next, each one pulling off a turkey leg. The crunch of the skin as the legs dislocated made Angelina's mouth water. "I think that's going to be the best turkey I've ever had, Anne." The golden-brown bird, caramelized in beer and brown sugar, was already taking on the appearance of a roadkill carcass mauled by vultures.

Edgar and Harold were next up. Harold wrapped his chubby little arms around Angelina's waist. "Thank you, Dr. Arbonne. It really means a lot for you to include me."

"Harold, I've always included you," Jude said defensively.

"Yes, sir, you have been gracious in all of your events. But we've never had a proper Thanksgiving dinner, bein' as you're not from around … America, and all."

Angelina giggled. "Other countries celebrate Thanksgiving, too, don't they?"

"Yes, ma'am, some celebrate the harvest. But it's always something different and never quite the same as home. Anyways, I just appreciate it, is all. The holidays can be mighty lonely."

"Well, you're always part of our family, Harold." She kissed his chubby cheek. "And you'll have to get used to it now that I'm around, because Emmaline and I celebrate Thanksgiving every year."

A tear rolled down his face as he beamed up at her, and he tried to catch it before she noticed. Angelina pretended like she didn't see it, allowing him to save face.

Everyone was seated, furiously chewing and chatting while Jude and Angelina looked on at them.

"Can I fix you a plate? Or what's on your mind? Something's on your mind," Jude asked, curious at what Angelina was about to say. She took his hands in hers.

"Look at them, Jude. We're all together, happy, relaxed. Call me crazy, but what if we went ahead and got married today? Here. After pie."

"You want to get married after pie?" Jude's face betrayed the rest of his demure exterior.

"Why not? Today might be the calm before the storm, for all we know. We don't know what the future is going to hold, so why not make today the most perfect it could possibly be? Edgar was going to officiate, anyway. And besides, Emmaline already has a wedding date today. What do you think?"

Jude wrapped his arms around her waist and pressed her up against the refrigerator, knocking off half of Emmaline's magnets. "I'm in."

Chapter

Twenty-Nine

All through lunch, Angelina and Jude kept sneaking knowing glances at each other, grinning, giggling, and hiding their faces at the secret between them. The only one to actively notice was John, who was at the end of the table and otherwise bored. Harold was sitting across from him, who was not much for small talk and just thrilled to be included.

With no one to keep him company while Anne and Emmaline chatted about this and that, he narrowed his gaze between Jude and Angelina several times, trying to telepathically crack their mystery. Angelina spotted him observing them several times, and each time she blushed and looked away.

Emmaline pinched Anne's cheeks. Anne politely tried to dodge her, but to no avail as they were sitting side by side. "I know you from somewhere, sweetheart. Do you volunteer here a lot?"

"No, ma'am, I can't say that I do. Everybody tells me I have one of those faces, though. The kind everybody thinks they know from somewhere. I'm getting used to it." Angelina nodded a silent "thank you" to her.

Emmaline sat back, pleased with Anne's response. "That must be it. Or it could be me. My memory is all chutes and ladders nowadays."

"Well, I bet you don't forget pie. Edgar made a lovely pumpkin cream cheese, a cherry, and a Derby. Which would you like?" Anne stood up, gathering as many empty plates from everyone as she could carry.

"Oh, honey, I can't possibly choose. I'll have all three." She sidled back up to Ludwig, who was doing nothing to discourage her advances. "With a slice of this scrumptious thing, as well."

"I'll bet you were a real heartbreaker back in the day, weren't you?" Ludwig wrapped his arm around her shoulders, allowing her to snuggle even closer to him.

"And a backbreaker, too. I'll dust the cobwebs off for you, you sexy piece of man. You just say the words."

"Emmaline! Ludwig, I am so sorry. She's not usually this feisty."

"There's not usually a titillating sex god in my presence, either. Child, you don't worry about me and mine." She motioned to Jude, who was doing his best to be respectful of his fiancée and not burst out laughing. "You need to take care of that one before he explodes all over this table."

Angelina sat there with her mouth agape, utterly embarrassed and unsure of how to respond. Jude took over, coming to her rescue.

"Actually, we have an announcement we'd like to make. We were talking earlier, and we'd be honored if you'd let us have our wedding ceremony here this afternoon, Emmaline. Everyone we would've invited is already here, and frankly, we don't want to wait any longer."

John was cutting pie slices in the kitchen. "I

knew it! I knew something was up with you two!"

Angelina looked at Edgar for approval. His onyx glitter eyes smiled in approval, and then turned wide with fear at the realization. "My Queen! I don't have anything ready! I was going to write a special poem for the occasion!"

"You're Edgar Allan Poe. Just wing it; I trust you completely. We have our own vows, also, so no pressure." She patted his arm.

Emmaline clapped her hands together ecstatically. "I love weddings! Oh, Angie, I don't have anything white. How will we fix this?" She thought long and hard, the wheels very slowly cranking in her mind until the lightbulb went off. "I know! We'll make you a tissue dress!"

Everyone rushed through their pies, eager for the patchwork wedding that was about to unfold. Edgar had resigned himself to the window, pie and notebook in hand, and started furiously scribbling and subsequently marking out entries over and over.

"Annie, dear, get my craft box from the closet. We've got a dress to make." Emmaline dragged Angelina into the bedroom and slammed the door.

After about forty-five minutes, Anne and Emmaline re-emerged from the bedroom looking quite pleased with themselves. Emmaline had always been the type to save tissue papers from every gift she'd ever received, not wanting to reinvest the money in something so frivolous. Consequently, she had about four large, color-coded boxes of tissue paper that traveled with her wherever she moved.

Jude and Ludwig had rearranged the furniture, while John had done his best to build a makeshift altar over the beaded curtains under Anne's rapid direction, using a handful of Emmaline's scarves.

"Everybody take your places!" Anne squeaked. She pinned a small sprig boutonniere of baby's breath, wrapped together with dental floss and tape, onto Jude. Then, she turned the TV on and shuffled through the classical channels until she found music similar enough to substitute for the "Bridal Chorus."

"Seriously?" Ludwig said. "You could've asked me."

"There's no piano here. What're you going to do, play the champagne glasses?"

"Well, I don't know, but I'd at least like to be

considered." He huffed, faking hurt.

"If we'd had more than an hour to plan, I would've suggested that you load your piano on top of the shuttle bus for just such an occasion before we left. But, times as they are, we've got to resort to digital music instead. You're walking Angelina down the aisle, and then you stand here after you drop her off," she barked, positioning Ludwig directly beside Jude as his best man.

"I think you missed your calling as a wedding planner. At the very least, a drill sergeant."

Anne ignored him. "John, you're walking Emmaline." She moved two chairs to be on one side, and a single chair on the other, creating a miniature aisle for Angelina to walk between. Satisfied, she said, "At the next change in music, we start." Harold took his place in the single chair.

Edgar and Jude stayed at the altar, while Anne lined John and Emmaline up, then herself, and then Ludwig. He lightly tapped on the door, and Angelina poked her head out.

"You about ready to become the official Queen?" She nodded, and there was a swishing of tissues behind her.

When the music changed, the memorable notes of *Für Elise* floated throughout the room. Ludwig laughed and punched Anne's shoulder lightly. "Ha. Psych."

"Nobody says that anymore. Grow up." She nudged John to begin walking. When he and Emmaline got to the counter and turned towards the door, Anne slowly began her walk, looking back at Ludwig and mentally telling him when to go. He just grinned at her and yawned.

Angelina swished out of the bedroom in her tissue dress, and Ludwig looked her up and down, his face a combination of awe and appreciation. She was wearing layers upon layers of taped white tissue, folded and fashioned as a skirt stylish enough for a runway, with a white satin camisole as the bodice. Baby's breath was pinned into her tresses, highlighting the preciousness of the moment.

"You look radiant, my Queen." Ludwig bowed slightly before extending his arm to her. "If I didn't know you were wearing wrapping paper, I'd think you paid a million dollars for that dress. They did an excellent job."

Angelina hadn't been nervous until just then, just when they turned the corner and she saw first her aunt beaming at her. Angelina hoped that Emmaline would remember at least a little bit of today, to carry with her always.

Then, her eyes traveled to the man she loved. Jude looked as nervous and excited as she was. He clasped and unclasped his hands repeatedly as they walked towards him, struggling to maintain his usually calm composure. She noticed he was biting his lips together to keep from smiling too widely, but it wasn't working. This, in turn, made her smile wider at his adorableness. Ludwig kissed her cheek, before stepping to the side to fulfill his dual position of best man.

He took her hands in his, and her nervousness disappeared.

"Ladies and gentlemen, we gather here upon this most glorious of days to celebrate the eternal union of Jude and Angelina. 'Till death do you part' is not an option for them, for their love knows no time, no boundaries, no barriers in this life or the next. Jude was made for Angelina, as Angelina was made for Jude. Their love and friendship for each other is eternal, youthful, and vigorous in its dedication. Jude, would you like to say your vows?"

Jude cleared his throat, his cheeks blushing. "I don't have anything to say that won't sound cheesy and overdone. I can't promise that you'll always be happy with me, but I can promise I will do my best to never disappoint you. I don't know what the future will bring, but I know that I want you in it.

"I don't know how much time we'll have, how many years or decades or centuries, but I can promise that I want to spend them all with you as your friend, your lover, your husband, and your confidant."

Everyone was crying, but none as much as Edgar. His chin was noticeably quivering as he wiped away tears. "Angelina," he said, barely above a whisper as he struggled to keep his voice in check.

"Two months ago, I was aimless and lost, traveling day to day throughout my life, unknowing of what I was missing. Then I met you, and everything changed immediately for the better.

"I feel like I've loved you a thousand lifetimes. My one regret is that I didn't know you until this one. You are my inspiration, my soul, and my favorite person."

Jude pulled her into his arms and kissed her. "Not yet! Not yet!" Edgar said through his sobs. "Jude, do you—"

Jude pulled back, resting his forehead on Angelina's. They smiled at each other, and together said, "We do." Angelina's arms went around Jude's neck as he dipped her, and their small family applauded loudly.

Nobody noticed the vibrating of the six beaded curtains except Edgar, who was standing directly in front of them. His mind dizzy with emotions, he only assumed that he'd bumped into the arbor, and thought nothing more of it.

Chapter

Thirty

By nightfall, they were headed back home to the palatial venue. While Anne and Edgar chatted excitedly about the day's events, Jude and Angelina had grown noticeably quiet. They were sitting in the back row, away from prying eyes and concealed by the darkness. The mood between them had become more intense and electrified, and they could not keep their hands to themselves. Angelina didn't bother to speak, because nothing she wanted to say was appropriate in earshot of their present company. She knew instinctually that Jude held the same sentiments.

By the time the shuttle bus rolled to a stop, Angelina was in Jude's lap and they were making out ravenously like high school kids under the bleachers.

"Hey, guys, you can literally get a room now," Ludwig said, hanging his head around the sliding door. "Harold wants to get parked and go to bed."

The insatiable pair clambered out of the shuttle bus, laughing and stumbling through the door. Angelina took off in a full run, with Jude hot on her heels.

By the time he caught up to her, his mood had changed. More carnal, primal masculinity filled the space around him, electrifying Angelina's skin. She was drunk off him, and energy surged through her skin as he approached her. Swirling clouds of tornados rimmed his gray diamond eyes, his desire fully washing over him.

Angelina pulled his cherry lips into hers, kissing him passionately. She ripped his shirt off, running her hands along his toned abs and tracing over his scar. He sighed into her, and, with the click of the door closing, succumbed to his wife's touch and everything he'd truly desired for the last 2,400 years.

Afterwards, Angelina slept for five solid days.

"Dude, did you break your wife already?" Ludwig
chided on the fifth day. "She's been out cold all week."
He flipped a burger on the grill. The three men were
on the back patio, relaxing in the evening sundown,
despite the chill in the air.

Anne and John had returned to New Zealand
temporarily, and would come back by Christmas. The
tentative plan was that the group would meet back up
and, after New Year's, embark upon trying to find the
others like them to prepare for this so-called war the
Wudges adamantly insisted was fixing to happen. Jude
was still highly skeptical of the situation, even though
Anne, Angelina, and Edgar were very much on board
with helping the Wudges with their quest.

The Wudges had not made another appearance
since Angelina's coronation. Jude assumed they were
still holed up in one of his trees, trying to rebuild their
life, which was fine with him. He was gracious enough
to allow them free housing, at least, these strange little
forest people. In thanks, there were tiny, fresh
bouquets of flowers placed at the bottom of the patio
stairs like sacrificial offerings every morning.

Marie had also not been seen since the coronation, which wasn't completely out of character for her.

Jude grinned lasciviously. "I did tell her to watch what she ate at Thanksgiving, because she didn't know how her system was going to handle it yet. She responded by going back for seconds."

"That's what we Americans do on Thanksgiving. It's the only proper way to celebrate," Edgar added.

"You know what they say. Happy queen, intact spleen," Ludwig said.

"That's not a saying. Nobody says that. I've got to go catch up on some paperwork. Gentlemen," Jude said, saluting his two brothers and turning to leave. He was nearly knocked out of the way when the glass door burst open, revealing Marie's short frame behind it. "And not a moment too soon, I see." He rolled his eyes at her and left. She stuck her tongue out at him before zeroing in on Ludwig.

"Wiggy! Did you make me a cheeseburger? You've always made the best burgers!" Ludwig's posture stiffened, and his eyes glazed over with irritation. He ignored her, until she walked up behind him and wrapped her hands around his chest, possessively feeling his rippling torso beneath his shirt.

"I had thoroughly—and I cannot express this enough—strongly desired that your presence was no longer with us."

"Oh, Wiggy, I know you don't mean that. It's me you think about when you keep yourself company at night."

"Unhand me, you repugnant leech!" Ludwig slammed down his spatula and stormed down the stairs and towards the river, trying to get away from her.

"Wiggy! Wiggy! Come back!" She ripped her heels off and bolted after him.

Edgar, alone on the patio, popped his earbuds in and started eating his burger.

Angelina woke up alone in their darkly colorful room. The brightness of the room's mosaics and decor in ceruleans, fuchsias, and creams were now turned to deep shades of navy, grays, and royal purples in the waning sunlight. The purple canopy flowed down from each of the posts, dancing in the wind through the opened balcony doors. Far off in the distance, faint shouts could be heard.

She swung her legs over the side of the bed, her bare feet hitting the marbled floor. Angelina smiled to herself, reliving her wedding night in blissful detail. She was satiated, but only for the time being.

She looked around the room at their crumpled clothes on the ground, the shredded tissue papers and the ripped camisole. Angelina moved to stand, and the bed squeaked along with her motion. It hadn't done that before.

She slipped on some pajama pants and a robe, and padded into the bathroom. Splashing water on her face to wake herself up, Angelina looked in the mirror at her eyes, their luminescence shining back at her. Did she feel any different? She was excited and full of energy, but she couldn't necessarily attribute that entirely to being a vampire and not to being a newlywed to the sexiest man she'd ever seen.

She looked herself over, noticing that her vision

was sharper than it had been. Before, she'd worn reading glasses occasionally. Hadn't Jude said the blood corrected minor ailments? And beheadings. Certainly beheadings.

He had been right about her diet, too. Angelina hadn't doubted him for a minute, but she wasn't about to miss Thanksgiving dinner, either. She couldn't remember how often he said he ate, so she'd have to get further notes on that. She wasn't hungry, but she was incredibly thirsty and felt like she could drink no less than ten gallons of ice-cold water.

Angelina opened the door, the smell of charred meats meeting her nostrils. She crept down the long, darkened hallway, letting her nose guide her footsteps. The mansion was completely cold and silent, its overcast shadows reaching out to her, like she'd gotten trapped in the most perfect gothic novel imaginable.

The pale strands of the watercolor sunset were streaming through the windows lining the patio. Angelina noticed smoke tendrils rising from the grill. She went to the refrigerator and grabbed three bottles of chilled water before going outside.

Down by the river, Ludwig and Marie were shouting loudly and making wild, furious gestures towards one another. The remains of what looked like it had once been a juicy hamburger crisped on the grill, so burnt that it had shriveled and was near to slipping beneath the grate to its ember-laden death. Two hot dogs on the side were now charred so profusely that they were closer to the size of Vienna sausages. Marie's heels lay beside the propane tank.

Angelina spotted Edgar and pulled up a chair beside him. He didn't acknowledge her presence at first. He was wearing red basketball shorts and a black tank top, and Angelina wondered how he wasn't cold. He was also sporting black flip-flops, his feet lounging on top of the iron table. Angelina couldn't help but notice how long his toes were, like fingers curling under the dawn of the sky. His eyes were closed as his head bobbed up and down, enchanted by whatever melody was streaming through his earbuds.

Edgar, feeling a shift in the air at Angelina's movements towards him, finally opened his eyes. "My Queen! How are you feeling?"

"Pretty thirsty, but otherwise I'm good. What're you listening to?"

He removed both of his earbuds and scrolled through his phone to show her his playlist.

"Needtobreathe. Their music really warms my soul to its depths."

"I totally get that. I didn't peg you for a Christian rock kind of guy."

"Art knows no classification except that of feeling."

Angelina looked down towards the river, its rushes drowned out by Ludwig and Marie's anger.

"Can you not just give me another chance, Wiggy? I know you still love me." She held her arms out openly, embracing his atmosphere. Ludwig, in turn, picked up a volleyball and slapped it hard, aiming it directly towards her head.

"It has nothing to do with whether or not I love you. The fact is that I can't trust you! Flynn didn't destroy us. I didn't destroy us. You, YOU single-handedly betrayed me. You destroyed us. And now, because of you we both have to spend an eternity with that fact!" Marie dodged the first volleyball, only for the second to hit her in her thigh. She angrily picked it up and launched it back at him with the speed and precision of a jaguar.

"Do you think they'll get back together? She seems to want him pretty badly."

"No, they won't. Observe their body language. She's wide open, and he's reserved. His body is saying what she refuses to accept, in that he's completely closed off to her. I know my brother. He's only loyal to those who are loyal to him. He doesn't forget betrayal easily. In time, he may forgive her, but he'll never trust her again."

"How did they meet? I'm still trying to wrap my head around everything not being what I thought it was, for, you know, centuries."

"Ah yes, my Queen. That's another story for another night, and requires much detail. You should always seek to learn and understand beyond your envisioning of reality.

"The thing with Marie is that she's a tragic, shattered soul. She's been so desperate for attention her whole life that now she's like pure poison. She knows just enough about practically everything to draw someone into her, get them interested and talking. By then, they're enamored and so completely enchanted by her Marie-ness that before long they don't even realize she's been quiet the whole time while they've poured their heart out to her and thus gotten themselves sewn into her sticky silken web.

"Except when they do realize it, she's already bored and spinning the next web to trap the next kill. All the while, they're just dangling there, mummified and helpless.

"She cracked Jude's heart and decimated Ludwig's. Neither man has been the same since. She destroys everything she touches, and she hasn't come to terms with that, yet."

"And what about you, Edgar? What of your love interests?"

He crossed his arms over his chest and rubbed his chin, contemplating. "I'm a romantic at heart, now and forevermore. I have loved more loves than love itself has known, but my truest love has been that of the written word. To be a writer is to document the human spirit."

"You're a champion of words, Edgar. I'm incredibly humbled and honored to call you, my friend."

He smiled and closed his eyes, soaking in her words one by one, his head nodding up and down slightly. "As am I, my Queen. Sometimes my thoughts get muddled, but I suppose that's how I always was—a little mad in my normal life, too. A writer's job is to find the peculiarities in the truth."

"Peculiarities in the truth," she repeated. "You have no doubts that the Wudges are telling the truth? You seemed rather invested in their story."

"Yes, my Queen. Stories keep us company when we feel alone. They remind us that we're not unique, but a fiber in the common thread of life. I should always seek to see the unseen, hear the unheard, know the unknown. Writers weave the unwoven together, until a fiction becomes a fact and vice versa.

"I do not find it so unusual that Jude was unaware of others like him. Odd, perhaps, but not entirely impossible. Why, just this week I had dinner with Anne Frank, Marie Antoinette, and Ludwig van Beethoven, which many, including yourself, would seem unthinkable.

"So we shall go forth, and we will find these 'others' that have been spoken of. Perhaps they'll help us, or perhaps they'll think we're quite absurd. I've been called worse, and I rather find comfort in the name of madness. What do you think, my Queen?"

"I think you and I will be great friends, Edgar." She stood up to hug his shoulders, and kissed his cheek. "Now, if you'll excuse me, I'm going to go find my husband."

Epilogue

Poveglia, Italy. December.

She stood on the dilapidated dock, the sound of waves gently lapping against the brick. On a clear day, Venice was just visible to the north. Today, there weren't even boats circling about like vultures. Sometimes the tourists and locals got brave, but she was quick to set them in their place.

She breathed in deep, the repugnance filling her nostrils. Closing her eyes, she smiled.

She playfully skipped over the dilapidated wooden planks laying in the walk, running a stick along the chain-link fence. *clink* *clink* *clink*

"I wonder what bones I shall be brought today," she pondered loudly to no one in particular. "A femur, perhaps, or a mandible?"

Her scales of flesh were hardly visible beneath her filthy exterior when her bare, dirty feet hit the sand. It oozed between her toes as she sang to herself. *"From dust you were born, and to dust you shall return."*

Broken shells and rotten wood struck and scratched her exposed soles as she continued on, searching. She leaned down, picking up a rounded, osseous stick before realizing its uselessness. "The charred bones that the depths dredge up are never in good enough condition."

She tossed it to the side and squatted down to rummage through a pile of freshly washed-up debris. Broken bottles, plastic rings, various other pieces of garbage, and dirty, swollen diapers fell meaninglessly from her fingers as she scrounged.

One at a time, they all deserve what is coming to them. A smile crossed her face. *Oh yes, they deserve it, indeed.*

Finally, she saw something sticking out that looked promising enough. She pushed the filth aside and reached for it.

The yellowed ivory bone trembled when her fingers touched it. Her hand withdrew automatically, hesitating before reaching over a second time. She snatched the bone up, afraid it would run away from her. Greedily, she eyed it in her open palm. Only a metacarpal, but it would have to do for now.

It shivered in her hand again, along with her entire body. She gasped, realizing that it wasn't the bone making the vibrations. Quickly, she plunged her hand down beside her, as far as she could into the mucky sand. Against her palm, the ground purred beneath her.

Her eyes shot up towards the asylum window, the one she knew he'd be at. Her marbled irises, as teal as seafoam, shrank at the sight of him, from both fear and adoration. Their gaze met, and her desire to be beside him in this moment of moments intensified. She shoved the bone into her pocket and proceeded to run.

Down the overgrown, dilapidated halls she ran, the tendrils of her hair flying wild behind her like starving black asps. Her maniacal laughter filled the empty hallways, reverberating off of the graffiti and decaying stucco walls.

Hopping over a collapsed part of the floor, she spread her arms out. The feeling of the heat in the air flowed around her and through her dress, a pale, outdated smock, nearly as thin as a feather.

She looked down at her arms and legs, marbled with the grime from her outings. *Just the way he likes her.*

Her heart beat out of her chest as she pushed the door open, equally afraid and elated at what waited for her on the other side.

He turned from the window to watch her as she entered. His skin was like mercury, his eyes like dying embers. His hair flowed thick and dark down his shoulders, like cooled lava. The sight of him never wared on her.

"Has he talked yet, Stavros? Can he feel it, too?" she asked hesitantly.

Stavros was silent, still eyeing her as Ovid spoke. "Not yet. He refuses to look at us."

His eyes landed on her empty palms. He knew the importance as well as she did. "Did you have a productive day, Daiora?"

"A metacarpal only. It will be enough for now, but I must keep searching. I don't want to use my stores."

Stavros shifted his gaze towards the table in the darkened corner, kicking the leg of it with his silver-tipped boot.

The young Wudgling shook in his glass cage. He was sitting in the corner, his knees pulled up and his arms crossed over his chest, trying to contain his sadness. No taller than a soda can standing up, in his curled-up form he was now the size of a tangerine. His head was leaning against the cage, his eyes closed.

The Wudgling's birch shoes lay in splinters at his feet, to remind him of how far he'd fallen. His moss-woven garments were unraveled and strewn about the cage. Daiora removed a tiny glass vial from around her neck as she approached.

"My sweet pet, do you still believe your papa will come for you? Surely today of all days, you must realize the end is near."

The Wudgling could barely open his eyes to look at her. He was so weak and malnourished, his normally slick green hair had turned to yellowed, dry straw. The only clothing he had were the clumps of moss he'd placed across his tiny body.

"Tell us where the keys are, my pet. Tell us where they hide."

The sickly Wudgling shivered in his cage despite the heat and humidity. "I ... I don't know."

Daiora's emerald eyes flared into reptilian slits at his insolence.

"Calm yourself, Daiora," Stavros said flatly, devoid of affection for her. "We need him."

"Yes, of course. Would you like some sunlight, my pet? Some nourishment, perhaps?" She taunted him with nutrition, trying to garner a response. The Wudgling moved his head, only just.

Daiora took a small cup from the table, filling it with a few drops of milk and honey. On top, she sprinkled some of the contents of her vial, a fine, white dust. She mixed the concoction together and drew some into an eyedropper.

"Here you go, little Wudgling, to make you grow up big and strong." She held the dropper towards his mouth through the cage. He weakly stuck his tongue out, each drop soaking into it.

"Do you know the one they call Queen? The one with the scar around her neck?" Daiora thought back to the vow she'd made to herself to finish that one off personally.

The Wudgling shook his head. "There is no queen that I know of."

Ovid snickered in the corner. "Fool, there is always a queen."

"Yes, the King is useless without his Queen." Daiora lowered her voice in the most calming manner she could muster. "Tell us what you know, and I will give you a thimble full of milk and honey to soothe your aching belly."

The Wudgling reached down to adjust some moss over his bare toes. "I don't know anything else. I've never even seen any of them. Please, I beg you, sit me in the sun for a moment."

"Why would I do that, Wudgling? So you can regain your strength and disappear from us? Tell us where the keys are!" Daiora hissed at him scathingly. The Wudgling's cage rattled at the sound of her voice. Only it continued on to the table, then the asylum. Then the island.

The trio leaned down on their hands and knees, their palms flush with the decrepit floor as the vibrations rang up through their bodies and throughout every corner of the grounds they were on.

"It is happening."

to be continued ...

Subject: ATTN: Conference Night Rumors

My Dearest Society Members,

I apologize that this email finds you later than expected. It was not my intention, but the last month has been extremely hectic, to say the least.

Many of you were a little aghast at our visitors this year, and I wanted to address the thoughts that must be swirling around the events of the second night. The kind People of Wudge have humbly asked for our help in retrieving their son, and in doing so they have unearthed some newfound revelations, which we were all previously unaware of.

There is an evil, a darkness so unfathomably vile and wicked, that we have not encountered it before. They seek to conquer and destroy those who are not their own, and they have nearly wiped the People of Wudge out of existence. They must be stopped. We must be the ones to stop them. We are unclear of the extent of the requirements it will take to do so, but we will investigate further and keep you updated.

We have also been informed that there are others like us, other immortals. You can imagine what a shock it was for us to learn that we are, in fact, not alone. We are unclear of the circumstances surrounding the others like us and their creation, but this too we will investigate and keep you updated on.

The People of Wudge assure us that they can locate the others, with our help acquiring travel arrangements. All six of the entire Society Council have agreed to go and meet with whoever our paths lead us to find along this journey.

In regard to the Society Council, Queen Angelina's coronation and turning were held four days before Thanksgiving, in a small ceremony. No major side effects were noted, and the turning was a success.

Subsequently, the wedding of King Jude and Queen Angelina was held in an intimate and impromptu ceremony on Thanksgiving Day, officiated by our beloved Edgar. Those in attendance were John, Harold, and Angelina's Aunt Emmaline. I served as the Maid of Honor, and Ludwig served as the Best Man.

That is the long and short of the last few weeks. We will be out of office in the coming months, as we travel to meet with these individuals.

I say this now, not as your Vice President, but as your friend and ally. My family, you are all aware of my personal feelings regarding the extermination of any race or species. I humbly and graciously ask you to rally alongside us in this upcoming battle. You are under no obligations or binding contracts to do so, but it would personally mean the world to me to have my family beside me on the battlefield.

We stand for what is right. We stand for what is good. We are the M.O.E.

Heartfelt regards,

Anne, V.P. of the Society of M.O.E.

P.S. It is with deepest regrets that I say this. The Society Yearbook will not be done this year, due to previously mentioned issues. But I will still be sending out all of the acquired photos in a large attachment later this afternoon.

Join the Society of M.O.E!!!

If you'd like to receive updates, information character inspirations and exclusive content, please consider subscribing to my ***The Story Behind the Story*** newsletter!

https://www.patreon.com/theamandalewis

If you'd like to receive free e-mail updates when new releases come out, please subscribe at:

https://www.bookbub.com/profile/amanda-lewis

Also by Amanda Lewis

The Levander Brothers Series

The Weight of Birds (2020 Silver Medal Winner, Contemporary Christian Romance, Reader's Favorite Awards)

Still Waters: Peter's Story

A History of Vampires Series

A History of Vampires – A New Queen

A History of Vampires – Legends & Lore (Pre-order now!)

Goodwater Ranch Series

The Cowboy – A Goodwater Ranch Romance

The Movie Star – A Goodwater Ranch Romance (Pre-order now!)

A Note from the Author

I'm still writing the third book in the *Levander Brothers,* I promise I am! I don't want to put it out until I feel like it's fabulous in its own right.

Ya'll might've noticed I diverged slightly into the world of the paranormal with this book. ;p

I couldn't help it. Even before I wrote *Still Waters,* Jude came to me. I was at work one day, and all of a sudden in my mind I'm transported to New Orleans. He's there, in Café du Monde, and Marie and Ludwig are bickering in the corner.

It's a strange thing, being a writer. Characters make themselves known out of nowhere, and it's really hard to explain with out sounding insane. If you're a writer, you know what I mean.

If not, the best way I can try to explain it is when you're driving down the road, thinking of all the things you should've said in a given situation. Now add a name, and a face, and a personality to that conversation, and there ya go. Write it down somewhere, and think about what would happen next. Congratulations, you're a writer now, and you've got the foundation to a story.

I digress. So, there I am, across from a vampire king, who's also the humblest man I've ever met. Oh, except for the part where he altered history a bit. I hope you enjoyed the first part of the story! Please consider leaving an honest review, and thank you for reading!

Acknowledgements

Thank you to God for giving me the gift of writing, first and foremost. Thank you to my husband, family, and friends, who have all been supportive in letting me do my own thing.

A huge THANK YOU to my readers! Thank you so, so, so much for all of your kind words and support since I got started!

Thank you to my editor Mark, who makes me look like I know what I'm doing. :)

Thank you to Craig, Erin, and the countless other kings and queens of the indie publishing community, for helping to make us all look like we know what we're doing!

Thank you to my fellow indies, for support, encouragement and a place to feel welcomed.

Last but not least, thank you to Neville, my fur baby and faithful sidekick. :)

Printed in Great Britain
by Amazon

36348104R00229